HUNTERS of Chaos

**DON'T MISS ANY
OF THE EXCITEMENT!**

Hunters of Chaos

Circle of Lies

HUNTERS of Chaos

By Crystal Velasquez

ALADDIN
NEW YORK LONDON TORONTO SYDNEY NEW DELHI

ALADDIN

An imprint of Simon & Schuster Children's Publishing Division

1230 Avenue of the Americas, New York, New York 10020

First Aladdin paperback edition February 2016

Text copyright © 2015 by Working Partners Ltd.

Cover illustration copyright © 2015 by Wylie Beckert

Also available in an Aladdin hardcover edition.

All rights reserved, including the right of reproduction in whole or in part in any form.

ALADDIN is a trademark of Simon & Schuster, Inc., and related logo is a registered trademark of Simon & Schuster, Inc.

For information about special discounts for bulk purchases, please contact Simon & Schuster Special Sales at 1-866-506-1949 or business@simonandschuster.com.

The Simon & Schuster Speakers Bureau can bring authors to your live event. For more information or to book an event contact the Simon & Schuster Speakers Bureau at 1-866-248-3049 or visit our website at www.simonspeakers.com.

Book designed by Laura Lyn DiSiena

The text of this book was set in Warnock Pro.

Manufactured in the United States of America 0116 OFF

2 4 6 8 10 9 7 5 3 1

The Library of Congress has cataloged the hardcover edition as follows:

Velasquez, Crystal.

Hunters of Chaos / by Crystal Velasquez.—First Aladdin hardcover edition.

pages cm

Summary: "Four girls discover that they are part of a timeless battle that pits good against evil. They have the ability to turn into large cats and an ancient duty to protect civilization from evil demons who want to rule"—Provided by publisher.

ISBN 978-1-4814-2452-3 (hc)—ISBN 978-1-4814-2453-0 (pbk)—ISBN 978-1-4814-2454-7 (eBook)

[1. Shapeshifting—Fiction. 2. Demonology—Fiction. 3. Good and evil—Fiction.] I. Title.

PZ7.V4877Hu 2015

[Fic]—dc23

2014030041

PROLOGUE

My muscles burn as the thick green jungle vines speed by in a blur. But I also feel strong and fluid, like liquid metal, or water coursing down a riverbed. I can run all night, and I have to. The thing I'm chasing—if I don't stop it, death will follow. I feel this in my gut. If I slow down, this creature of darkness will get away.

Though the canopy of dense leaves blocks out the night sky, I don't need moonlight to see. All my senses are on high alert as I bound over fallen trees and rocks. I inhale deeply, smelling everything around me—each wet leaf, every animal that has ever crossed this path. But the musty scent of fresh blood and decay rises above all. The scent of evil.

It's just ahead, so close I can almost taste it.

I cut through some underbrush, the branches scratching at my neck, and come to a clearing beside a rushing river. Without hesitation, I leap across in one smooth motion.

Only when I land gracefully on the other side do I stop to glance back. The river is at least fifteen feet wide. How did I make it across so easily? How? Something is definitely wrong.

I know my prey is speeding away into the dark, its scent fading fast. I should keep running. But I also need to see myself, to look into my own eyes and know that I'm still me. I inch toward the water, leaning forward, stretching my neck. My face is just about to come into view when—

chapter 1

I WOKE WITH A START.

The front doorbell was ringing. The sound must have pulled me out of my dream, which had been about . . . well, I couldn't quite remember. But my legs felt sore, as if I'd been running a marathon in my sleep, and for a moment my room looked strange. For some reason, I'd been expecting plants and mud instead of lavender walls and thick gray carpet. My desk near the window was still covered in schoolbooks and glittery pens. The door to my closet hung halfway open, the insides as messy as ever. My aunt had been begging me for days to straighten it up, but I knew she would cut me some slack. Though my parents had died when I was barely old enough to remember them, Aunt Teppy never stopped trying to make it up to me. My aunt and uncle, Tepin and Mec Navarro, never had kids of their own, but they were better parents than most of the people in our little corner of suburbia. Without them,

I'd be in some awful orphanage or bouncing from one foster **home** to the next. Instead I lived in a two-story house on a **quiet** block in Cleveland. I had my own room, all the books **and** music I could want, and two people who loved me. I always heard adults say that kids don't know how to appreciate what they have. Not me: I was lucky and I knew it.

A soft knock sounded at my door. "Come in," I called.

Aunt Teppy peeked her head in and smiled. "Up and at 'em," she said. "Breakfast is ready. I made your favorite, but your uncle said to tell you if you're not downstairs by ten fifteen, your pancakes are fair game."

I looked over at the digital clock next to my bed: 10:12 a.m.

"You tell him I said hands off!" I cried, throwing my covers back and swinging my feet to the floor.

"All right," she answered, shrugging. "But he looks pretty hungry. . . ." She tsked as if my short stack was already history. Then she retreated into the hallway, closing my door with a grin.

I knew this game was just a ploy they used to keep me from sleeping till noon all summer, but it worked every time. I shot out of bed and pulled on some sweats and slippers. After I ran to the bathroom and brushed my teeth, I sped down the stairs, the smell of warm syrup urging me on. I skidded to a stop in the hallway right in front of my uncle, who had been looking down at his watch and counting the seconds. "Ten fourteen. You made it." He cocked one eyebrow. "This time."

I laughed as I moved past him and entered the kitchen, my slippers making a *shh shh* sound against the tiled floor.

"Morning, sleepyhead," Aunt Teppy said when she saw me.

"Morning," I replied. I stopped to give her a quick peck on the cheek and parked myself in a chair across the island. She had her dark brown hair tied back in a loose ponytail, and she wore jeans and a formfitting white T-shirt. A glass of milk and a plate of warm pancakes were on the counter, waiting for me. She'd added a smiley face made of blueberries. I grinned.

"Eat up," she said. "You're getting too skinny. Honey, don't you think Ana is getting too skinny?"

Uncle Mec had followed me into the kitchen and now sat at the small round table by the window, the morning paper spread open before him. He lifted his graying black eyebrows and shrugged. "She looks just right to me," he said. "No one would complain if you ran a brush through that hair, though."

I smirked and ran my fingers through my tangled mop of inky black hair. "You guys just don't appreciate my punk rock style." I turned around, poured an almost illegal amount of maple syrup on my breakfast, and dug in. "Anyway, hair brushing is for school days," I said through a forkful of pancake. "I'm on vacation."

"Well, good manners are for all year round," my aunt answered. "No talking with your mouth full."

I pretended to use sign language, flashing her a series of ridiculous made-up gestures until she reached over and put the fork in my hand. "No signing with your hands full," she said, grinning. Aunt Teppy had this way of looking at me as if I was a source of constant amusement, even when I was just being myself. I took a gulp of milk and said, "Fine. But do I have to eat with *him* staring at me like that?"

Aunt Teppy followed my gaze to the hand-carved mask that hung on the wall near the island. It was a square wooden face with holes for eyes and what looked like a row of brown fangs bared in a permanent grimace.

"Oh, he won't bother you. Will you, Balam?" she cooed to the mask. "Isn't he just wonderful? What a find."

She was always bringing home special finds like "Balam." Unlike most of the homes in the area, which were decorated with store-bought art, ours was full of interesting Mayan artifacts that Uncle Mec and Aunt Teppy had collected on their travels or bought at auctions. They were pretty proud of our Mayan ancestry. Uncle Mec's full name—Mecatl—even meant "lineage," so I guess he sort of had to be into the culture. But he'd done a good job of passing that pride down to me. Every time they bought a new piece, they'd tell me its history and what it meant, and each story was cooler than the last. That's how I knew the mask in the kitchen was made of cedar wood and represented magical transformation. That didn't make it any less creepy, though. I angled my chair away from the mask and tried my best to ignore it.

"Was that the doorbell I heard before?" I said.

"Oh, right." Aunt Teppy tapped her forehead. "I almost forgot." She circled around the kitchen island and picked up a stack of mail from the basket by the front door. "It was Laura from across the street. The mailman put our mail in her box again." She took a seat at the table next to my uncle and began her daily ritual of sorting through the mail with a sigh. "I swear, if I get one more Publishers Clearing House envelope, I'll scream! Don't they know how *annoying* . . ." As her gaze stalled on a creamy white envelope, her voice trailed off and the kitchen grew pin-drop quiet.

Aunt Teppy held up the envelope and frowned. She was usually on the serious side, but the look on her face now worried me. Her skin had paled, and she seemed stunned, as if the envelope had spoken to her.

"Something wrong?" I asked.

She glanced up at me, her mouth hanging open for a second. "I, uh, no," she said at last. "Not exactly."

I rose from my chair to get a better look, and was surprised to see my own name written across the front in elaborate black calligraphy. In the space where you usually see a return address was an embossed gold seal that said **TEMPLE ACADEMY**.

"For me?" I said. "What is it?"

Instead of answering, Aunt Teppy turned the envelope around so that it faced Uncle Mec. "Honey," she said. "Hon?"

He looked up from his newspaper, squinting his eyes at first as he read my name. Then when his eyes landed on the seal, they widened. "Is it time already?" he asked.

She nodded sadly. "I knew it would happen eventually. I just didn't think . . ."

"You didn't think what?" I urged. "What is Temple Academy?" Anything that had them this wigged couldn't possibly be good. But they remained silent, ashen faced.

"C'mon, you guys. You're really freaking me out now," I said.

At last my aunt handed me the envelope and said, "Open it."

On a scale of one to ten, my curiosity level was at about a hundred, so I tore into the envelope and pulled out a piece of heavy cream-colored paper, folded into three perfectly equal sections. "Dear Ana Cetzal," it began.

We are pleased to inform you that you have been accepted into Temple Academy's matriculating class for the upcoming school year. As I'm sure you know, this is an honor bestowed on very few. . . .

I looked up at my aunt and uncle, more confused than ever. "What is this?" I asked, holding up the letter. "Are you shipping me off to boarding school or something? Is this your way of saying that you're sick of me?" I could hear the panic in my voice, but I couldn't help it.

"No, of course not!" Aunt Teppy cried at once, rushing forward to pull me into a lung-crushing hug. "We could never get sick of you."

I glanced at Uncle Mec, who said, "Eh," lifting one hand and teetering it back and forth like a seesaw.

"Mec!"

"Oh, she knows I'm just playing with her. She knows she's my favorite kid in the whole world, right, *niña*?"

I shrugged—as much as I could, anyway, while still wrapped in my aunt's bear hug—and gave him half a smile. "I guess so. But what is this?"

Finally Aunt Teppy released me and guided me to a chair next to my uncle's. She patted my hand on the smooth blue surface of the table. I know most people had white or wood kitchen tables, but we had an electric-blue one—Maya blue— to represent Chaahk, the Mayan god of rain and agriculture. Aunt Teppy once told me that having blue near the kitchen meant that our cupboards would never be bare. "We should have told you sooner," she said. "But Temple Academy is where both your parents went to school. It was coed back then, but it's an all-girls school now."

I held my breath. I never asked my aunt and uncle too many questions about my parents because I was afraid they'd think I didn't accept *them* as my parents. Plus, Aunt Teppy always looked so sad when I mentioned the sister she'd lost. But now that she'd brought it up, I couldn't wait to soak in any information she offered me.

"Really?" I said.

Aunt Teppy smiled. "Yes. They often said that other than

having you, their time at Temple was the best time of their lives."

I tried to picture teenage versions of my parents running through dim school hallways hand in hand, laughing, sneaking kisses beneath stairwells. If that was their beginning, then it was mine, too, in a way.

"Anyway," my aunt continued, "they swore that if they ever had kids, they would send them to Temple. And just after you were born, they established a trust to cover your education there."

I closed my eyes and shook my head. "Wait a minute, wait a minute. Are you saying I'm a trust-fund kid? You mean to tell me that I've been washing dishes and taking out the trash to earn an allowance when all this time I've had a bunch of money stashed somewhere with my name on it?"

"Well, no," Uncle Mec broke in. "Technically, it doesn't have *your* name on it. It's been earmarked specifically for Temple Academy."

"Oh," I said, not sure how to feel about that. I'd always thought I'd go to school with the rest of my friends. None of us were poor, but we were not exactly rich, either. Only, it turned out I was a little less not-rich than I'd thought—even if I could only use those riches for one thing. "But why didn't you guys tell me sooner?"

The two of them shared a guilty glance before Aunt Teppy said, "I think we were in denial. If it were up to me, you'd live with us until you were old and gray." She picked up the letter again and read it over. It might have just been the angle of her head in the sunlight, but I think she was tearing up. Uncle Mec just kept gazing out the window and sighing.

"And what if I refuse to go?" I asked. "What then?"

"Well, then your aunt and I would take the money and buy that yacht we've had our eye on at last!" said Uncle Mec.

My aunt rolled her eyes without even looking his way. "What he means to say is, we'd have to ask the lawyer about that. But really, this is what your mom and dad wanted for you, *niña*."

"But if this place is so great," I said, "why do the two of you look like I was just drafted into the army or something?"

They shared another long glance and my uncle shifted uncomfortably in his chair. "Listen, Ana," Uncle Mec said, his voice not quite as confident as he probably hoped it sounded. "We didn't mean to give you the wrong impression. We're just two selfish old people who want to keep you close to us. But this"—he held up the letter—"is good news, not bad. Temple Academy can offer you opportunities you'd never get at the local school. That is, if . . ." This time he trailed off and looked helplessly at my aunt. He seemed worried. If I hadn't been staring at them so hard, I would have missed the almost imperceptible shake of Aunt Teppy's head.

"*If?*" I demanded. "If *what*?"

But Aunt Teppy had plastered on a smile and brushed past my question. "There's nothing to worry about, Ana. You are going to do wonderfully at Temple. It's in your genes! Now—I'm sure you had an exciting day planned of lying around in your pajamas and watching game shows, but instead let's go shopping to buy you all the things you'll need. According to this letter, you have to be there in two weeks, so we don't have much time."

"But, but what about—?" I tried.

Aunt Teppy clapped her hands. "Chop chop, Ana. Hurry up and finish your breakfast. Big day ahead." She rushed out of the kitchen then, and my uncle quietly rose from his chair to follow her, giving my arm a squeeze before he left.

I took a seat in front of my now cold pancakes to try to finish my breakfast. I had eaten the bottom half of the circle, so the blueberry smile was gone. All that remained were two blue eyes staring back at me, looking just as lost as I felt.

Two weeks passed in a blur and suddenly it was the night before I had to leave for Temple Academy. The weather seemed to feel as uneasy as I did. A storm had raged outside the house all day, rattling our windows and lighting up the darkness with occasional bursts of lightning. And there was so much rain, I started to wonder if I'd have to swim to the airport the next day.

I looked around my room for the millionth time. Was it possible that in just a few hours, I wouldn't be sleeping here anymore? I'd be somewhere in New Mexico surrounded by strangers and, if every movie I'd ever seen about boarding schools was to be believed, sharing a room with a clique of girls who would spend their time plotting my demise.

I opened my suitcase again and took out the ratty stuffed cat I'd had since I was little. It was kind of my security blanket. But if I was going to be surrounded by snobby mean girls who'd make fun of me over every little thing, I didn't want to give them any ammunition. *Sorry, Whiskers.* I put him back on my bookshelf. I picked up the small photo album I'd placed in the side compartment of the suitcase and sat on the edge of my bed, flipping through it until I came across a picture of my parents.

In the picture they were in a park, knee-deep in snow. They had one long red-and-black scarf wrapped around both their necks. Mom, her long black hair tucked into a pink wool cap with a white pom-pom on top, was kissing Dad's cheek. His eyes were closed, snowflakes settling into his lashes, and he had this silly grin on his face. It was a little blurry and off center, maybe because snowflakes were landing on the lens. But I could see that they had been young in the photo, early twenties, maybe. It was weird that I knew so little about my own parents. I knew that I looked like my mom, and Uncle Mec always said that I laughed just like my dad. But other than that, I didn't know the first thing about them—except that for some reason, they'd wanted me to go to Temple Academy. Was that really where they met? I wondered.

Just then I heard three soft knocks. My door creaked open slowly and Aunt Teppy peeked around the edge. "Mind if I come in?" she said.

I waved her in and kept looking down at the photo. She came and sat next to me on the bed and looked down too. "Aw, that's a great one," she said, taking the album from my hands and laying it across her lap. "I think I actually took this picture. I remember we had so much fun that day." Her voice broke a little on the last word and tears filled her eyes and slid down her cheek. This, exactly this, was why I never asked about my parents.

"I'm sorry, Aunt Teppy," I said, getting up to grab a box of tissues from my nightstand. I handed her one. "I know you miss them. I'll put the album away."

But she waved me off like I was being silly. "No, no, it's not that," she said, dabbing at her nose with the tissue. "I mean, it *is.* But it isn't only that. We're just going to miss you *so much.*" She offered me a weak smile. "You've made us so happy, Ana."

"Jeez, Aunt Teppy, I'm not dying," I said. "Just going to school. You'll see me again in, like, two months, you know." I tried for a light tone to cheer her up. But the truth is, I was just as sad. I'd miss them like crazy.

Aunt Teppy laughed a little. "I know," she said, then cleared her throat. "But until then, I have a present for you."

She reached into her pocket and pulled something out. In her hand she held a leather necklace with a turquoise Mayan jaguar carving hanging from the end. It was a little bit smaller than my palm.

"This jaguar is very special to me and to our people," she said. "I want you to promise to wear it all the time so that your uncle and I will always be close to your heart."

I couldn't help cringing a little. Talk about giving any mean girls ammunition to make fun of me. Nothing says, *I fit in here*, like a Mayan jaguar carving hanging from my neck. But I could see how important it was to my aunt, so I took the necklace from her and pulled it over my head. The carving was lighter than it looked, and the surface felt oddly cool against my skin. But I still hoped it wouldn't be too hot in New Mexico for me to throw on a pretty scarf to hide my newest piece of jewelry.

I felt guilty for even having that thought. She and Uncle Mec were super into the whole Mayan thing, and they always tried to make it clear how important it was for me to know about my Mayan heritage and to take pride in it. And I did. I actually loved hearing about the ancient warriors and seeing all the art they left behind. Knowing that I was connected to this whole civilization that archaeologists spent a lifetime studying was kind of cool. But, honestly, that all seemed like such a long time ago. What did those dusty relics in the history museum have to do with my life now? Other than the fact that my last name—Cetzal—was Mayan, I just didn't feel the connection. But for my aunt's sake, I kept that to myself.

"Thanks," I said. "It's awesome."

"I'm glad you like it," she answered. "There's one more thing." She stood up and went out into the hall. When she came back into my room, she was carrying a large gift-wrapped box. She sat next to me on the bed again and handed me the present.

"What—what is this?" I asked as I took it from her.

"Something every student should have." She smiled knowingly.

I ripped open the box to find a brand-new shiny silver laptop. For a moment I was speechless. "But—but are you sure?" I managed finally. "These cost so much—"

Aunt Teppy held up her hand to silence my protests. "You're worth every penny," she said. "And we've already had someone install all the software you might need."

I put the laptop aside and flung my arms around her. "Thank you," I said, my voice a bit shaky. We held on to each other like that for a long time before she gently pulled away and stood up. She glanced around the room, the same way I had been for days. "Well, I suppose I should let you finish packing. We have to get an early start tomorrow, so don't stay up too late, okay?"

"I won't."

She leaned down to kiss me on my forehead, then cupped my face in her hands. As I looked into her eyes, I thought I saw something more than run-of-the-mill sadness. There was unease there, a hint of fear that I could swear I'd seen in my uncle's eyes every time I said the words "Temple Academy."

"I'm worried about you guys," I said. "What will you do without me?"

Aunt Teppy smiled. "We'll be just fine," she replied. "Don't worry about us."

But that night as I lay in my bed, listening to the sounds of the storm outside, I did nothing *but* worry.

chapter 2

WHEN THE AIRPORT TAXI STOPPED AT THE END OF THE Temple Academy driveway, I put one foot out of the car and paused, suddenly frozen in fear. For some reason I'd expected New Mexico to be just like Ohio—same cookie-cutter streets and houses, just different address numbers. But getting out of the taxi felt like stepping into a science-fiction movie. For one thing, it was hot in a way that Cleveland never was, not even in the summer. There wasn't a single house for miles in any direction, and the only roads I saw weren't even paved—they were just dirt, the dust from them rising up into the faint blue sky like puffs of gray cloud. All around me were towering mountain ranges and jagged rock cliffs that looked as if they were made of red clay. I might as well have been on the moon. "This is where you wanted to go, right?" a gruff voice said from the front seat.

"What?" I said, swinging my head around to see the driver staring at me with bored eyes.

"You don't seem too sure you're in the right place. Do you need to call somebody? Your mom, maybe?"

I shook my head. "No, I'm in the right place . . . I think. I'm just not sure I want to stay."

The driver turned to peer out of the passenger-side window at the school. He took off his worn baseball hat to reveal a slightly sunburned bald scalp and wiped his forehead with his arm. "Doesn't look so bad to me," he said, leaning back in his seat.

He was right, actually. Against the otherworldly backdrop of the mountains, the school itself looked like an oasis of normalcy. The cream-colored facade of the main building was nestled in a valley of lush greenery. Large French windows revealed a homey lobby area with overstuffed blue and brown sofas. The elegant columns on either side of the entrance seemed almost humble compared to the steep cliffs that hemmed in the campus. Even the sign out front with the Temple Academy crest on it was downright friendly—no large scary block letters or intimidating gold calligraphy, just simple lettering in an arc over a picture of an open book. Through the large windows I could see other students roaming around in groups of three and four. None of them looked particularly homicidal and they definitely weren't as alien as the rest of New Mexico. Taking it all in, I felt a wave of relief. Like me, Temple Academy didn't look like it belonged here. So at least we had that in common.

"Going or staying?" the driver prodded, tapping his meter,

although the school had arranged for the car to pick me up and paid him in advance.

I took a deep breath. "Staying." With that I brought my other foot out to join the first and stood up. My legs were shaky as I moved toward the trunk to get my luggage. But before the driver even had a chance to open it, the ground suddenly rumbled and shook beneath me, like *it* wasn't so sure about my decision to stay here. I yelped and clung to the side of the car. What was happening? The trees in front of the school swayed and brushed against the windowpanes, and the water in the fountain off to the side rippled as if someone had been skipping rocks across its surface.

"What's going on?" I cried, still hugging the rear of the car as if it were my stuffed cat, Whiskers.

The driver, who had climbed out of his seat, pressed a button on his key chain and the trunk popped open with a snick. He furrowed his brows at me and let out a grunt. "What?" he asked.

"The—the—" But by then it was over, I realized. I leaned against the trunk and sighed. *Did he seriously not notice that?* Maybe earthquakes were so common here, a huge rumble like that barely registered. It's possible that it would seem normal to me eventually. But I seriously doubted I would ever stop noticing the *ground moving. Great,* I thought. *One more thing to get used to.*

After the driver dragged my suitcase out of the trunk and onto the walkway, he wished me luck and drove off, waving his baseball cap out the window as he went. I waved back as if I were saying good-bye to an old friend or a favorite uncle instead of a total stranger. It sure beat thinking about the fact that I was now completely alone.

With a sigh, I turned and made my way past the columns into the warm glow of the lobby. For a moment I just stood there, not sure where to go next. Everyone else seemed to know exactly where they were going and what they were supposed to do. Was I the only new girl? It was a terrifying thought.

"Ana Cetzal!" a loud voice boomed. I looked up to see a tall blond woman in a chic summery dress and low heels striding toward me. She seemed to be around the same age as Aunt Teppy, but with golden skin and fewer laugh lines around the eyes. When she got closer, she held out her hand. As we shook, she smiled sweetly. "We've been expecting you," she said. "I'm Principal Ferris. How was your flight in? Did you have any trouble getting here?"

I shook my head. "No, it was pretty cool. They showed movies on the plane." I immediately cringed inside. Had that been a dumb thing to say?

But Principal Ferris didn't seem bothered. "That's wonderful!" she said, letting my hand go and clapping hers together. "Now, let's get you all settled in, shall we?"

"Sure," I said, shrugging.

"Splendid. This way, please."

Silently, I followed her through the lobby and out a back

21

door at the far end. We stepped into the sunshine onto a path that split off in five different directions, each one leading to what looked like a miniature version of the main building. Perfectly manicured grass and precise rows of flowers filled the spaces between the paths. The paths came together at the lobby door, intersecting in a wide paved circle with curved benches all along the perimeter. I'd bet that from the air this whole place looked like an elaborate crop circle.

"These are our five dorms," Principal Ferris said in her cheery voice. "Each one is named after an important person in Temple Academy's history. You'll be staying in Radcliff Hall, named after one of the founders of this school."

She looked at me expectantly, as if I should be thoroughly impressed by this revelation. I tried my best to make her happy. She was being so nice to me; I didn't want to let her down. "Wow!" I said, faking enthusiasm. "That's . . ." *Don't say cool. Don't say cool.* ". . . awesome." I sighed. I'd have to step up my vocabulary game for sure.

But the principal just smiled wider, seeming happy that I understood what an honor it was to be placed in this hall. We entered the circle and took the second path to our right, then walked up to the cozy-looking dorm building. After we passed through the heavy oak doors, I was even more surprised. Outside may have been all old-world charm and history, but inside—well, it looked like a West Elm showroom. The furniture was sleek and modern, with the occasional sparkly pillow thrown *just so* in the corner of an armchair. A flat-screen TV was mounted above a small fireplace, and a huge black-and-white photograph of Frida Kahlo took up half the wall behind the couch. I had to bite my lip to stop myself from screaming, *Cool!* I wasn't sure what I'd been expecting, but it wasn't this.

Principal Ferris seemed to note the surprise on my face. "Quite nice, isn't it? We renovated it recently, at the request of some of the girls, actually. History is important to us here at Temple Academy, but we saw no reason not to make the common areas a bit more modern."

"Good call," I said. "It's . . . exquisite." *There you go.* I mentally patted myself on the back.

"All the girls have access to this space," she continued, gesturing for me to follow her up a short flight of stairs. "Each dorm has what we call a dorm mother. Yours will be Mrs. O'Grady, who is a dear woman. She'll be around to keep an eye on you ladies."

"How many of us are there in this dorm?" I asked.

"Including you, there are approximately forty young ladies. But you'll only have to share a room with one." At the top of the stairs we came to a hallway with several doors. She knocked on the third one, which bore a small white block with the names **NICOLE VAN VOORHIES** and **ANA CETZAL** on it.

The door swung open and the most beautiful girl I'd ever seen in real life stood there, smiling at me. She had shining corn-silk-blond hair that was the stuff of shampoo commercials, straight white teeth, and makeup so flawless she looked like she belonged on a red carpet. *I have to room with her?* I thought miserably. It would be like a potato farmer rooming with Marilyn Monroe, and guess which one of us was the potato farmer?

"Is this my roommate?" she squealed.

Principal Ferris laughed. "Yes, I told you she would be arriving today. Nicole, I'd like you to meet Ana. I expect you to make her feel right at home."

"Naturellement!" Nicole cried, grabbing my hand and pulling me into the room. She gave me a quick hug. "Oh, God, totally! I'm so glad you're finally here. I've had this room to myself for two whole weeks already. Privacy is nice, but after a while . . . bo-ring. Am I right?"

I didn't know what to say. Up until this moment I'd always had my own room. I'd had friends over sometimes, but between music, books, and my thoughts, I'd never been bored when hanging out alone. *Should I have been?*

"Totally," I agreed, nodding hard.

"Wait till you see how big our closet is," she said. "Come on, I'll show you." She reached behind me, grabbed the handle of my small suitcase, and rolled it away.

I looked back at Principal Ferris, who gave Nicole the same head shake and smile Aunt Teppy usually gave me. "Well," she said, "I can see I'm leaving you in capable hands. There's a welcome packet in your desk with more information for you. And Nicole can fill you in on anything else. But feel free to find me if you need anything. Okay, Ana?"

I nodded. "Okay. Thank you, Principal Ferris."

She gave me one last warm smile and retreated down the hall, humming to herself.

Reluctantly, I closed the door and followed the sound of Nicole's chatter to our shared walk-in closet. *Seriously?* I didn't even have a walk-in closet at home.

"The left side is mine," Nicole said, gesturing to the long rack of what looked like brand-new clothes and a shelf stacked with shoe boxes. "The right side is all yours."

I looked from the huge empty half of the closet to my pathetically small suitcase. "Um, I don't think I'll need a whole side," I muttered.

Nicole seemed momentarily confused. "This isn't all you brought, is it? I know my mom didn't want me lugging four suitcases around the airport, so she shipped the rest of my things in boxes. Thank God, too. I wouldn't have had the heart to fold my Carolina Herrera dress." She reached out and lovingly stroked a gorgeous designer gown made of some kind of shimmery fabric that looked like vanilla ice cream.

"This is all I brought," I said, suddenly feeling underdressed and underpacked.

To Nicole's credit, if she was appalled, she hid it well. She shook her head and said, "Well, you don't need a million pieces. You probably just brought the essential ones. Less is more. Am I right?"

I had a feeling I'd be answering that question a lot and that the answer was always supposed to be yes. But now as I unpacked my neatly rolled T-shirts and Old Navy jeans, it seemed to dawn on her that maybe, for the first time ever, she was wrong. Very, very wrong. Her side of the closet screamed New York Fashion Week, and mine screamed Cleveland mall. Suddenly I felt kind of dumb for not having seen this coming. When I flashed back to everyone I'd seen in the lobby, it occurred to me that they hadn't all been just like me. Not that I was any kind of fashionista, but I could read labels as well as anybody, and I knew that one girl had been wearing a Donna Karan tank top, and one of the purses I'd seen had been Louis Vuitton. Nicole's side of the closet was a who's who of every designer I'd ever heard mentioned on *Fashion Police*. Until now, I'd never met anyone who had even one piece of designer clothing—not a real one, anyway. But designer clothing was all Nicole seemed to own!

I shouldn't be surprised. It didn't take a genius to figure out that a school that only the rich could afford would be filled with rich kids.

And me, now.

"Um, Ana, don't take this the wrong way, but . . . did you bring anything a little less . . . casual?"

I didn't want to tell her that my idea of dressing up was wearing a belt with my jeans. My expression must have said it all, because she looked at me with real sympathy for a moment, like I was a lost puppy she'd come across in the woods.

"You know what?" she said. "Don't even worry about it. Actually, this is a good thing. You can be my little protégée!"

I wasn't sure I liked the sound of that. I almost protested. But then I thought about how out of place I already felt. Maybe I could use a little training. It couldn't hurt.

I grinned at Nicole. "Okay, sure. Help me, Obi-Wan. You're my only hope!"

Her nose crinkled in confusion. I guess she wasn't a *Star Wars* fan. "You're so weird," she said. "I love it! Now, I think we're about the same size. So let's get you into something a little more sophisticated." She rifled through the rack, her wooden hangers snapping against one another, until she came across a beautiful silk skirt with orange flowers blooming along the hem. Then she pulled out a sky-blue sleeveless mock turtleneck from a pile of folded tops on a shelf. "Perfect!" she said. "You don't want to be too matchy-matchy." She pushed the ensemble into my chest. "Go ahead. Try it on. I won't look."

She turned her back and whistled a game-show theme song while I kicked off my sneakers and socks, peeled off my road-weary jeans and cotton T-shirt, and pulled on the designer duds, grateful that the turtleneck allowed me to keep my jaguar a secret for a little longer. I couldn't even see myself yet and already I felt like a million bucks.

"You can turn around now," I said. I held out my arms. "So, what do you think?"

Nicole nodded, her eyes twinkling. "Getting there," she said. "But we've got to do something about that hair."

I could practically hear Uncle Mec say, *Told you that you should have run a brush through it.* For a moment I missed him so much I thought I might cry. So it was a relief when Nicole pulled me back into the room and sat me down on a chair facing away from her. After she dug my brush out of my suitcase— she later informed me the one I was using was all wrong, of course—she brushed my hair until there wasn't a single tangle left. Then she took it in her hands, twisting and patting and twisting some more. Finally she disappeared into the closet again and returned with a pair of pretty beige Jimmy Choo flats with little blue satin bows near the toe. "Six and a half, right?"

"How did you know that?"

She shrugged. "It's a gift. Lucky for you, we're the same size there, too."

I slipped my feet into the shoes and stood up.

"Oh. My. God," Nicole said. "Major upgrade. Ma-jor." She dragged me over to the closet again, but instead of entering, she closed the door to reveal a full-length mirror. "Look how pretty you are!" she gushed.

I had to admit, I really was. She'd styled my hair into a sleek side braid that hung over my shoulder, and the light blue shirt popped against my jet-black hair. Even the skirt was flattering on me, and I never wore skirts. *I could get used to this,* I thought. "Nicole," I said. "You're a miracle worker."

She fluttered her hand and said, "Pshaw," but it was obvious that she agreed. "Well, now that you're ready to be seen in public, let's get out there! I'm dying to show you around."

"You mean there's more?" I asked. How big was this place?

"Are you kidding?" she answered. "Wait till you see. Let's go." She grabbed a small Michael Kors bag and slung it over her head so the strap rested in a diagonal line across her chest. In her peasant blouse, dark blue True Religion jeans, and strappy sandals, she managed to look casual and glamorous at the same time. How did she do that?

When we were almost at the door, I stopped and said, "Hey, Nicole?"

She turned and raised her eyebrows.

"I just wanted to say, thanks for doing all this. I mean, I know I'm probably not the kind of roommate you expected. But you've been really"—there was no other word for it—"cool. So thanks."

Nicole smiled, flashing her brilliantly white teeth. "Not even," she said. "We're going to be great friends, you and me."

"You think so?"

"*Naturellement.*" She winked and floated out of the room.

I smiled. I still felt like a strange girl in a strange place, and Nicole wasn't like anyone I'd ever known. But at least I had a friend, and that felt kind of nice.

"Going or staying, Ana!" Nicole called from down the hall.

Staying, I thought.

chapter 3

MAYBE I WAS HALLUCINATING. MAYBE I'D GOTTEN SICK ON the plane and this whole thing was some kind of crazy fever dream. What else could possibly have explained the jet sitting in the middle of the school grounds?

I was all set to tell my new roommate that she should probably take me to the nurse, when she walked right up to what I was sure had to be a mirage and knocked on its shimmering metal side. *Thunk thunk thunk.*

"You mean to tell me that thing is real?" I said, blinking in disbelief.

Nicole crinkled her perfect nose. "I know, right? I told you this place was sick."

"And students can actually use it?" For a brief shining moment, I pictured myself hopping in the plane and flying it right back to Ohio, where things made sense.

"Not exactly," Nicole said, bursting my bubble. She rolled

her eyes. "Supposedly it's only for emergencies, and you need all kinds of permission. But I happen to know that Tammy Winston used it last year to fly home and get a nose job. She denies it, of course. Claims she went home for her grandma's funeral, but when she came back her nose was all pointy, like she'd had part of it shaved right off."

"Hey!" a deep voice shouted from the end of the short runway. "I told you already. This area is off limits unless you are flying somewhere!"

I turned to see a short, olive-skinned man with a scruffy gray beard stalking toward us. His saggy knees, which peeked out of the bottom of a pair of khaki shorts, dimpled with each step, his shoes slapping against the pavement. As he approached, his gaze landed on me, and he stopped short. I watched as his eyes narrowed a bit and he tilted his head. For a moment he almost smiled, as if he'd seen an old friend in an unexpected place. But he quickly shook it off and turned toward Nicole, glaring at her hand, which was still resting on the jet.

Finally she lifted both her hands in the air and backed away until she was standing next to me. "All right, all right. Relax, Antonio. Don't have an aneurysm. I was just showing the new girl your pride and joy."

Antonio grunted, took a white rag out of his back pocket, and started polishing the spot where Nicole's hand had been. He muttered under his breath in what I think was Italian.

31

Nicole leaned toward me and whispered, "He's the pilot. He's been here for, like, ever."

I shot a glance at Antonio. If he had been here for that long, he had to have known my mom. Maybe that's why he'd looked like he recognized me.

Nicole squeezed my arm and shook her head before I could say good-bye to Antonio, or maybe ask him a question about my parents. She pointed at his back and swirled her index finger in a circle near her ear—snarky sign language for, *Don't bother. He's crazy.* She grabbed my arm and pulled me away from the landing strip. "Come on, Ana. I want to show you the stables."

If I had been drinking anything, I'd have spit it out when she said that. "Stables? As in for horses?"

Nicole just laughed and pinched my cheek as if I were an adorable two-year-old. "Aw, you're so cute," she said. "You don't know anything!"

After I followed Nicole around some winding pathways lined with flowers, we reached a dark wood structure with an open entryway on either side. I could see rows and rows of horses in separate stalls, some drinking out of buckets of water, some neighing and stomping their hooves. I'd expected it to smell like a gross combo of manure and . . . well, horse, in there, but instead it smelled like freshly cut grass and apples. There was a group of girls in the last stall, crowded around a chestnut-brown mare. The one brushing the horse's mane was wearing a chic riding outfit, right down to the black leather boots.

"Oh my God, Jessica!" Nicole squealed, rushing forward with her arms wide open. "When did you get here?"

Jessica stopped brushing the horse and greeted Nicole with a smile. The two of them hugged and made kissing sounds on either side of the other girl's face, though their lips never made actual contact. "Just got here this morning," Jessica said, tucking a loose strand of auburn hair behind her ear. "But Mother insisted that I get in some riding practice right away. You know how it is."

"Do I," Nicole answered. "My mom had me get here two weeks ago so I could prep for classes before they even started."

"Nightmare," declared a girl with dark brown skin and round, expressive eyes. As she wrapped one of her black hair twists around her finger, she shook her head as if the thought of getting to school two weeks early was the worst thing she could imagine. She wore a white knit jumpsuit that I was pretty sure I'd seen Rihanna wear once on the cover of *Teen Vogue*.

Nicole shrugged. "It isn't so bad now that my new roomie is finally here. Ladies"—she put her hand on my back and prodded me forward—"meet Ana."

I noticed that the other girls took a beat before reacting, as if they were waiting for a cue from Nicole. But after she smiled, they did too, and crowded closer, introducing themselves and shooting all kinds of questions at me. Where was I from? What did my parents do? Where did I spend my summers? I wasn't sure how to answer. I had a feeling that telling them I spent my summers in Ohio taking swimming classes at the Y and going to museums with my aunt and uncle wouldn't exactly impress. Before I could figure out how to respond, a petite brunette with sharp features who'd been standing in the back came forward, cradling a Chihuahua in a pink, rhinestone-encrusted collar. Nicole gave my shoulder a subtle nudge and rubbed the side of her nose as if she was scratching an itch. But her sly smile let me know that the brunette was none other than Tammy Winston.

"Forget where you spend your summers," Tammy said with a slight Southern twang. "I want to know where you got that skirt. It's gorgeous. Is it vintage?"

I shot Nicole a nervous look. "Oh, this?" I said, smoothing my now sweaty palms over the smooth fabric. "Actually, Nicole—"

"—asked her the same thing when I saw it," Nicole broke in. "But duh, of course it's from the new Vivienne Westwood collection."

The rest of the girls regarded me with renewed interest. "Good taste," Tammy said. "I might just have to go raid your closet now."

I swallowed the lump that instantly formed in my throat. If she raided my pathetic side of the closet, the jig would most definitely be up.

"Sorry, Tammy," Nicole said in a singsong voice. "No time

for that right now. My new bestie and I have a campus tour to finish. See you girls later, m'kay? Ciao."

Nicole spun on her heel and strutted out of the stable, her bouncy blond hair swinging behind her. She didn't even glance backward, but I knew she wanted me to follow her. I turned awkwardly to the group. "Um, it was nice meeting all of you."

Jessica, who had gone back to brushing her horse's mane, smiled and said, "You too. Welcome to Temple, Ana."

I caught up to Nicole just outside the stables. "Hey, thanks for saving me back there," I said. "You didn't have to."

"Are you kidding?" Nicole answered, slowing her pace a bit. "Ana, those girls are piranhas. If they'd known you were rocking my hand-me-downs, they'd have chewed you up and spit you out."

"I . . . really? I don't know. They didn't seem that bad to me."

"You'll have to trust me on this one," Nicole said. "You're lucky I was there. I mean, Jessica's okay, considering. . . ."

"Considering what?"

Nicole finally broke her stride and faced me. "Well," she said, taking a quick peek over her shoulder then leaning toward me with big blue eyes. "You didn't hear this from me, but Jessica's only at this school because back home she was way too boy crazy. So her parents figured how much trouble could she get into at an all-girls school in the middle of the desert, you know? Good thing her family is loaded, because she's not the brightest bulb in the box."

"Oh," I said dumbly. I thought back to how happy Nicole had seemed to see Jessica—the hug, the air kisses. Had that all been an act?

"And Tanya," she went on, talking about the girl in the white jumpsuit, "her mom used to be a model. But you would never know it looking at her, am I right?"

"I don't know. I thought she was pretty."

Nicole made a huffing sound. "With those pores?"

It went on like that as she continued to show me around the school. Every time we passed someone, Nicole introduced her as a close friend and then whispered a piece of gossip about her as soon as she was out of earshot. Already I knew that Maria's parents, both high-powered lawyers, were going through a messy divorce. Sindu had been adopted. Tracy had gotten caught cheating on a test once and had almost been kicked out of Temple. Diane's family was rich only because her dad had won the lottery, which is why she had such awful taste in clothes, according to Nicole.

The whole time she spoke, I stayed quiet. Maybe it was corny, but Aunt Teppy had always told me not to say anything behind someone's back that you wouldn't say to her face. But Nicole clearly didn't feel that way. I considered calling her out on how mean she was being. But then I remembered how nice she had been to me all day, how she had lent me her clothes and let everyone believe they were mine. She couldn't be all bad. Besides, if the other girls really were piranhas like she said, maybe it was good that my new "bestie" was a shark. How lost would I have felt without her?

So I tuned out the gossip and just focused on the gorgeous place I'd be living for the next school year. In addition to the horse stables and the jet, there was an Olympic-size pool, an outdoor track, a kennel for students' pets, hiking trails, and tennis courts. Even the cafeteria looked more like a five-star restaurant. Had my mom and dad really gone here? And had they actually fit in? I doubted that I ever would.

Nicole was about to show me the library when Katy Perry's voice sang out from her pocket, and she whipped out a smartphone. "*Bonjour,*" Nicole answered. After a pause, her eyes went round and her mouth dropped open as if she'd just heard something especially juicy. "Shut. Up. Oh my God, she didn't!" she cried. "Tell me *every*thing."

I slowly drifted away from Nicole, figuring she'd come find me when she was done. I wandered around the back of the library, past a row of trees, and came to a wide grassy field opposite a set of metal risers. A group of girls sat on the highest row with books open on their laps. I was wondering what they could be studying since classes hadn't started yet when a male voice shouted, "Watch out!"

I turned in the direction of the voice and saw a small orange ball hurtling toward my head. Without even thinking, I shot my hand up and caught it.

"Nice catch," the boy who'd shouted said.

Wait—the *boy*? What was a boy doing here? *An extremely cute boy.*

He seemed to be around my age and had unblemished golden skin and sun-streaked blond hair, neatly trimmed to frame his thin face. His eyes were a color I couldn't quite define—some mixture of blue and green—and his smile was easy and sincere. *Whoa,* I thought, feeling my knees buckle. I'd thought the jet would be the most amazing thing I'd see all day, but I guess I was wrong.

"You've got good reflexes," he said. "Have you thought about going out for the lacrosse team?" I must have been staring at him in a strange way, because he furrowed his brows at me. "What? Why are you looking at me like that?"

"Sorry. I didn't mean to." I shook my head and handed him the lacrosse ball. "It's just, I wasn't expecting to see any boys here. Isn't this an all-girls school?"

"Oh, that," he said. "You must be new. You've met Principal Ferris, right?"

I nodded.

"Well, she's my mom. We live here. Since my mother's the principal, I have special permission to go to Temple. The public school at the far end of the valley lets me play on their boys' teams. I'm Jason, by the way." He stuck the lacrosse ball under his left arm and reached out to shake my hand. As soon as my palm touched his, the girls in the bleachers stirred. When I turned to look, I caught them ogling us for a second, and then they all bowed their heads and started flipping pages—all except for one pretty Asian girl who sat with her back straight and her head held high. We locked eyes as if she were daring me to a staring contest. I lost. *Oh, now I get it,* I thought as I blinked and turned away. They were studying, all right. They just weren't studying books. From their spot on the risers, they had a perfect view of Jason as he practiced tossing lacrosse balls into the net.

"I'm Ana Cetzal," I said, focusing on Jason and doing my best to ignore our audience. "And you're right—I am new. I just got here today, actually. My roommate has been showing me around."

Jason started tossing the orange ball from hand to hand. "Too bad," he said. "I was just about to offer to do that."

He smiled, and my heart fluttered in my chest like a strip of paper in a breeze. No wonder the bleacher girls were openly stalking him. As the only boy at Temple, he probably got plenty of looks. But he also happened to be completely crush-worthy, turning those looks into stares.

And I had to admit he had my total attention. I almost told him he was free to give me the rest of the tour since my guide had gotten sidetracked. But just as I opened my mouth, Nicole came running up, slightly out of breath.

"There you are!" she cried.

And here's the part where the cute guy becomes entranced by Marilyn Monroe, and the potato farmer disappears into the background. But when Jason saw Nicole approaching, he scowled.

"Oh, hey, Jason," Nicole said as she threw her arm around my shoulders. "I see you've met Ana. You're not breaking hearts with those baby blues already, are you?" I'd never seen a girl do this in real life, but Nicole batted her eyelashes.

It was clearly a practiced move, meant to turn any boy into butter. But instead Jason's face turned to stone. He glanced back at me. "This is your roommate?" he said, hiking a thumb toward Nicole.

I nodded again, and his eyes filled with anger and pity. Whatever warm fuzzies we'd had between us evaporated like steam. But I was pretty sure the anger wasn't directed at me. He shot an icy glance at Nicole, then said, "Good luck, Ana," and quickly jogged across the athletic field.

"Wow, what was that all about?" I asked Nicole. "Did you two have a fight or something?"

Nicole flipped her hair behind her shoulder and gave me a grin. "Who, me and Jason? Don't be silly. We're like this." She wrapped her index and middle fingers around each other. "It must have been because of you. He's just shy around new people."

I gave Nicole a skeptical sideways glance. Granted, I'd only just met Jason, but he hadn't seemed shy at all. Pointing that out would have only hurt her feelings, though. "Well, if shyness makes a person seem angry," I said instead, "that girl over there must be the shyest person on campus. She's been glaring at me ever since I started talking to Jason." I gestured subtly to the queen bee of the bleacher girls, who had gone back to monitoring Jason's every move.

Nicole looked toward the bleachers and nodded knowingly. "Yeah. That's Lin Yang. You'll want to watch your step around her. She's spoiled rotten and is a major brat."

I glanced back at Lin and the group of girls surrounding her. "Then why does she seem to have so many friends?"

"Those leeches? They're not really her friends," Nicole answered matter-of-factly. "They just suck up to her because her parents are sort of famous and they have more money than God. Lin's used to getting her way, though, so if she's got her eye on Jason, I'd back off if I were you. You don't want to be on her bad side."

Anyone—especially someone I didn't even know—deciding who I could or could not be friends with rubbed me the wrong way. But I didn't want to make any waves before I'd even settled in. For now it seemed safer to just change the subject.

"Should we finish the tour?" I asked.

"You know, I think we *have* finished," Nicole replied. "I've already shown you the most awesome stuff. I only skipped the boring things—the library, the museum, the classrooms—and you're going to see all that when classes start anyway. Besides, you must be starving. What do you say we head back to our room, order some food, and have a

Vampire Diaries marathon? Damon is so hot, am I right?"

Even though I'd never actually seen the show, I nodded. After the long plane ride, the earthquake, and the gossip-filled tour around my strange new home, going back to the room to just relax and eat with my roommate sounded like heaven. "Let's do it," I cried, genuinely excited.

Only, instead of the one-on-one roommate bonding I'd been expecting, Nicole made it a party by inviting the rest of the girls who lived on our floor of the dorm. Since the *Vampire Diaries* marathon went on so long, everyone changed into their pj's and the whole thing turned into a big slumber party. It was actually fun, and my dorm mates all seemed nice enough. But I found myself feeling nervous all over again. I was wearing mismatched Hello Kitty pants and a tank top, and they were wearing La Perla silk pajamas.

For the rest of the night I did my best to mimic their casually chic vibe. I wasn't sure I would ever fit in with this group, but as we dug into our slices of pizza and watched the show, I realized that I wanted to fit in.

And if I played my cards right as Nicole's protégée, I just might.

chapter 4

THE NEXT MORNING, WHILE NICOLE GRUMBLED ABOUT having to wear our school uniforms, I put mine on with a sigh of relief. At last I looked just like everyone else. But as we filed into the spacious auditorium for assembly, I gazed out at the sea of knee-high socks, blue and gray pleated skirts, and crisp white shirts and felt sad. It would be so easy to lose myself in this crowd. Only the jaguar, which I wore around my neck, as I'd promised Aunt Teppy I would, reminded me that I was still me—Ana Cetzal. Subconsciously, I reached up and rubbed it between my fingers.

"Welcome, students!" Principal Ferris called out from the podium once we'd all settled into our seats. Her smile was as bright and cheerful as the day she'd shown me to my room, and she wore a formfitting beige pantsuit with delicate pearl-drop earrings. *So she's Jason's mom*, I thought, searching for similarities. I glanced around, hoping to catch a glimpse of him, but the room was too packed.

"It's wonderful to see so many familiar faces, and a few new ones too." Principal Ferris scanned the crowd and smiled right at me for a moment. "I trust you all have made the most of your summer vacation. Show of hands—how many of you read the books on our recommended summer reading list?"

When one girl up front enthusiastically raised her hand, Nicole tittered beside me and whispered, "Brownnoser."

I pretended I hadn't heard her.

"Now, normally I would use this first morning assembly to discuss our goals for the year," Principal Ferris continued. "But I have exciting news that I simply can't wait to share."

"Probably just another big alumni donation. Happens all the time," Nicole mumbled, adding an exaggerated yawn. But what Principal Ferris said next made me sit up and take notice.

"As you know, we experienced a minor earthquake yesterday afternoon."

So I wasn't crazy! The ground *did* shake yesterday.

"Well, as one of our teachers discovered last night while walking the grounds," Principal Ferris continued, "the earthquake collapsed a cliff side on the north end of the campus near one of the hiking trails and revealed something rather astonishing: an ancient temple carved into the rock!"

The room erupted into gasps and whispered conversations. Even the teachers, who'd been standing on the sidelines like stone sentries, seemed to come to life at the announcement.

"Though we obviously haven't had time to verify this definitively, we do suspect that the temple is Anasazi in origin. As I'm sure Ms. Benitez could tell you"—she gestured to a pleasant-looking woman with shoulder-length brown hair and wire-rimmed glasses hanging from a long chain around her neck—"it has long been known that the Anasazi people were active in this area as far back as fifteen hundred BC, but this is the first indication that they may have lived right here on what is now Temple Academy! Needless to say, this is quite a coup. Temple has always valued the history of the many cultures that have enriched our lives, but now we can say that our fine campus is also an actual archaeological site."

She started clapping, smiling from ear to ear, and we clapped along with her. I wished Uncle Mec and Aunt Teppy were there with me. They would have been more interested in the uncovered temple than anyone. I wondered what they were doing right then. I zoned out for a minute, trying to picture them sitting at our blue kitchen table, poring over the newspaper together, drinking fair-trade coffee. By the time I refocused, Principal Ferris was waving a tall, dark-haired man with gray patches of hair over his ears onto the stage. I'd never seen him before—not even in the welcome packet, which featured pictures of every member of the faculty.

"I am delighted to introduce a very special guest speaker, Dr. Richard Logan, who will be the lead archaeologist working on the site. Please give Dr. Logan a warm Temple Academy

45

welcome." Once again, she led us in a round of applause as Dr. Logan replaced her behind the podium and adjusted the microphone so that it angled up toward his chiseled face.

"Thank you, Principal Ferris," he said. "And thank you all for the welcome." He straightened his tie and shook his head, as if he still couldn't believe what had happened. "I must tell you," he began, "the news of this temple's discovery was so exciting that I hopped on a plane last night so that I could arrive here first thing this morning. As Principal Ferris mentioned, the Anasazi—or Pueblo peoples, as they are sometimes called—did once populate the Southwest in significant numbers. But to find an actual temple, well . . ." He shook his head again and smiled, revealing a row of perfect white teeth. "It's a rare and extremely important find."

He nodded to someone standing on the left of the stage—his assistant, I guessed—who used a remote to roll down a large screen from the ceiling, then pressed a few keys on a laptop. Suddenly a picture appeared on the screen behind Dr. Logan's head: an entire city carved out of sand-colored rock beneath a jet-black ledge.

"What you see here is the Cliff Palace, located in the Mesa Verde National Park in Colorado, discovered in 1888. Notice how the structures were built into the cliff, which we believe was done to protect them from the elements and from outsiders."

He went on to talk about how the Anasazi were known as

the "Basket Makers." He said they were farmers and pioneers in building irrigation systems. He showed slide after slide of all the treasures they had left behind—the pictures they'd drawn on cave walls, the bowls decorated with intricate designs, the baskets woven tight enough to hold water. Then a final slide came up, this one of what the earthquake had uncovered on the far side of the campus. I could only see pieces of it since so much was still buried in rock and soil, but the parts I could see were incredible. It looked almost like the pictures that Uncle Mec had shown me of the Mayan ruins of Chichen Itza in Mexico. There were heavy stone stairs leading up and out of sight and skulls etched into the base, like a warning.

Dr. Logan nodded once more to his assistant, who typed something on his laptop and pointed the remote control. The screen darkened and ascended back into the ceiling. "The Pueblo people may have begun as humble farmers," Dr. Logan said, "but I think you'll find this temple indicates that they aspired to greater levels of spiritual enlightenment and power. I can only hope this excavation proves enlightening for us all."

We applauded as Principal Ferris rejoined Dr. Logan on stage and shook his hand. She then stepped up to the podium and waited until we quieted down. "Thank you, Dr. Logan, for that fascinating insight. I'm sure all our students will be interested in seeing how the excavation unfolds. And now for one last piece of school business before I bring this assembly to a close." Her lips tightened the slightest bit and her normally eighty-watt smile dimmed to a low sixty. "I'm afraid there have been reports from several students of small items that have gone missing from their bags. I truly hope this is simply a misunderstanding and these things have been misplaced. But if that is not the case, let me make our school policy perfectly clear: Any student caught stealing will be immediately and permanently *expelled.* No exceptions. Is that understood?" When no one made a sound, she gave a curt nod and said, "Good."

I wondered who would need to steal anything when all the students seemed incredibly wealthy. Were there other *normal* students like me? And if so, was one of them jeopardizing her position here by stealing? I hoped not.

At last we were dismissed and I made it to my very first class: history with Ms. Benitez. Thankfully, Nicole and Jessica were in the same class, so they led me through the hallways, saving me from wandering around aimlessly, or even worse, using the welcome-packet map. As I sat down in an old-fashioned wooden desk near the center of the room, all I could hear anyone talk about was the Anasazi site.

"Seriously, how major is that temple?" said Lorna, one of the girls Nicole had introduced me to the day before. "Do you think this could be on the news?"

"Probably," Nicole answered, sounding unimpressed. "You heard Dr. Logan. The site is a 'rare and extremely important find.'"

"Well, I think Dr. Logan is the rare and important find,"

said Jessica, pulling her red hair up into a ponytail. "How cute is he?"

"So cute I'm thinking about becoming an archaeologist," said Sindu. "If that's what archaeologists look like, sign me up!" They all dissolved into giggles.

Are they really all gaga over Dr. Logan? I thought. Maybe it had been a mistake to make Temple an all-girls school. They were clearly so unused to seeing boys around that any guy looked like Ryan Gosling to them—even a geeky-looking grown-up like Dr. Logan.

Ms. Benitez, who had walked into the room and now stood at the front of the class, listening to all this talk with an amused look on her face, said, "Well, ladies, I'm glad you're all so interested in this—for whatever reason." She raised an eyebrow at Jessica, who bit her lip bashfully. "So, why don't we go take a closer look?"

A few minutes later we were all walking in the soft reddish dirt that surrounded the unearthed temple. Dr. Logan and his team had cordoned it off with ropes and yellow cautionary tape, and there were two women dusting off the steps with small brushes. With every swipe, the line of skulls came into clearer focus. I wondered if maybe they should have been trying to cover them up instead. I knew that ancient Mayans believed that skulls represented fallen enemies and would grant them eternal life. But what did they mean for the Anasazi?

I asked Ms. Benitez, and she looked thrilled that I was

actually interested. "Excellent question," she said. "There could be many meanings behind the skull images. Some say they were a means of honoring their ancestors and calling on their spirits. Some say they were simply meant to scare off outsiders. What do you think the skulls mean?"

"I think they mean a bunch of people died of boredom here," said someone behind us. We turned to find Nicole and a group of her friends blinking innocently at Ms. Benitez, as if none of them had said a word. But as soon as the history teacher turned back toward the ruin, a sly smile spread across Nicole's face and she winked at me. Meanwhile, a few of her friends pulled out their cell phones and started texting. I didn't get it. The biggest archaeological event in a century was happening right in front of them, and they couldn't have been less interested.

At the risk of forever being labeled a nerd, I caught up to Ms. Benitez and whispered, "I'm sorry about that. I'm sure they didn't mean it."

"I'm sure they did," Ms. Benitez said with a weary smile. "But don't be sorry. I'm used to it. Not many kids your age get how exciting and relevant the past can be. Not many adults, either."

"How do you deal?" I asked. "Doesn't it make you want to quit and, I don't know, run off to Hawaii or something?"

Ms. Benitez let out a surprised laugh. "I admit, Hawaii sounds tempting sometimes. And trying to make others appreciate history the way I do can be frustrating. But that just makes having a student like you all the more rewarding." She stopped walking then and tilted her head in my direction. Her brown eyes were filled with such warmth that for a moment I thought she might hug me. "I'm so glad you're here, Ana."

I was startled. She hadn't even taken attendance yet before she brought the class outside, so how did she know my name already? Maybe I was the only kid she hadn't taught before, but she was gazing at me as if she had known me for years, instead of only a few minutes. Either she was psychic, or she had been expecting me. But I shook off that crazy thought as quickly as it had come. *Paranoid much?* a voice that sounded a lot like Nicole's echoed in my head. *She's probably just psyched that someone here isn't bored to tears.* Besides, according to the letter they'd sent to the house, Temple Academy was an exclusive place and they didn't admit many new students each year. So maybe my arrival had been a bigger deal than I knew.

We all watched the excavation team for a while longer, until Ms. Benitez announced that it was time to return to the classroom. She fell to the back to wrangle the stragglers, so I found myself walking ahead. Somehow I ended up next to Nicole and a group of the girls who'd spent the past twenty minutes texting.

"Lin, your bag is killer. Is it Coach?" Nicole said to a pretty Chinese American girl with shiny black hair pulled up into an elegant chignon. Her bangs swept across her forehead at a perfect forty-five-degree angle, and I had a feeling the diamond studs in her ears and the bracelet circling her wrist were real. Even in her school uniform, she looked like she belonged on a red carpet in Paris.

But when Lin turned to glare at Nicole with eyes that were so brown they were nearly black, I recognized her immediately. It was the same girl who had been spying on Jason from the bleachers. She lifted the bag that had been resting in the crook of her arm and let out a harsh puff of air, as if Nicole had just insulted her in the worst way. "*Coach?* Please. Coach is so over. Anyone can get a Coach bag these days. This is a limited-edition Marchesa."

"Oh, totally." Nicole scrambled for words, clearly trying to save face. "I was just kidding about Coach. Gag, am I right? What I meant was, how did you score the new Marchesa? Isn't there, like, a two-year waiting list?"

Lin flashed a smug smile. "When your father is the ambassador to China and your mother is China's most successful actress, there *is* no waiting list."

While the other girls oohed and aahed over Lin's designer bag and expensive jewelry. I had to turn away so no one would see me roll my eyes. This was the girl that Nicole had described just the day before as a spoiled-rotten brat who everyone sucked up to only because her parents had "more money than God." She'd said it with such disgust, and yet now it looked like Nicole was the biggest suck-up of them all. How many faces did my roommate have?

"Gee, Lin. Thanks for reminding us again who your parents are. I think it's been a whole five minutes. I'd almost forgotten!"

Lin looked coldly at the dark-skinned, athletic-looking girl to her left. I noted that, unlike Lin, she didn't have a single accessory on her body, and her hair hung in loose natural waves just past her shoulder blades. She hadn't even rolled the waistband of her skirt to show a little more leg like most of the girls had. I liked her instantly.

"You're just jealous, Doli," Lin told her. "My parents are famous and respected, while yours sell cheesy souvenirs on some rinky-dink Indian reservation. Deep down, you know you don't belong here."

"*I* don't belong here?" Doli raised her eyebrows and pointed one slim finger at her chest. She had been slouching a little, hunched in that way tall girls sometimes do when they want to seem less intimidating. But when she straightened her back and lifted her chin, she towered over Lin. "You must have been asleep during assembly today. That temple back there means I'm the *only* one who belongs here!"

"Oh, give me a break," Lin said, then sucked her teeth and flicked her hand dismissively. "I was wide awake during Dr. Hottie's speech, and he said the temple was Anasazi, not Navajo."

Doli, completely unfazed, sighed as if she were tired of explaining the obvious. "The Anasazi were an ancient people who lived on this land. In other words, they were my ancestors. Anasazi literally means 'ancient ones' in Navajo."

I wished I'd had a camera to capture the look on Lin's face when Doli schooled her into silence. It was priceless. But Lin knew we were watching her, so after a few seconds she twisted her lips into a snarl and narrowed her dark eyes. "How nice for you," she said in the iciest voice she could muster, then turned and sauntered away.

"Wait up, Lin," Nicole called, jogging after her like a puppy, along with the rest of Lin's entourage.

Doli just shook her head. "That girl has her nose so high in the air, she's going to get a nosebleed. Good thing Nicole will be right there to clean it up."

I knew I shouldn't laugh. Nicole was my friend—at least I thought so—and I was sure there was probably some unwritten rule about always having your roommate's back. But I couldn't help smiling. Especially since Doli was the first down-to-earth person I'd seen since I got here—except, maybe, for Jason. She noticed me fighting not to laugh and smiled back at me. Maybe I didn't have to work so hard at making friends after all.

When classes finally ended for the day, I trailed everyone else out of the academic building and toward the pathways to the dorms. We were still pretty far away when the sky darkened and thunder boomed like a cannon. Suddenly the clouds opened up and rain started pouring down in sheets. Lightning cracked overhead and for a second everything was bathed in light. It was just like the storm on my last night in Ohio.

The other girls around me screamed and ran to take cover under the nearest oak tree. I knew that was absolutely the worst thing you could do during a lightning storm, but in this rain, I thought I might drown before I ever reached the dorm. So I joined the others under the large tree, sandwiched between Lin and Nicole.

"Doesn't anybody have an umbrella?" Lin whined. Nicole frantically rifled through her bag for an umbrella I knew she didn't have. She glanced at Lin and shook her head apologetically. "This is ridiculous," Lin continued. "I'm calling Principal Ferris. If she doesn't want a diplomat's daughter getting sick because she was forced to walk in the rain between classes, she'll have to send Jason over with an umbrella."

"Why don't you just call your daddy?" Doli called from the other side of the tree. "He's so high and mighty. I'm sure he can make it stop raining so your precious Marchesa won't get wet." She laughed.

"Why don't you mind your own business, Doli? Better yet, call *your* daddy. I'm sure there's some anti-rain dance he can do."

"Watch it, Yang," Doli snapped.

Lin rolled her eyes but kept her mouth shut. She may have been mean, but she wasn't stupid. Instead of pushing her luck with Doli, she pulled out her smartphone. But as soon as she unlocked the screen and started dialing a number, the phone sizzled like bacon and died, the screen going black as the sky.

Her eyes bulged as she tapped the phone's surface in vain. "What is this? Ugh!"

"Maybe it got wet," I offered. "It only takes a drop or two of water and—"

She stared at me. "You're the new girl, right?" she interrupted.

"The name's Ana, actually."

Her gaze turned cool and she lifted her nose in the air. "You know, thunderstorms are really rare this time of year, New Girl. But we've been having all kinds of weird things happen lately. First there was the earthquake yesterday, now this. It all seemed to start when *you* showed up."

I sputtered. "You—you *must* be joking."

She gave me an evil-looking half smile. "Am I? You show up here with this demonic-looking lion necklace—"

"It's a jaguar!"

"—around your neck and suddenly the ground is splitting open and we're stuck in a monsoon. How do we know you're not carrying some kind of ancient Aztec curse or something?"

All the girls huddled under the tree laughed, and the person laughing the loudest was Nicole. That stung more than I wanted to admit. I could feel the heat rising up the back of my neck and flashing through my cheeks. But I wouldn't give in to embarrassment and let Lin walk all over me. Doli had stood up to Lin and survived, which meant I could too.

"It's not Aztec," I said.

Lin stopped laughing long enough to sneer at me. "What was that, New Girl?"

"It's not Aztec," I repeated, strengthening my voice. "The necklace—and my ancestors—were *Mayan*, actually."

"Like it matters." Lin shrugged. "They were all savages anyway."

For a moment I saw red. How *dare* she say something like that to me? If Uncle Mec and Aunt Teppy were here, they'd be furious. I backed away from the tree so I could look at the other girls gathered there, fully expecting to see outrage on their faces. But the only one who would even make eye contact with me was Doli, who gave me a sympathetic look. The others didn't seem to care at all.

The only thing I could do was pretend that I didn't either.

When the rain finally let up, I headed back to the dorm, feeling lonelier than I ever had before. Was that how they all saw me—as an outsider, a savage? I was glad that Nicole had gone somewhere to gossip with her friends so I had the room to myself for a while. I didn't want to give her the satisfaction of seeing me cry in front of her. I stood outside my room, looking at the small white name tag that told the world Nicole and I were roommates and, according to her, besties. *So much for that*, I thought. Just then I heard the heavy footsteps of someone climbing the stairs. I looked up and found Doli standing at the end of the hallway. The corner of her mouth lifted into a half smile. She gave me a look that said she knew what I was going through because she'd gone through it too. But neither of us uttered a word.

Eventually other footsteps sounded on the stairs, and Doli continued up another flight to her floor. I entered my room alone, grateful to finally be away from everyone. At that moment the only two people in the world I wanted to talk to were my aunt and uncle. I took my phone out of my book bag, where I'd stashed it before classes started. I pressed power and waited patiently as it came to life. Only when I saw the screen, which showed that I had no missed calls or text messages, did I realize that I hadn't heard from Uncle Mec or Aunt Teppy since I'd gotten to New Mexico—not even to make sure my flight was okay. *Strange,* I thought. That wasn't like them at all. I checked the time: 3:15 p.m. That meant it was 5:15 in Ohio. They were probably still driving home from work and wouldn't answer their cell phones in the car. So I opened my laptop and sent them a quick e-mail.

> *Hola, Tio y Tia,*
> I'm here! The flight was great, and everyone here is so friendly. I have a ton of new friends already. We even had a slumber party. The campus is out of this world. I can see why Mom and Dad liked it here. You could have warned me about the earthquakes, though. How do you not mention that the freaking ground moves? But even the earthquakes

have turned out to be cool. You might see this on the news, but after the one yesterday, they found an Anasazi temple right here at Temple. Ha! A temple at Temple. Funny, huh? Anyway, I miss you guys. Hope you're doing all right without your favorite kid around. Got to go hang out with my new friends now. They all love my jaguar necklace, by the way.
Les quiero,
Ana

I hit send before I could feel too bad about lying to my family. What good would it have done them to know what a rotten day I'd had? It's not like they could hop on a plane and come get me, and sulking wasn't my style. Besides, Lin may have been a pain, but she wasn't the only one who lived in this dorm. I cracked my door open and heard the sounds of other girls hanging out in the common room. They had turned on the TV, and I could smell the aroma of popcorn wafting up from the kitchen. Aunt Teppy always told me that the best revenge against people who are trying to make you miserable is to be happy. And that's just what I planned to be. I closed the door behind me and headed to the common room to join my new friends.

chapter 5

BACK IN MY OLD SCHOOL, WE WERE LUCKY TO GET WAXY pizza and frozen fish sticks for lunch. Now I sat at a table stocked with spicy tuna sushi rolls and ramen soup. And there wasn't a plastic spork in sight—only real silver spoons and forks, individually wrapped in cloth napkins, and porcelain chopsticks. But none of that was as weird as the fact that I was sitting with Nicole, Lin, and the rest of their friends. They'd invited me to lunch that day as if nothing had happened the day before.

"Are you sure you want to hang out with a 'savage' like me?" I'd said when Nicole asked.

She laughed it off like I was being silly. "Are you still on that? You've got to learn to take a joke, Ana." She jerked her head, gesturing for me to follow her.

I wish I could say that I held out for an apology. But I was bummed that I still hadn't heard from my aunt and uncle— *Have they forgotten about me already?*—and the thought of eating alone only made me feel worse. The good news was, Lin was just as rude to the rest of her friends as she'd been to me, and none of them seemed to take it too seriously. Maybe I *had* overreacted. Still, the longer I listened to them talk, the less I felt like I'd ever truly be a part of their group.

"Are you going to spend Christmas in Aspen again this year?" Tanya asked Lin. "My parents are buying a chalet there. We could meet up over break."

"Doubtful," Lin answered. "Aspen has been done to death. Besides, it looks like my mother will be filming her next movie in Shanghai, so I'll be there. I'll have to spend hours on set with that awful craft-services food." She rolled her eyes as if the whole thing was such a bother.

"I'd kill to be either one of you," Tammy chimed in, picking up a California roll with her chopsticks. "I'll be in boring old Beverly Hills, as usual."

"What about you, Ana?" Jessica asked, turning to me. "Where did you say you were from again?"

I hesitated, racking my brain for anything that would sound more glamorous than "Cleveland." "Oh, um, I live on the East Coast," I said. *Well, near it, anyway.*

"I love New York City. Have you been shopping at Henri Bendel?"

I had never heard of this Henri person, let alone shopped at his store. I did my best imitation of a Lin shrug. "Who hasn't?"

Before they could ask me anything else, I excused myself to go get a bowl of red-bean ice cream from the dessert bar. I guessed chocolate chip cookies would have been too common. By the time I got back, the conversation had moved on to tennis lessons and charity balls, and of course more talk about Lin's famous mother and diplomat father—Nicole and the others listening with rapt attention. I breathed a sigh of relief. Lin's self-centered babble may have been annoying, but it also took the pressure off me. It was exhausting trying to fit in with these girls, and I wasn't sure how much longer I could keep it up.

Again I wondered how my own mom and dad had managed to do it. Had they lied their way through, pretending to be wealthy East Coast socialites? Or had Temple just been very different back then? I tried to picture them sitting in this fancy dining room together, cloth napkins folded over their laps, heavy polished silverware in their hands. But maybe when they were here it had been a normal school cafeteria with hard white benches and plastic utensils. Maybe instead of drinking tea from delicate china cups, they'd had cardboard cartons of milk with cartoony pictures of cows on them. Or maybe it hadn't been different at all, and my mother and father were just like the girls that surrounded me now—privileged, shallow, and completely alien to me. It was possible that the picture of them sharing a scarf in the falling snow was the lie. All I knew was that the harder I tried to picture my parents here, the blurrier their faces became. I thought coming to Temple Academy would bring me closer to them, but they felt further away than ever.

That afternoon, when classes were done for the day, instead of walking back to the dorm with everyone else, I told Nicole I had forgotten my book and had to go back to math class. But really I just wanted to get away and take a walk on my own. I let my mind wander as I made my way around the paths and across the athletic field until I felt my black shoes sinking into soft red earth. When I looked up I realized I'd come to the site of the Anasazi temple.

A team of archaeologists was hard at work, clearing away fallen rock and tagging objects as they pulled them from the dirt. Dr. Logan stood off to the side in a pair of jeans, the sleeves of his button-down shirt rolled up to the elbows. Though his boots were caked with dirt, his teeth were still so white, I probably could have seen them from space. When he noticed me, he smiled and waved me over. I ducked under the yellow cautionary tape and joined him at the base of the temple.

"You were one of the students from Ms. Benitez's class that came yesterday, right?" When I nodded, he said, "I knew it. I never forget a face. Couldn't stay away, huh? Well, I don't blame you. This is fascinating stuff. Just look at what we found this morning." He bent down and picked up a clay bowl that had black interlocking diamond designs covering the surface.

"When most people think of ancient civilizations, they picture simple folk whose only concern was function. Not so!" he cried, pointing his index finger toward the sky. "They were artists, too, and cared about aesthetics as well as utility."

I nodded again, almost entranced by the intricate patterns. When I finally looked away, my eyes landed on a fat gray vase that was shaped like a teardrop. There were figures carved into the side, though I couldn't make out what they were. "What about that one?" I asked, pointing to the vase.

Dr. Logan looked at the artifact, then looked back at me with a shrewd stare. "Ah. Good eye, Miss . . ."

"Cetzal," I supplied. "Ana Cetzal."

He studied me for a moment, then said, "You've picked out a very important piece, Miss Cetzal." He stooped to pick up the vase, blowing away a bit of dust at its neck. As he brought it closer, the abstract form I'd seen began to take shape.

"It's a cat," I said, surprised to find a common household pet on such an old piece of art.

"Very good," said Dr. Logan. "But that should be no surprise. Many cultures have worshipped cats as gods or conduits to the spirit world. Ancient Egyptians, for example, and the Ashanti people of West Africa. Like them, the Anasazi believed that cats represented enormous power."

"Even regular house cats?"

"I believe so, yes. But notice the elongated limbs here and the thick tail," Dr. Logan said, pointing to different parts of the drawing. "This particular piece more likely is an early rendering of one of the great wildcats—a lion, perhaps, or a jaguar."

My hand flew to my neck, tracing the curves of the turquoise jaguar hanging right below my collarbone.

Just then a flicker of movement off to the right of the temple caught my attention. It was a sleek black cat with blazing green eyes. As I watched, it disappeared into a nearby bush. I had to follow it. I'd always loved cats, though Uncle Mec had never let me have a real one because he was allergic. But I'd heard we were allowed to keep pets here at school, so maybe this cat could be mine—at least while I was in New Mexico.

"Thanks for showing me this, Dr. Logan," I said. "I should get going."

He nodded. "Of course, Miss Cetzal. Come back anytime." He gave me another big smile, then went to talk to one of the other archaeologists.

I made a beeline for the low shrubs where I had last seen the beautiful black cat. I couldn't go through the tangle of twigs and weedy branches as the cat had, so I circled around until I was on the other side of the line of bushes facing the jogging path. "Here, kitty, kitty," I called. Then I hunched over and made kissing sounds as I walked along, scanning the bushes for a flash of green. My lips were still puckered when I ran right into someone's legs.

"Should I leave you and the bushes alone?" Jason said, giving me a curious smile.

Well, that figures, I thought. I hadn't seen him all day, so of course he'd catch me blowing kisses to a shrub.

"Um, it's not what it looks like, I swear. I . . . I thought I saw a cat," I said, wishing I could vanish the way the cat had.

"Uh-huh, I believe you," he responded, then shook his head and mouthed, *No, I don't.*

I chuckled. "Fine. You got me. My name is Ana Cetzal and I am in love with this plant."

"Well, the first step is admitting you have a problem."

I smirked at him, holding back a laugh. Why did he make me feel so giddy, even when he was making fun of me? "What are you doing here, anyway?" I asked. "Hiding out from your many admirers?"

He blushed, which I hadn't even known boys could do. "Actually, I was just jogging around the valley when I decided to come check out the Anasazi site. I hear they have a lot more of it uncovered now."

"I just came from there," I said, pleased to find we had a common interest.

"So you've seen it," he said. "How cool is it that they found it right here at Temple?"

"Very cool," I agreed. "But I was starting to think I was the only one who thought so. My class couldn't even be bothered to stop texting and check it out."

"That's crazy," Jason said. "Don't think I'm a total geek but . . . after the site was discovered, my mom asked me to look up some facts about the Anasazi on the Internet, and now I'm kind of obsessed."

"Well, the first step is admitting you have a problem." I smiled.

"No, seriously. They were awesome! Did you know that they migrated a bunch of times over hundreds of years, from here all the way down to Mexico, but all their settlements were along the exact same meridian, one hundred eight? They didn't have compasses or anything, though. No one knows how they did it."

"Really? Is this school on that meridian?"

Jason shrugged. "Beats me, but I wouldn't be surprised. It's like they were magic or something."

I laughed. "Come on. Magic? You don't really believe in that, do you?"

"Honestly? I don't know," he said, scratching the top of his head. "Archaeologists have found wood in their cliff cities that could have only come from trees that were at least fifty miles away. Nobody can figure out how they did that without cars. So you tell me."

"Well, they probably just . . . I mean, maybe they . . ." I trailed off. I had no idea. "Okay, fine. They were magic."

"What? You believe in magic?" Jason said. "What a freak."

I knew he was joking, but his words brought to mind what Lin had said to me the day before. "You're not the only one who thinks I'm a freak. This girl Lin said the earthquake and yesterday's thunderstorm were my fault since they arrived around the same time I did. She said maybe I was carrying around some ancient Aztec curse."

"Lin Yang? Don't pay any attention to her. She's just jealous."

"Of me? Why?" I asked. "Her father is a diplomat and her mother is some kind of movie star. She has everything."

"Yeah, but she's been at this school for a while and nothing much has happened. But you show up, and things start getting interesting."

Before those final words were even out of his mouth, the ground began to tremble beneath our feet, and the trees swayed as if they were being shaken by invisible giant hands. Another earthquake! I screamed and latched on to Jason's arm until it was over. When the rumbling finally stopped, Jason glanced down at his arm, which my hand was still clutching for dear life. He looked up, into my eyes, smiled, and said, "See what I mean? When you're around, the earth moves."

chapter 6

"GET THOSE LEGS UP, LADIES! NICE AND HIGH. No dawdling, Patrice! Pick up the pace, Tammy! Go, go, go!"

I listened to Coach Connolly's voice blare through the megaphone as I rounded the track during PE class. I'd only done one lap and already my lungs were burning in my chest and sweat poured down my back. The blazing sun seemed to be sitting right on my shoulders. But I kept my legs pumping and focused on keeping pace with the rest of the girls. I wasn't exactly a track star, but at least I wasn't dead last. There were five girls behind me, some barely jogging, with their arms up and hands hanging limp, like a T. rex's. Way out in the lead was Doli, who ran as though she'd been born running, taking long, graceful strides and easily leaping over the hurdles that were spaced several feet apart on the straightaway. I noticed Coach Connolly keeping track of Doli's time on a stopwatch.

When we'd all completed two laps, the coach blew the

whistle hanging around her neck and told us to gather on the grassy area inside the track.

"That was a good run, ladies," she said. "Those of you who ran *around* the hurdles instead of *over* them"—she raised her eyebrows and shot some of the girls a knowing look—"don't think you got away with anything. You'll do extra laps next time. In ten minutes we'll do two-person relay races. But for now, pair off for buddy stretches. Face each other with your legs extended in a V, feet touching. Hold hands and pull back and forth like you're rowing a boat. You should feel it in your hamstrings."

She blew the whistle again, and immediately the others began turning to one another, pairing off one by one with their friends. Within seconds everyone was taken except Doli and me. She approached with a confident smile. "Hey. Ana, right?"

"Yeah. And you're Doli?"

She nodded. "That's me. Looks like we're the only ones left. Want to be my partner?"

"Sure," I said, relieved that I'd found a buddy, even if it was only for buddy stretches.

We got into position, pressing the soles of our sneakers together and rowing back and forth. "So are your ancestors really Mayan?" Doli asked as she pulled me toward her. My face must have registered surprise—*Does everyone know everything about me?* But she laughed and said, "I heard you tell Lin the other day."

"Oh, right." I shook my head and rowed backward. "Then I guess you know the earthquake and that thunderstorm were both all my fault too. Lin says I'm cursed."

"Classic Lin," said Doli, frowning. "I wouldn't worry about her or what she thinks. She's not the kind of friend you want anyway."

"What do you mean?"

Doli squinted her eyes against the sun as she met my gaze. She seemed to be sizing me up, deciding if she could trust me. Finally she released my hands and folded in her long legs. "I know it seems like I give Lin a hard time, but that's only because she gives me one. She knows I'm here on scholarship, and she never lets me forget it."

"Really?" I said, shocked. I'd thought I was the only one who wasn't rich. "Is it an athletic scholarship? I saw Coach Connolly timing you."

"Well, track is why Temple recruited me. Coach works with me whenever she can to get me ready for the meets. I may even try for the Olympics someday. But the scholarship was a total surprise. You can't believe much of what comes out of Lin's mouth, but she was right that my parents live on a Navajo reservation. Last year, after I got the letter inviting me to Temple, I found out that this Navajo charity had given me a full scholarship. Good thing, too, since there's no way we could have come close to affording it otherwise. The whole thing really freaked me out, though, since I hadn't even applied. But my parents were so happy, I didn't question it. And here I am."

I was floored.

"The same thing happened to me," I said quietly.

"You got a full scholarship from a Navajo charity?" Doli raised one eyebrow skeptically.

"No." I looked down and picked at the blades of grass in front of me. "I got one from my parents. They left me the money for tuition . . . in their will."

Doli's face fell. "I'm so sorry," she said. "I didn't know."

"That's all right." I shrugged one shoulder. "I live with my aunt and uncle now, and they're great. My parents died a long time ago, when I was really little. I don't even remember them, to tell you the truth. But I know they wanted me to come to Temple Academy. So here *I* am."

"Huh," Doli said, swiping her forehead with her arm. "I guess that makes two things we have in common."

"Two?"

"Your necklace. It's a cat, right?"

I hadn't realized that when I'd bent over to do the stretches, the necklace had fallen out of my T-shirt and was resting against my chest. I cradled it in my palm, the turquoise carving cool even in this heat. "It's a jaguar. My aunt and uncle gave it to me. Aunt Teppy told me never to take it off so they could always be with me." Feeling like I had just said something unforgivably lame, I added, "It's a Mayan thing."

But Doli just nodded seriously as if she understood completely. She reached into her own T-shirt and pulled out a necklace. I couldn't hide my surprise. She had an accessory after all. Dangling from the end of a thin leather loop was a small carving of a cat in midleap. "Must be a Navajo thing too, because my parents also gave me a cat to wear. Only, this one's a puma."

"Why did they give you a puma?" I asked.

"They said it was to keep me safe. My people believe that pumas are protectors—guardians. But really I think they just wanted to give me something that would make me feel close to them."

"Your mom and dad must miss you a lot. How far away is the reservation?"

"That's just it!" Doli laughed. "It isn't far at all. The reservation is right outside the Temple Academy grounds. If I had a pair of binoculars, I could probably see my parents from my room."

I laughed with her for a second, but my longing must have been written all over my face. Doli stood up and gazed down at me. "What's the matter?"

"Nothing." I ripped more blades of grass from the ground, shredding them into confetti. "I just wish my aunt and uncle were that close by. They're all the way in Ohio, and I miss them like crazy."

It was a risk telling her these things. Not only had I revealed that I was from glamour-free Ohio, but I'd exposed myself as the homesick kid I was instead of the independent New York debutante I'd been pretending to be. But Doli and I had so much in common; somehow I knew she wouldn't hold it against me.

She drew her lips in with that same look of compassion I'd seen earlier in the hallway of the dorm. For a few moments we let the silence stretch out between us, until Coach Connolly blew her whistle. At last Doli reached down and clamped her hand around my forearm. With one strong tug, she pulled me to my feet. "Come on, Ana," she said. "Let's team up for this relay race and show these girls how it's done."

After class ended and we'd showered and changed back into our uniforms, Doli and I walked out of the locker rooms together. She was practically bouncing up and down, she was so excited. "Did you see how we left those other teams in the dust?" she said. "Tammy hadn't even finished her first lap when you crossed the finish line."

It was true. We made a pretty powerful team. Even I found it hard not to gloat. "Aw, give the other girls a break," I said with a laugh. "I was the only one with a future Olympian on my team."

"True, true," said Doli, taking a bow, her arms spread wide. "But I think I'll wait till later to sign autographs, if you don't mind. Right now, I need food! Want to get something to eat?"

"More than anything," I replied. All that running had worked up my appetite. "But do we have to go to the dining room? My legs are so shaky, I'm not sure I could make it that far. Not to mention I'm not in the mood for sushi or Cornish game hen. Doesn't this place have any regular food?"

Doli laughed. "No problem. There's food in the kitchen back at Radcliff, and I know how to cook a little bit. How do grilled cheese sandwiches sound?"

"Like heaven!"

We walked back to the dorm, chatting like old friends the whole way. It felt good to find someone I could really talk to. After Doli made the sandwiches, we sat in the kitchen devouring them and talking about life at Temple until we heard someone clearing her throat.

I looked up to see Nicole standing in the doorway with her arms crossed, an annoyed expression on her face. "There you are, Ana. I've been looking for you. Why didn't you come eat with us in the dining room?"

When I didn't respond right away, Doli jumped in. "We had a real craving for grilled cheese after our relay races. You should have seen it. We rocked that—"

"Excuse you, but I was talking to Ana," Nicole said, sneering. "Don't you have some studying to do, Doli? You've got to maintain that C average if you want to keep your scholarship, right?"

I was mortified. I couldn't believe how awful my roommate

was being to my new friend. I registered a glimmer of hurt in Doli's eyes, but she quickly steeled herself, snatched up the rest of her sandwich, and rose to leave.

"Doli, wait," I called. "You don't have to go—"

But she was already halfway up the stairs. "I'll see you later, Ana," she called without turning back.

After she had gone, I glared at Nicole, waiting for the apology I was sure would come. But she said nothing.

"What is wrong with you?" I cried after a moment. "Why were you so rude just now?"

Nicole blinked in surprise, touching her hand to her chest. "*Moi?* Rude? I don't think so. You were the rude one for standing us up. I mean, seriously. Major faux pas, Ana, ditching us for Doli Haskie of all people. What are you *doing*?"

"I was having a nice lunch with a friend until you showed up," I snapped. Having lost my appetite, I dumped the rest of my sandwich in the trash, circled around Nicole, and sped up the stairs to my room. But of course it wasn't *my* room, it was *our* room, and she was right on my heels.

"Don't you get it?" she continued. "I'm trying to help you. Hanging out with Doli is social suicide."

"Says who?"

"Says Lin Yang. She can't stand Doli, and that's enough to make her a pariah on this campus. Haven't you even noticed how hardly anyone talks to her besides her juvenile delinquent roommate, Shani?"

I flashed back to gym class, when everyone was pairing up. Was that why only she and I were left standing? I'd thought the other girls were intimidated since she was so much better at track. But maybe that hadn't been the reason. Maybe thanks to Lin, Doli had needed a buddy just as much as I had.

"Shani's some kind of nutcase who's been kicked out of eight different boarding schools, so it figures that she'd like Doli. But you don't have an excuse. Besides," Nicole went on, "that girl doesn't even belong here."

"What's that supposed to mean?" I said, feeling the control I had over my anger begin to slip.

Nicole opened her mouth to say something, then seemed to think better of it and closed it again. Finally she crossed her arms and said, "If you don't know, I'm not going to spell it out for you. But you should do yourself a favor and take my advice: Stay away from Doli. I wouldn't steer you wrong. You're my protégée!"

"So this is you looking out for me?" I shot back.

"*Naturellement!*"

"Well, thanks, but no thanks."

Nicole sighed as if she were an underappreciated mother. "Fine," she said. "Do what you want. But don't say I didn't warn you."

I wanted to tell her that I didn't need her warnings or her advice about who my friends should be, but instead I just turned away. I could tell that arguing with Nicole about this was pointless. Good thing I had to go to my next class soon. I decided to quickly check my e-mail to see if my aunt and uncle had written me back, and then I would leave the room and stay gone for as long as I could. But when I sat down in my chair and moved to open my laptop, I noticed a square white envelope on the desk. It had the school's insignia on the front with my name written in blue ink beneath it.

"What's this?" I asked, picking it up.

Nicole, who had been checking her outfit in the full-length mirror on our closet door, turned to see what I was holding. "Oh, yeah," she said. "Our weirdo history teacher dropped it off for you. Looks like *she* wants to be your new BFF too!" She giggled in that snide way that lets you know someone is laughing *at* you, not *with* you.

I ignored her and tore open the envelope. Inside, I found a plain white card with a neatly printed note in blue ink.

Ana,

I hope you have enjoyed your time on campus so far. This evening I am holding a small reception for a select group of students to be held at the school's private museum. As the museum curator, I would like to acknowledge certain exceptional individuals who have much to contribute to the school. I would love for you to attend and allow me to properly welcome

you to Temple Academy. Please join us at the
museum at 8:00 p.m. I look forward to seeing
you then.
Sincerely,
Ms. Benitez

This is weird, I thought. Why would Ms. Benitez invite
me to a special reception? What made her think I was so
exceptional? I hadn't done anything yet, unless you counted
winning a relay race in gym class. But since, according to my
roommate, I was on the verge of becoming the new campus
outcast, I figured it might be a good opportunity to make
some friends besides Nicole. At this point, what did I have
to lose? I tucked the card into my book bag and left for class
without saying another word.

chapter 7

THE PRIVATE MUSEUM, LOCATED RIGHT NEXT TO THE tennis courts, was smaller than I'd imagined. Maybe because I'd been to the Cleveland Museum of Art so many times, I'd been expecting a massive entryway facing an even larger pool of water. But compared to the rest of the buildings on campus, this one was modest, except for the tall black steel gate that blocked the entrance. The gate was twice my height and had sharp spires at the top of each bar.

I peeked at my phone to check the time. I was ten minutes early. I hadn't wanted to wait around in my room with Nicole for one more minute. Besides, I was grateful to have something to distract me from the fact that I still hadn't heard back from my aunt and uncle.

I rang the buzzer outside and waited patiently. A few seconds later Ms. Benitez came out of the glass double doors and unlatched the gate.

"Ana! I'm so pleased you could make it," she said, and this time she did give me a quick hug. "Right this way."

She walked me back through the entrance into a dimly lit lobby with hard marble floors. Already I could hear the clink of glasses and the low hum of voices coming from an adjoining room. I looked up to find Ms. Benitez staring at my necklace. "That is a stunning jaguar carving," she said.

"Thanks. My aunt gave it to me." And just like that, a surge of homesickness hit me so hard that I teared up. How embarrassing. It was the last thing I wanted to do in front of this teacher who seemed to think I was exceptional, but I couldn't help it.

Ms. Benitez furrowed her brow in concern. She laid a comforting hand on my back. "Ana? Is something wrong?"

I swiped away a tear. "I'm sorry," I said, getting ahold of myself. "It's just . . . I e-mailed my aunt and uncle days ago and I still haven't heard back from them. I don't get it, because Aunt Teppy is good about checking her e-mail. I'm sure she got my message."

Ms. Benitez's dark eyes warmed with sympathy. "You know, Ana, many families don't contact students here during the first week because they know how busy you'll all be settling in."

"Yeah, not my family. Back home they checked on me all the time, even when I was sleeping. You've heard the term 'helicopter parents,' right? Well, it was invented for my aunt and uncle." Ms. Benitez laughed, but I couldn't join in. To me, nothing about this was funny. "It's like they've forgotten all about me," I said, feeling the tears threatening to spring up again.

"Oh, I'm sure that isn't true," Ms. Benitez replied, putting her arm around my shoulders and walking me toward the sounds of the party. "Anyone who would give you such a precious Mayan artifact to wear must love you very much indeed."

I glanced up at her in surprise. "You know something about Mayan art?"

"Quite a bit, actually," she answered with a smile. "I also know the Navarro family, especially your uncle Mecatl and your aunt Tepin."

I jerked my head back, rocked by this revelation. "You do? How?"

"We share a common interest in Mayan heritage. They have outbid me at more than one auction for priceless Mayan pieces like the one you're wearing around your neck. The fact that your aunt trusted you with such a special item means you must be very special to her too."

"If I'm so special to her, why hasn't she at least texted me to see how I'm doing?"

"Well, maybe she's just trying to give you room to thrive on your own."

I grunted, unconvinced. "If this is her tough-love way of making me miss them less, it isn't working."

Ms. Benitez squeezed me closer to her. "It's perfectly normal to be homesick, Ana. But you'll see. In time, Temple will feel like home. You *belong* here."

She said it with such confidence, I almost believed her.

"Now, please help yourself to refreshments and mingle with the other students. I'll be right back."

She gave my back a final pat, and smiled in a way that did make me feel like I belonged. But as I entered the reception room, all my doubts came flooding back. Hovering by the snack table, nibbling on chips and looking unbelievably bored, was Lin Yang, dressed to the nines, of course. When she saw me, her mouth fell open, and she eyed me with obvious distaste. I hadn't been able to bear asking Nicole to let me borrow her clothes again, not after the argument we'd had. So I was wearing my own jeans, a plain, red long-sleeved T-shirt, and a belt. I had brushed my hair for the occasion, but that was as fancy as I could get. The look on Lin's face said that it wasn't good enough.

Thankfully, on the other side of the room I spotted Doli, talking to a girl I didn't know. They both had on jeans, too. I made a beeline for them right away. "Am I relieved to see you!" I cried. "Is this everybody? I thought there would be more people here."

"Me too," said Doli. "It's good to know Shani and I weren't the only ones who got this bizarre invite, though. Oh, you guys haven't met yet, have you? Ana Cetzal, this is my roommate, Shani Massri."

I said hi, and Shani nodded and gave me a big smile. She had skin the color of red shale and a hank of blue hair hanging over her left eye. Tiny hoop earrings climbed all the way up the edge of her right ear. When she said, "What's up?" and waved, I noticed that she had a drawing of a complicated tangle of flowers on the top of her hand, one of the leafy vines traveling up her index finger all the way to the nail.

"Whoa, cool flower. Your parents actually let you get a tattoo?"

Shani's smile turned sly. "They insisted."

At my look of disbelief, she licked her thumb and rubbed the edge of her hand. Part of a vine disappeared. "It's temporary," she explained. "A henna tattoo. My mom did it for me the night before I came here and said it would last about a month. I just think it looks awesome, but she says henna on top of a person's hand is supposed to protect them or whatever."

"It's an Egyptian thing," Doli added with a smile. "I've been begging her to do one for me. Maybe a bluebird."

"Why a bluebird?" I asked.

"Doli means bluebird in Navajo," she answered. "I keep telling Shani how cool it would be to have a tattoo of one on my shoulder, but she claims she doesn't know how."

"And I keep telling you that I'm all about apps, not tatts," Shani said. "You're looking at the next Mark Zuckerberg, not an Egyptian Kat Von D. Besides, if you're going to get a tattoo that represents your name, you should go with your last name." She looked at me. "Haskie means warrior in Navajo. Now *that* would be sick."

"Not to change the subject," I cut in, "but what are we really doing here?" I lowered my voice. "And why is Lin here?"

"Your guess is as good as mine," Doli said.

Shani leaned in. "I hear she's been giving you grief. She's been torturing us for at least a year. So maybe this is some kind of intervention. About time!"

We all laughed. But when I glanced over at Lin, standing by herself, I felt like we were treating her just as badly as she'd treated us. Slowly I made my way to the snack table and grabbed a chip and a can of soda. Doli and Shani reluctantly followed and did the same.

"Hey, Lin," I forced myself to say.

She took a few seconds before saying, "Hello." Afterward we just stood, crunching in silence. It was the definition of awkward. Ms. Benitez came back in then, and she could not have reappeared at a better time.

"Ladies, I'm so glad to see you all here tonight," she began. "I've recently acquired some new pieces that I'm excited to show you." With that she waved us into the next room, which had copper plates in glass cases, oil paintings on the wall, and different-colored vases on freestanding podiums. She told us a little about each one, beaming with pride at having secured some of the harder to find pieces. "Many of these were gifted to the museum by former students," she explained. "We're very lucky to have them. In fact, our collection is so sought after that while we do display most of the items, we keep the most valuable ones in a large safe in the basement. As a special treat, I'm going to show them to you four now. Oh! I forgot. One of the lights has blown down there. I'll get a flashlight. Just give me one moment."

With that she ducked into an office at the end of the hallway and started rifling through a set of desk drawers. Meanwhile, the rest of us turned to one another, exchanging looks of total confusion.

"The basement?" Shani said. "Um, am I the only one who's afraid Ms. Benitez is a crazy ax murderer who's about to kill us and stuff us in the safe?"

Doli clutched my arm. "Oh my God, we didn't even tell anyone where we were going tonight. We're going to be on that show *Vanished* about people who just up and disappear."

"You guys are overreacting," I whispered. "Ms. Benitez is no ax murderer. She's just . . . trying to be nice. She likes us." Even I could hear the uncertainty in my voice.

Lin huffed. "So she drags us to a creepy museum basement in the middle of the night for a tour we didn't ask for? If that's what she does for people she likes, I wish she hated me."

"Give her time," Shani blurted.

We heard Ms. Benitez close the door to the office. "Found one," she called, holding up a flashlight. She waved us forward. "Come along, ladies."

Despite our hesitation, we boarded the freight elevator and rode down in uncomfortable silence. Only when we exited into the basement did Ms. Benitez speak.

"I'm sure you're all wondering why I chose the four of you, what you have in common."

"Other than the fact that we've been kidnapped?" cracked Lin under her breath.

"What was that?" Ms. Benitez asked.

"Nothing," Lin said, and bit back a nervous laugh.

Ms. Benitez walked farther into the basement and turned a corner, where we found a huge fireproof door. She turned to face us. "You are each fortunate to be descendants of important ancient civilizations. We are thrilled to have representatives from your fascinating cultures enrolled here at Temple."

"Oh brother," Lin mumbled, and rolled her eyes.

Lin was being a pill, as usual, but for once I sort of knew how she felt. Here I thought Ms. Benitez had seen something unique in our characters, but I should've known better. I was proud of my heritage, but why did I always have to be the representative for the entire Mayan civilization when all I wanted to be was myself?

"Each of your families," Ms. Benitez continued, "has donated a highly valuable item to the museum. I thought you might like to see how very special they are."

Baffled, I glanced at the other girls. Had they known about this? Judging by the confused looks on their faces, no. I racked my brain, but I couldn't remember Aunt Teppy or Uncle Mec mentioning anything about donating an artifact to the school. Why hadn't they told me?

Ms. Benitez turned to the door and typed in a long, num-bered code. There was a high-pitched beep and the door creaked open. Ms. Benitez entered and gestured for us to follow.

"Good-bye, cruel world," Shani whispered so only we could hear.

We found ourselves in a small room within the safe. Ms. Benitez pointed to a golden fan spread open on a black metal stand. Covering the silk folds were pictures of moun-taintops and bonsai trees. "This authentic Chinese fan was donated by your family, Lin. And this . . ." She walked to the opposite side of the room, where a beautiful woven rug hung from the wall. "This rug was donated by your parents, Doli."

"What?" she cried. "That makes no sense." She sped to the rug and examined it closely. "Why would they donate this? This rug is a family heirloom! And if it's worth any money . . ." She cast a glance at Lin, as if she knew what she was about to say would be held against her later. "My family can't afford to give it away. They're struggling. Why would they have given it to you?"

Ms. Benitez hurried to explain that the rug was just a loan. "It will be here at the school as long as you're here."

Doli frowned, clearly still puzzled. But she stayed quiet. To her credit, so did Lin.

"Shani, if you look in the corner behind you, you'll see your family's donation."

We all turned around. There to the left of the door we'd

entered through was a six-foot-high statue of a sphinx on a thick onyx platform. Shani, always quick with a joke, was rendered speechless.

"Like all sphinxes, it has the head of a man and the body of a lion. But usually the lion is lying down. A sphinx that is in a standing position, like this one, is quite rare."

I looked around the rest of the room but didn't see any more art pieces. "What about mine?" I asked. "What did my family donate?"

Ms. Benitez smiled and walked to the wall opposite the woven rug and flipped a switch. The back half of the room that had been draped in darkness came to light. There in the far corner was an object on a low pedestal. All four of us joined Ms. Benitez around it. It was a square vase with a large cat on each side. It occurred to me that the cats resembled the stylized one I'd seen on the vase at the Anasazi temple. The lid of this vase was shaped like a bat and was fastened to the base by four brightly colored stones.

"Are those real gems?" I asked.

"Oh, yes," said Ms. Benitez. "Rubies and emeralds, to be exact."

I couldn't have been more shocked. I thought I'd seen every piece my aunt and uncle had ever bought. "I've never seen this vase before," I said. "It looks like it's worth a fortune. Why would they have donated it?"

"I can't say for sure," Ms. Benitez responded. "But they were quite insistent that the vase accompany you to the school."

"Wait. You mean it showed up at the same time I did?"

She nodded. "Ladies, you should all be so proud of your respective cultures. All of the ancient civilizations that live on in you were known for having great power. In fact, many ancient peoples believed that power could be stored in inanimate objects and could be used for both good and evil. Now, if you follow me into the main room, I have one more very special object to show you."

She turned toward the open door at the end of the foyer and walked into the utter darkness beyond.

The four of us looked at one another with wild eyes. *What the . . . ?* Maybe Shani was right and Ms. Benitez was nuts. But as weirded out as I felt, I was also curious. I followed her into the room, with Doli, Shani, and Lin right behind me.

Once our eyes had adjusted to the blackness, I could see Ms. Benitez taking out a row of tall white candles and lining them up on a table. "Sorry it's so dark," she said. "I remembered the flashlight but forgot the batteries. We'll have to create light the old-fashioned way." She struck a match and lit the candles one by one. Soon the room was filled with a soft yellow glow.

She blew out the match and walked over to a protective glass case, which she opened with a key. Slowly, she pulled out a golden orb. I could have sworn it was pulsing with light, but that was probably just the reflection of the candles. "Come closer, girls," she said.

We inched toward her. I wasn't sure what Ms. Benitez was holding, but at least it wasn't an ax. As I neared, I could see there were etchings on the orb. "What is that thing?" I asked.

"In ancient times your ancestors were very powerful. If you look closely, you'll see that this orb outlines the territories of your people." She pointed each one out to us, tracing her finger along the thin lines. "Go ahead, take a closer look," she said, handing the orb to Lin. "Each of you take a turn and see if you can point out the territory of your ancestors that I just showed you."

Lin gazed at the orb for a few seconds, then touched one finger to the area that represented China. A tremor seemed to pass through her body and her face paled. She quickly passed the orb to Doli and took a step back. Lin seemed shaken, but when she noticed me watching her, she rolled her eyes and said, "Okay, I'm done. Can I go now? Some of us need our beauty sleep."

"Not yet," said Ms. Benitez. "We're almost done here. Just wait till everyone's had her turn."

While Ms. Benitez spoke, I watched as Doli took the globe from Lin and pressed her finger to the Navajo territory. It seemed like she, too, couldn't wait to pass the orb to Shani.

After Shani touched her finger to Egypt, she held the orb out to me, her eyes dark and serious. I hesitated, suddenly not sure if I wanted to touch the orb, but Shani pushed it into my stomach, and I had no choice but to wrap my hands around it. I lifted it up and touched the territory that had belonged to the ancient Mayans. Almost immediately, I felt a tingle race up my arm. It was like the pins-and-needles feeling you get when your arm has been asleep for a long time and is finally waking up. I caught Doli's eye and she stared back, bobbing her head the slightest bit, and I knew: She'd felt the strange sensation too.

After the bizarre round of hot potato, Ms. Benitez replaced the orb in the glass case and led us out of the basement and back to the museum's entrance. Before she pulled open the door to let us out, she stopped and gave us each a long look. "Girls, I really want you to take from tonight that your ancestry makes you powerful. And don't forget that, if anything . . . well, unusual should happen. All right, you should get back to the dorms. It's late. Thank you so much for coming."

With that she ushered us out the door and closed it behind us. I glanced at Lin and she swirled her finger near her ear. This time I couldn't argue. Ms. Benitez may not have been an ax murderer, but this evening she seemed completely insane.

Once we were safely outside the gates and far enough away from the museum that we felt free to talk, I said, "Unusual? What could be more unusual than what just happened?"

"I'm drawing a blank," said Doli.

"That's because that was the weirdest, most bizarro event to happen in the history of the world. Like, ever," said Shani. "And I'm speaking as someone who's seen what Doli looks like when she wakes up in the morning." She shuddered as if she'd seen something hideous.

Doli lightly punched Shani's arm. "How long were we in there, anyway? It felt like years."

I pulled out my phone and checked the time. It was only 9:15. I showed the digital clock to the other girls.

"Aw, are you kidding me?" said Lin. "I missed *Revenge* for *that*? Now *I* want revenge."

We all laughed. Who knew Lin could be funny? We walked the rest of the way back to the dorm in a semifriendly silence. Right before we went in, Shani turned to us and said, "I vote we keep what happened tonight to ourselves. At least until I've had some serious therapy and can make sense of it."

"Deal," I said, throwing my hand out, palm down. Shani slapped her hand on top of mine.

"Deal," Lin and Doli added in unison, adding their hands to the pile. I couldn't help but smile. Maybe we'd be at war with Lin again the next day. But for now, the super-weird evening had turned us into allies. At least until the sun rose and made this all seem like a bad dream.

chapter 8

BECAUSE I COULDN'T PUT IT OFF FOREVER, I WENT BACK to the room I shared with Nicole. As I stood in the hallway, preparing for round two with my roommate, I took a few deep breaths and tried to calm down. I felt odd, as though I'd eaten something that didn't agree with me. But dinner had been hours ago. Why would my stomach wait until now to revolt?

No. I wasn't sick. But I wasn't well, either. For starters, the lights in the hallways were so bright that I had to squint my eyes against the glare. And my nose seemed to be working overtime. I could smell everything—from the fruity scent of Nicole's mango shampoo to the faint hint of toothpaste and the remains of the grilled cheese sandwich that now lay at the bottom of the trash can downstairs. It was overwhelming. I rushed into my room to escape the almost painful sensory overload.

But inside the room was a whole different pain—in the

form of a beautiful blonde named Nicole. I'd been hoping maybe she'd be asleep when I got back, but she was wide awake and lying on her bed, flipping through a magazine. When I entered, she sat up and put the magazine on her lap. "So," she said, tossing her hair behind her shoulder, "how was Ms. Benitez's little party? Are you two sorority sisters now, or what? She's cray cray, you know. She can't find friends her own age, so she hangs out with teenagers. Total loser. But maybe you want that in a BFF." She gave me a toothy grin, like a shark who smelled blood in the water.

Suddenly I wasn't just annoyed with my roommate; I was disgusted by her. It took all my strength not to get up in her face and hiss something awful. *What is happening to me?* I thought. Was I becoming like Nicole in the worst possible way? I hoped not.

I turned away from her, deciding to ignore her jabs. Instead I'd do something constructive—I'd e-mail my aunt and uncle again. Better yet, I'd Skype them. Right before I left home I'd downloaded Skype onto Aunt Teppy's computer, but she'd found the whole thing confusing. After a half hour of me try-ing to show her how it worked, she'd said, "What's wrong with a good old-fashioned phone call?" I was sure that by now she'd figured it out, though. At least, I hoped she had. I needed to see their faces and hear my aunt's voice. I grabbed my laptop off my desk and opened it, and was immediately hit with the overpowering smell of mocha latte, Nicole's favorite drink. I looked down and saw light brown liquid pooled into the spaces between the letters of the keyboard, dried stains forming on the mouse pad.

"Wh-what happened here?" I sputtered, shocked. "Did you spill coffee all over my laptop?"

Nicole craned her neck to see her handiwork. "Oh, yeah. Sorry about that. It's just, the laptop was open on your bed, and I'm *such* a klutz that I tripped over the computer cord you left on the floor. You should really be more careful with that. I could've broken my leg, and a cast is so *not* the look for fall. The worst part is, I wasted a perfectly good mocha latte. Tragic, am I right?" She chuckled as if it were nothing and went back to her magazine.

I saw red. "You've ruined my laptop and you're worried about your cup of *coffee*?"

Nicole's head shot up when she heard the anger in my voice. "Chill, Ana. What's the big deal? Have the IT guy look at it, and if he can't fix it, just buy a new laptop."

"Are you insane?" I yelled. "Laptops are expensive! I don't have that kind of money. This laptop was a gift from my aunt."

Unfazed, Nicole put the magazine aside and stood up, widening her satisfied grin. "Come on now, Ana," she said. "You don't have to be coy with me. Lin texted me about what happened at the museum tonight. I know that your family donated a priceless piece of art to the school. Did you honestly think I wouldn't find out about it?"

At her words, I felt the tiniest stab of betrayal in my chest. I couldn't believe Lin had told her. I knew we weren't exactly friends, but things had definitely felt friendly between us by the time we got back to Radcliff Hall. She'd sworn, just like the rest of us, to keep what happened at the museum to herself. Lin wouldn't break her promise less than five minutes after making it, would she? But I immediately answered my own question. *Of course she would, and she obviously did.* I was naive to think our one hour of friendship had changed anything.

"What does my family's donation have to do with my laptop?" I asked.

Nicole scoffed as if astonished by my brazenness. "Here I was feeling sorry for you because you had nothing. I even let you borrow my clothes. But if your family could just give something as valuable as that vase away, then they must be loaded! They're probably richer than any of our families."

"That's ridiculous," I retorted, my anger simmering to a boil. "My family isn't loaded. They're just . . . normal. And they happen to collect Mayan art because they care about our heritage."

Nicole narrowed her eyes at me and closed the distance between us. "Whatever, Ana. You want to keep up this poor-little-orphan-from-the-sticks act? Fine. But don't expect any more sympathy from—"

Without a second thought I reared my arm back then

whipped it forward, swiping at Nicole with my fingernails. I felt a deep growl rumble up from my chest. Nicole dodged the blow just in time and my fingers sailed harmlessly past her pretty face. Had she been standing two inches closer, though . . .

I stepped back in horror. *I just attacked my roommate!*

Nicole slowly backed away too, covering her cheek with her hand as if I'd made contact and had left a nasty scar there. She was clearly in shock. "Have you even read your welcome packet?" she asked. "Temple has a no-tolerance policy when it comes to physical violence. Assault is grounds for permanent expulsion. If I told anyone what you just did—"

"No," I said in almost a whisper. "Please don't. It was a mistake. An accident. I didn't mean to. . . . I'm so sorry."

I reached out to touch her arm, but she flinched and backed farther away. Keeping both eyes on me, she grabbed a pillow from her bed and hugged it to her body like a shield. "I need some time to think. But I'd feel more comfortable if you slept somewhere else tonight."

I opened my mouth to plead my case one more time, but the grip she held on the pillow told me that she wouldn't change her mind. All I could hope for was that she wouldn't report me. As quickly as I could, I gathered up my own pillow and blanket and stacked my soiled computer on top. With any luck, I could wipe it off and get it running so I could reach my aunt and uncle and ask them to help me make sense of everything that had happened since I arrived.

The second I entered the hallway, Nicole slammed the door shut behind me and I heard the snick of a lock. I hadn't even noticed that we had a lock; we'd never used it before, and I didn't have a key. I squinted my eyes against the overhead light and made my way to the stairs.

I figured I would go to the common room and sleep on the couch. It wouldn't be comfortable or private, but at least I'd be away from anyone I could hurt. I replayed the scene in my mind—Nicole's sneering face, my hand lashing out. The image played over and over again in my head, like a Vine. I'd never, ever, in my entire life attacked anyone. I'd never even been in a shoving match. *So what were you thinking?* I shouted at myself silently.

But that was just it: I hadn't been thinking at all. That swipe felt more like some protective instinct taking over, the same way people's hands shoot out when they're about to fall, or the way your eyes snap shut when something flies at your face.

I headed down the stairs toward the common room and ran into Doli on her way up. She already had on her pj's— shorts and an old T-shirt. She held a toothbrush in one hand and an apple from the kitchen in the other. I was standing a few feet away, but I could smell the apple as if it were right under my nose. "Hey, Ana," Doli said, all smiles. But after taking in the pile I was holding in my arms and my defeated stance, her face tightened in concern. "What's going on?"

I told her what had happened with Nicole and how I'd

been banished from our room. "I don't even blame her," I said. "I'm going to sleep on the couch tonight. Maybe every night."

Doli groaned and gave me a sympathetic look. "No, you're not. You're coming with me. You can stay in our room. Shani has a sleeping bag you can use."

"That's nice, but really. You don't have to—," I tried.

But Doli grabbed my pile of belongings and started up the stairs. "You coming or what?" she called over her shoulder.

Shani and Doli's room was cozy and warm. Pictures of their families and friends were tacked onto corkboards over their beds, and they'd set the dimmer switch to its lowest setting, filling the room with a warm golden light. I was grateful that neither Doli nor Shani was the type of girl who used perfume. My nose was so sensitive right then, I didn't think I could have taken it. I sank into the plush gray carpet covering the floor, pulled my legs into my chest, and lowered my head to my knees.

"Ooh, that's not a happy camper," Shani said when she saw me. "What happened?"

"Eh, she tried to kill Nicole," Doli said matter-of-factly.

"Is that all?" Shani answered.

I looked up at them in disbelief, only to see that they were both smiling. "It's not funny, you guys! I could have really hurt her," I said.

Shani turned in her chair and lifted her bare feet onto the edge of her bed. "Okay, what did she do that made you so mad?"

I repeated the story, leaving nothing out. When I got to the part about how Nicole had broken my computer and didn't even care, Shani exploded.

"She did *what*?"

Doli slid my ruined laptop onto Shani's desk. "Exhibit A."

"Sacrilege!" Shani cried as she opened the laptop and turned it over in her hands. Drops of mocha latte dripped onto her desk. "I would have taken a swipe at her for this too."

"I'm not even sure that's why I did it," I said miserably. "It was like my hand acted on its own."

"Sounds like she had it coming, so don't feel so bad," Shani said. "I don't know if Doli told you, but I used to be Nicole's roommate."

"You were?" I got up off the floor and took a seat on Doli's bed. "What happened?"

"Pretty much what's happening to you," she said. "She was cool in the beginning, but then her evil streak came out. The insults and gossiping about me I could take. But then she started 'accidentally' erasing my voice-mail messages and hiding my homework so that I'd get in trouble in class. Petty stuff like that. I could never prove it, but I knew it was her. I would have gotten her back myself, but I've already been kicked out of a bunch of schools for doing stuff like that, and

I wasn't about to let her be the reason I got expelled again. Finally I begged Principal Ferris to just let me change rooms, and that's when she put me in here with Doli."

"An upgrade of major proportions, wouldn't you say?" said Doli.

"I would, my friend," Shani replied, giving her a fist bump.

"So I'm just the next victim." I bobbed my head, understanding the situation now.

"Guess so. But hey, look on the bright side: I happen to be something of a computer whiz, and I think I can fix your laptop. Plus, I know how we can get Nicole back without hurting a hair on her pretty little head."

I wish I could say I took the high road, but right then, revenge sounded pretty sweet.

"Do tell," I said eagerly.

chapter 9

SOMETHING EVIL LURKS IN THE JUNGLE. I'VE BEEN STALKING *it for some time, and i'm finally getting close. The creature ahead can sense me slinking through the grass, swimming through shallow pools of stagnant water, closing in on my prey.*

In the distance, a stepped pyramid towers above the tree line, and the sound of many voices chanting as one keeps time with a steady drumbeat. Though the leaves still drip with rainwater, the sun breaks through the clouds and heat sizzles on my skin. In the warm light of day I pick up the thousand scents of the jungle—wet earth, half-eaten pomegranates, animals . . . and an overpowering stench more terrible than anything I've ever smelled before. It taints the very air and makes me wrinkle my nose in disgust. I crouch low, preparing to spring. Ahead of me is death and destruction. I must stop it!

A gentle roar sounds nearby, and suddenly a puma emerges from the thick foliage. I'm not afraid. Somehow I know the puma is there to help me. But why? I search for answers in its large yellow eyes, but it lowers its head and pads silently to a nearby puddle. The puma looks at me and I know to follow, to crane my neck down and peer into the water. A golden cat's face covered in black spots stares up at me. I'm a jaguar? My heart thumps in my chest. I think of my aunt—the turquoise necklace she gave me, the jaguar I promised to keep with me always. . . . Is this a dream? It has to be. But I can't wake up.

The puma bites gently at my back and runs off through the trees. I trail after, eyeing its tracks in the dirt. Soon I pick up the scent—the smell of pure evil. Whatever it is, we have to find it. I watch as the puma leaps over a fallen tree and ducks beneath a curtain of hanging vines. I mirror its every move, and when I break through to the other side, I come face-to-face with a two-hundred-pound tiger. The big cat chuffs and shakes its massive head as a female lion stalks into the clearing. How is this possible? Why are we all here? As if in response, the lion bares her teeth and lets out a powerful roar. It's time to continue the hunt.

But then the wind parts the canopy of leaves around us, and I spot something through the trees—a sight so hideous that I sway on my paws.

There, only ten feet away, stands a demon I've never seen before, but he is as familiar as flame. He stands upright, his muscular body almost human, but his feet and hands are knife-like talons and his head is that of a rabid jackal. His long snout is filled with tiny razor-sharp teeth and his red eyes glow like fire. He wears the golden headdress of an Egyptian god, but his waist is wrapped with disintegrating ribbons of filthy gauze, and black beetles scuttle around his feet. He leers at us with an evil grin and lifts one bony arm. A scale hangs from his clawed hand—on one side is a pristine white feather; on the other, a red and beating human heart. The smell of its blood permeates the air.

I recoil, but some part of me wants the blood. When I hear the lion roar again, I remember my sacred duty. This evil thing doesn't belong in the mortal world, and we have to destroy it. I round my back and lower onto my haunches, letting the blood-lust fill my limbs until I ache to strike. The tiger, the puma, and the lion all crouch alongside me, poised to attack.

But suddenly a dark-faced creature explodes out of the trees and blocks our path to the demon. It's a hyena, menacingly loping back and forth, saliva dripping from its jaw. But its mocking laughter and unsteady gaze inspire no fear—just a desire to tear and rip and kill.

We attack the hyena at once.

The small scavenger is no match for us. The tiger falls on the hyena first, its heavy paws tearing into one scrawny leg, while the lion swipes at its back, shedding rivers of blood that soak the damp earth. The puma buries its teeth in the interloper's chest, as if trying to devour its heart. And I . . . I climb onto the doomed hyena's back and search for its throat.

When we are done, the hyena's body lies in pieces before us and I look up at the demon with blood caked into the fur around my mouth. I'm thrilled at my conquest, exhilarated— and horrified at how good it feels to tear another animal limb from limb. . . .

"NO!" I cried, sitting straight up as I tore away from the dream. I was panting hard, desperately trying to catch my breath. For a moment I didn't know where I was. But then I saw the sleeping bag and remembered. I was on the floor of Shani and Doli's room. I peered up at them in their beds. They were both still sound asleep, though they were tossing and turning, kicking at their sheets.

I touched my fingers to my lips. *I could still taste the blood.*

I jumped up and crept out of the room. I needed to splash water on my face and drown the metallic taste that lingered on my tongue. I entered the empty bathroom and turned on the faucet in the nearest sink, filling my hands with cool water. *That's better,* I thought. But when I looked up at the mirror, for one terrifying second I could swear I saw a pair of huge, slitted yellow eyes staring back at me.

chapter 10

THE NEXT DAY, STILL SHAKEN FROM THE NIGHTMARE I'D had, I went around in a daze, going from one awkward situation to another. First I had to knock on my own door so that Nicole would let me in to retrieve my uniform. "I'm warning you—I've got campus security on speed dial," she said, watching me from the doorway as I gathered my things. Then came my first class, which of course was history with Ms. Benitez . . . and Nicole.

I didn't know how to be around either of them anymore. I couldn't blame Nicole for being afraid of me. Even in my sleep I was dangerous. I couldn't get the nightmare I'd had out of my mind. In the light of day I wanted to dismiss it as just a stupid dream. But it had felt so *real*.

At least I still liked Ms. Benitez and knew that she cared about me. But it was clear she had secrets, and I wasn't sure that I wanted to find out what they were. I could tell that Lin,

Doli, and Shani, who were all in her class too, felt the same way. But we kept our cool as Ms. Benitez launched into her lesson.

Five minutes into it, Principal Ferris tapped on the door and strolled in. Following behind her was Dr. Logan, looking relaxed in a light linen suit. Jessica immediately straightened in her chair, a cheesy grin on her face.

"Principal Ferris, Dr. Logan . . . what a surprise!" said Ms. Benitez with an uncertain smile. "To what do we owe the honor?"

"I'm so sorry to interrupt your lesson, Ms. Benitez," Principal Ferris replied in her usual chipper tone, "but we're visiting every classroom to make this announcement personally." She turned toward us now and clapped her hands together. "Ladies, as you all know, the excavation occurring on our campus has turned into quite the national sensation, thanks in part to Dr. Logan." She gave him an almost flirtatious smile and twirled her earring like a shy teenager. "We've decided that the discovery of this important archaeological site is the perfect opportunity for the school to become more involved with the community. So we will be holding an exhibition for the local residents a few nights from now. We hope that—"

Like a nightmarish déjà vu, the room began to tremble. Pieces of chalk clattered to the floor and the windows vibrated in their frames. It was another earthquake. *What is going on?* I thought. One was bad enough, but this was the third one in less than a week. I glanced at Lin, thinking she might look at me as if I were causing it. But her eyes were on the rattling windows and the swaying trees beyond. I noticed the way her hand gripped her chair. *She's afraid,* I realized.

"Everyone, under your desks," Ms. Benitez called, but before we could move a muscle, the shaking stopped.

Somewhere far off, on the other side of campus, the dogs in the kennel began to howl. My ears pricked, listening to the mournful sound, even as I wondered how I could possibly hear the dogs all the way from here. I glanced at Ms. Benitez and saw her cock her head. I realized with a start that she could hear them too!

She turned to Principal Ferris and Dr. Logan and offered a weak laugh. "I guess you see why an exhibition might not be a good idea."

The principal returned a blank stare. "I'm sorry," she said. "Why is that?"

Ms. Benitez spread her arms, gesturing outside. "The frequency of these earthquakes has made it necessary for the museum staff to spend extra time to secure the pieces already on display. Otherwise, they could be damaged by the aftershocks. I'm not sure three days is enough time to secure a whole new exhibit. Besides, the excavation is still in its early stages. Do you really think it's wise to open the site to the public when there are so many priceless artifacts still being found and openly displayed?"

Principal Ferris nodded, taking in the history teacher's position with disappointed eyes. She turned to Dr. Logan. "Those are valid points. Dr. Logan. What do you think?"

Dr. Logan cleared his throat and said, "I can certainly understand your concern, Ms. Benitez. I'm sure the team I brought with me would be happy to assist in securing the exhibit so that should the earth shift again, the new pieces won't. And no one is more protective of the artifacts than I am. Every measure will be taken to ensure their safety. But as you and I have discussed many times, Principal Ferris, it would be an injustice to keep them locked away, hidden from the public."

Shani lifted her eyebrows at me in surprise. *Do Principal Ferris and Dr. Logan even know about the treasures that Ms. Benitez has hidden away in the safe beneath the museum?* the look said. It seemed unlikely.

"And let's not forget that this very school rests only yards away from a thriving Native American community, descendants of the Anasazi people, who I'm sure would love to see what their ancestors have left behind."

I glanced at Doli, but she stared straight ahead and sank down into her seat, looking uncomfortable.

"I suppose you're right," said Ms. Benitez, but she was still wringing her hands, and her smile was laced with worry.

Personally, I thought the exhibit was a great idea. It would be good to finally be around *normal* people for a change—people who didn't think Old Navy was the seventh circle of hell and who didn't own private islands. Besides, Dr. Logan was right—everyone deserved to see firsthand how incredible the Anasazi were. As a history teacher, Ms. Benitez should understand that better than most. So why did she look so upset?

After the adults spoke alone in the hallway for a few minutes, Principal Ferris and Dr. Logan left to continue their tour of the school, and Ms. Benitez reentered the classroom without them. She seemed to have put any lingering doubts about the exhibit behind her for the moment.

"Class, we have been given a wonderful opportunity to participate in the exhibit being planned. We will be putting together a display about the Anasazi and their way of life. I will divide you into groups. Decide among yourselves what aspect of Anasazi culture you choose to highlight." Usually, when we were divided in groups to work, she had us turn to the girls immediately surrounding us. But not this time.

"I will call out names at random," she said, but we all knew there was nothing random about the fact that Lin, Shani, Doli, and I were all in the same group. Lin moaned, whining that her ambassador father felt strongly that she could make her own decisions about whom she chose to work with, and her actress mother blah blah blah . . . but Ms. Benitez cut her off.

"Time is of the essence, Lin. So let's table this for now. You're all dismissed to the library for the remainder of the period. Meet with your groups and get to work."

As soon as the four of us were huddled in one corner of the library, Lin let out a wistful sigh. I noticed her usual clique, which included Nicole, whispering excitedly at the next table and figured she probably wished she were working with her friends. But since that couldn't happen, Lin looked at each of us in turn and said, "So, I call this first meeting of the Ancient Civilization Superpowers to order." She brought her fist down on the table like a gavel. The librarian shushed her.

The tension was broken and we all laughed as quietly as we could.

"ACS for short," added Doli.

Shani whispered, "Could she have been any more obvious about wanting us to work together?"

"I feel like she's some kind of cultural groupie," said Doli.

"Ew," Lin added sagely.

While they talked, I opened my newly revamped laptop in front of me. I had volunteered to search for facts about the Anasazi so we could choose a topic. I did genuinely want to learn more about the Anasazi, but I also wanted Nicole to see that my laptop was alive and well, no thanks to her. After I clicked on the Internet icon on my desktop, the school's log-in page automatically popped up, requesting a Wi-Fi password.

I typed it in, and the Temple Academy website came on the screen with a flourish. Along the top of the page were pictures of the campus and students raising their hands in class. Beneath that were links to access class schedules, articles about Temple, a link to the museum collection, and faculty contact information. I was just about to go to Google when a link at the very bottom of the page caught my eye. "Temple Academy Archives."

Of course. Why hadn't I thought of this before? The school had records and photos of the previous classes of students, which meant somewhere in here there might be information about my mom and dad. Maybe even photos.

Doli, Lin, and Shani were still riffing about the Ancient Civilization Superpowers, so I figured I had a couple of minutes. I clicked on a photo link that said "Temple Academy 1985–1990." I did the math in my head—my parents would have been here at the time. I did my best to tune out Shani's jokes about us making matching spandex ACS superhero uniforms, and Lin's complaints about how dusty the table was and whom could she call about that? It was harder to drown out the sound of someone at Nicole's table whining that the money in her wallet had disappeared.

Nicole scoffed. "Just have your parents send you some more," she suggested. "And stop carrying so much cash. *Ew.* Cash is over."

The girl groaned. "But my parents are already mad at me

for spending my book money on that vintage Chanel jacket. . . ."

My skin pricked with annoyance, and I was pretty sure Nicole's Flowerbomb bath gel was giving me a headache. But when a list of photos from different classes popped up, I focused in on the archive, clicking through as quickly as I could, hoping to catch a glimpse of my parents as teenagers. Finally I came across a picture that looked incredibly familiar. It wasn't of my parents, though. . . . I gasped. Brown hair, kind eyes, glasses hanging from a chain . . . *Ms. Benitez*? But that was impossible! I mean, not that she showed up in the school's archived photos. That wasn't the weird thing. The strange part was that in the photo, she looked exactly the same as she did now.

According to the caption, the photo had been taken in 1985, nearly three decades ago. From her current appearance, I'd estimated her to be around forty years old—max. Was the woman in the photo her, or someone who just looked exactly like her? I didn't know what to make of it. But one thing was absolutely clear—

"*I LIKE BIG BUTTS AND I CANNOT LIE. . . .*"

The blaring music snapped me out of my thoughts. Where was it coming from? I looked over and saw Nicole fumbling in her purse. She pulled out the offending cell phone and looked at it in horror as Sir Mix-a-Lot yelled out, "*YOU OTHER BROTHERS CAN'T DENY. . . .*"

The librarian who had shushed Lin now stomped over to

the table just as Nicole was finally able to shut the phone off. But it was too late. The librarian held out her hand. Nicole slid the phone onto her palm as she turned twelve different shades of red. "You'll get it back when you *leave*," said the woman, clearly not amused.

When she was gone, Lin turned in her chair and said, "Ugh. That song is gross. Is that really your ringtone?"

"No!" Nicole whispered desperately. "I've never even *heard* it before. Someone must have hacked my phone."

My eyes immediately slid over to Shani, who gave me a knowing smile. I grinned back. This was the payback for the laptop. I fist-bumped her under the table, making a mental note to tell her later her new motto would have to be *Hacks and apps, not tatts.* She'd love it.

"Hey, how's that research coming?" Doli said, nudging my arm.

"Right," I said. "I'm on it." Reluctantly, I closed the photo archive. The mystery of the Ms. Benitez look-alike would have to wait.

chapter 11

IT'S AMAZING HOW QUICKLY A PLACE BECOMES FAMILIAR—
even one I'd thought was basically a different planet not so
long ago. I was proud of myself for getting to know the campus so well in such a short amount of time. I'd been there for
only five days and I'd already learned some of the shortcuts.
For example, I found out that if I left the academic building
from the east exit, I could cut through a section of the hiking
trails and come out near the athletic field. Going that way also
gave me a much-needed break from the other girls, most of
whom cared too much about their shoes to follow me through
the woods.

After my last class of the day, I took the shortcut again,
only this time the trees were alive with sounds I'd never heard
this clearly before. Had the birds always been that loud? Looking up at them through the bright green leaves, I saw an image

from my dream flash before my eyes. The thick jungle vines, the hyena's frightened stare as my jaws closed in on its neck. . . .

I shook the image away, blinking my eyes. *It was just a dream,* I reminded myself. *Just a terrible dream.*

I refocused my attention on the beautiful, clear day and the birds with their colorful wings. Beneath their excited chirping, I could have sworn I heard a boy's voice—and it sounded like he was cheering himself on. Sure enough, when I emerged onto the field, I was rewarded with the sight of Jason Ferris practicing lacrosse all by himself. He had a bucket of balls next to him and was using the lacrosse stick to shoot them into the net one by one. I smiled as I approached.

"Nice job!" I called. "But then I guess it's not hard to score when the goal isn't even guarded."

Jason wiped sweat from his face and smirked at me. "Sounds like a challenge," he said.

"You got that right." I dropped my bag and pounded my chest like an ape. "I even have my gym clothes with me, so I'm ready for you. There's only one little problem."

"What?"

"I don't *actually* know how to play."

Jason laughed. "All right. We can fix that. First let's get you suited up."

He led me into the clubhouse where all the sports equipment was stored. When I came out, in addition to my running shorts and T-shirt, I had protective pads on my elbows and knees, and a helmet over my head that was one size too big.

"Is all this really necessary?" I asked.

"Only for first timers like you," Jason answered. "Lacrosse can be brutal. Are you sure you want to play?"

"Bring it on."

After he showed me how to hold the lacrosse stick, he gave me a quick tutorial in the game. It sounded a little bit like soccer, except instead of kicking the ball with your feet, you catch it with the mesh at the end of the stick and fling it into the goal any way you can. *Easy.* That is, if you can get it past the goalie.

Since we didn't have a full team, we couldn't really work on defending or attacking, so we boiled it down to the essentials.

"I'll be goalie first," Jason said, "and you just try to get it past me. Then we'll switch, okay?"

I nodded, getting into position. I slid my right hand up a few inches from the top of the shaft and clamped my left hand a few inches from the bottom. I picked up one of the balls from the bucket and ran at Jason, zigzagging back and forth to psyche him out. I feinted left and when he mirrored me, I shot to my right, whirled, and sent the ball flying past his ear and into the net. Jason looked at me in disbelief. "Nice!" he exclaimed.

"Beginner's luck," I said. But we both knew it wasn't. I was good at this. I didn't make every goal, because Jason was a strong player. But I had speed, and my aim was dead on. When we switched, it turned out I wasn't a bad goalie, either.

Jason had played for years, so a few shots took me by surprise and got by me. But eight times out of ten, I seemed to sense where the ball would go and was right there to bat it away or block it with my body. I reacted to shifts in the ball's position with lightning-fast reflexes that surprised even me.

"Wow," Jason said when we had finished and were putting the equipment away. "You're really good. I mean, *really* good. Are you sure you've never played before?"

"Never, I swear." The truth was, my prowess at lacrosse came as a shock. I had been okay in sports back home, but something felt like it had shifted in my body over the past week. I felt more coordinated, more agile.

"I guess you're just a natural," Jason said, giving me a look of genuine admiration. "This is the best practice I've had in years! So thank you."

"Anytime," I replied, feeling proud of my newfound abilities.

We started walking back toward the dorm when he stopped suddenly and said, "Hey, I found something I wanted to show you." He reached into his pocket and pulled out a copper coin that looked centuries old. "I found it at the Anasazi temple."

"What?" I exclaimed. "Jason, you can't do that! This coin is part of an official archaeological dig. You shouldn't be taking things from there."

"Would you just look at it?" he pleaded. "Once you do, you'll see why I took it."

I hesitated, not wanting to touch the stolen goods, but my curiosity got the better of me. I held out my hand and he dropped the coin into my palm. It was a small copper coin, about an inch wide, the edges worn away like the heel of an old shoe.

"See here?" Jason said, pointing to some writing on the back. "I can't make out what it says, but I'm almost positive that's Latin. And see the face on the other side? The man has some kind of wreath on his head. I think this coin is from Ancient Rome!"

I took it between my thumb and index finger and held it up to the light. Jason was right. It did look like a Roman coin. "But that doesn't make any sense," I told him. "The Anasazi didn't know the Romans existed, or vice versa. The only way this coin could have ended up at the Anasazi temple is if . . . Oh, wow. Maybe they *did* know about each other."

Jason nodded thoughtfully. "Maybe. But there is another possibility." After a pause he said, "What if the Anasazi temple isn't really Anasazi at all?"

The thought blew my mind. "But . . . but they were so sure."

"People make mistakes," Jason said.

I handed him back the coin. "We have to go talk to Dr. Logan about this. He'll know what it means." When I noticed Jason bristle at the mention of the archaeologist's name, I paused. "What's the problem?"

Jason shuffled his feet. "I don't know," he mumbled. "I get

a weird vibe from the guy. I think we should ask someone else. . . ."

"Like whom?" I said, baffled by his response. "Dr. Logan's a world-renowned archaeologist who knows a lot about ancient civilizations, and you found the coin on the site his team is excavating. If he can't help us, who can?"

Jason slipped the coin back into his pocket. "Fine. But I want it on the record that I think the guy is a little weird."

I sighed. "Noted. But, Jason, we don't have a lot of options here. I think Dr. Logan is a nice guy who can help us figure this out. Now let's go!"

It took us a while to track Dr. Logan down at his temporary office in the History Department. And once we got there, Jason seemed even more unnerved.

"Relax, Jason. I talked to him just a couple of days ago. He's really nice. You'll see."

I knocked on the door.

"Enter!" Dr. Logan called from inside.

I twisted the doorknob and pushed the door open. Dr. Logan was sitting at a large oak desk with papers and markers strewn all over it. He had a pen nested behind his ear and was busily tagging points on a large map with thumbtacks.

"Hi, Dr. Logan. I hope we aren't bothering you," I said.

He looked up and smiled pleasantly, flashing those extra-white teeth. "Miss Cetzal. What a nice surprise. And Mr. Ferris, always a pleasure."

"Mm," Jason grunted.

"Please, excuse the mess. I'm tracing the origins of various artifacts to study migration patterns of ancient peoples and how it has affected lifestyle and language development across different hemispheres. It's a fascinating study. I hope to incorporate my findings into the work being done on the Anasazi temple. But never mind all that. What brings you to my office today?"

When Jason remained silent, I took the lead. "Well, it's about the temple, actually. We—I mean, Jason found something, and we were hoping you could tell us what it is."

"Of course," Dr. Logan said. "What did you find?"

I nudged Jason's arm and wagged my head at Dr. Logan. "Go on. Show him the coin," I said.

Jason sighed and pulled the coin out of his pocket once more. He handed it over to Dr. Logan, who seemed taken aback. "Remarkable!" he said, turning the coin over in his hand. "Where did you say you found this?"

"We didn't say," Jason muttered.

"He found it near the Anasazi temple, which seemed weird since the coin looks like it's Roman, and—"

"Oh, thank goodness you found my coin!" Dr. Logan interrupted.

Jason knitted his brows. "*Your* coin?"

Dr. Logan rose from his desk and shoved the coin into his own pocket. He then walked over to us, put one hand on each of our shoulders and guided us toward the door. "Yes, my coin," he repeated. "I must have dropped it while I was working at the site. I'm always carrying small items like that around with me in my pockets—coins, keys, et cetera—and sometimes one of them escapes." He laughed, but it sounded wooden and forced.

"You carry ancient Roman coins around in your pockets?" I asked, finding that hard to believe.

A hint of annoyance flashed across his face, but it was gone in an instant. "It's actually not that rare," he offered. "I carry it for luck—it's silly but we all have our little superstitions! Anyway, thank you so much for stopping by to return it. But I really should be getting back to work now. Good day."

With that, he practically shoved us into the hallway. As soon as we left the building, Jason turned to me. "*Weird,* right? Now do you see why I didn't want to come to him? Did you notice how surprised he looked when we first showed him the coin?"

I nodded slowly, thinking this over. Jason's eyes widened. "Then as soon as I say where I found it, suddenly he claims it's his? If it was such a prized possession, how come he didn't recognize it? And could he have pushed us out of his office any faster? I knew there was something super weird about that guy; I just couldn't put my finger on it. But now I think I know what it is: He's a liar."

"If he's lying about the coin being his, then he's a thief,

too," I added. I started up the path toward the dorms, and Jason fell into step beside me. "I'm sorry for insisting on going to him. You were right. Something's definitely fishy about him. Maybe we should tell your mom what happened."

Jason gave his head a quick shake. "I don't think so. She's been spending all this time with him, and when he's not around, she talks about him nonstop. *Dr. Logan this, Dr. Logan that.* I think she's half in love with him."

Ah, I thought. No wonder Jason seemed to dislike Dr. Logan even before we found out he was a liar and a thief. "What about your dad?" I asked.

"What about him?" Jason shrugged. "My parents got divorced three years ago. He's already remarried and living in Colorado."

"Wow. That must be hard on you."

"It's not so bad. I visit, especially over the summer, and his new wife is okay. I mostly worry about my mom, you know? I don't want her to be lonely. That's why I chose to go to Temple instead of some other school. If my dad wasn't going to be around to look out for Mom, I figured I should. Are your mom and dad still together?" he asked.

I debated telling him. Once you tell people you're an orphan, that becomes your whole story. And I wanted Jason to know there was more to me than that. But he had told me some pretty personal stuff, and it seemed only fair that I share something with him too. "Technically, yes, they're together," I said.

"But only because they both passed away when I was little."

Jason slowed his pace, looking down at his sneakers as he let his arm graze mine. Goose bumps raced along my skin. "I'm really sorry," he said.

I nodded at my shoes, watching them as they padded alongside Jason's as if they, too, were having a private conversation. "Thanks," I said finally. "But it's really okay. I live with my aunt and uncle now. They're still together and so in love it's almost gross." I gave Jason a smile, letting him know it was all right for him to smile too. This orphan story had as happy an ending as anyone could hope for.

I saw his lips curl up the tiniest bit. "Sounds like you have a really good home to go back to."

"I do. I just wish things were as good here."

Jason cast a concerned glance my way. "What do you mean?"

In brief, I told him about everything that had happened with Nicole and all the tension that had built up between her and her group, and me and mine—though I wasn't sure which team Lin was on just yet. She hated me one day and was okay with me the next. "Everybody's so different from my friends back home, especially Nicole. I just don't know if I'll ever fit with them."

Jason considered my words for a moment and then said, "Why would you want to? Truthfully, I've never liked Nicole; she just seems so fake and shallow. All she talks about is money and clothes and what mean gossip she can spread about someone else. She sets my teeth on edge. If you did fit in with her and her friends, I doubt *we* would be friends."

A warm feeling spread through my chest when he said we were friends. "Are you a good judge of character?" I asked.

"I haven't been wrong yet."

"So what do you think of Doli and Shani? Nicole told me to stay away from Doli, but she wouldn't explain why. What do you think?" We had just reached my dorm. I could see lights coming on in various windows as the sun began to fade into the horizon.

"Nicole's just jealous. Doli is nice, and so is Shani. A few months back I dropped my smartphone in the fountain and Shani fixed it for me in three minutes flat. She's cool." I panicked a little when he said that. Did he *like* Shani, like Shani? But then he turned to me and smiled shyly. "You seem cool too. *Really* cool." He reached down and squeezed my hand.

"Good night, Ana," he said, and walked on toward his home. Only when he disappeared around a bend in the path did I remember how to breathe.

chapter 12

A FEW DAYS LATER THE SCHOOL BUZZED WITH ACTIVITY. Principal Ferris had made it clear at morning assembly that she wanted everything to run like clockwork for the exhibition. So naturally everything was a mess. A storm had blown in that morning, making the school's lights flicker on and off, as if we were in a horror movie. Thanks to the rain, the temple itself was off limits, but plenty of people showed up anyway to see the artifacts that had been pulled from the site, along with the class projects about the Anasazi and the rest of the pieces in the Temple Museum, which was open to the public for the day. In fact, so many people had shown up that everyone in Ms. Benitez's history class had been called to the museum to serve as volunteers.

Nicole and her friends looked miserable, of course. They were manning the coat-check room, and griping about it every step of the way. All they had to do was take the guest's jacket and umbrella and hand the person a ticket, but Nicole moaned each time, like she'd been forced to do hard labor. I could hear her muttering from all the way across the room.

I, on the other hand, was in heaven. My job was to hand out brochures, while Shani and Doli acted as hostesses, welcoming guests and directing them through the exhibit. It felt so good to be around normal people again—my kind of normal, anyway. I was surrounded by average families dressed in basic cotton and denim, some of them pushing strollers or toting kids in Elmo T-shirts. Some had on costume jewelry and smelled of drugstore perfume. I couldn't have been happier. These were not the kind of folks who had private jets in their backyards or Roberto Cavalli on speed dial. In short, they were my people.

When I'd finished handing out all the brochures, I looked around to find Doli and saw that she, too, had found her people—literally. She was standing near the doorway talking to what looked like a group of Native Americans. Like Doli, they had dark wavy hair and catlike eyes. I hurried to her side.

"Is this your family?" I asked her.

Doli smiled. "No, my parents had to work tonight. But this family does live on the reservation."

I was so excited to meet someone from Doli's world back home. I turned to the woman nearest me. "Hello, it's nice to meet you."

The woman shook my hand and said, *"Yá'át'ééh."* At my

confused look, she sounded it out slowly for me: *yah*-ah-te. "That means hello in Navajo," she explained.

I tried repeating it in return and Doli nodded her head. "Not bad, Ana," she said. She turned back to finish a brief conversation in Navajo with the woman and her family, and they waved at me before heading farther into the museum.

"You didn't tell me you could speak Navajo!" I exclaimed.

Doli shrugged. "Of course I can," she answered. "I grew up on a Navajo reservation. It's my native language. Most of us there speak Navajo and English."

"That's so cool. What did she say to you just now?" I asked, gesturing to the woman from Doli's reservation as she walked away.

"She said she was glad she could come. They heard about the temple and are excited about it. She didn't think that the ancient Pueblo peoples were active here, so they are very interested in seeing what was found."

Even the local Navajo people hadn't known the Anasazi were active here? *Interesting.* I thought back to the Roman coin Jason found; was it possible that it really *hadn't* fallen out of Dr. Logan's pocket? I'd have to make it my mission to find out for sure.

For now, I followed the crowd around the museum, taking in the beauty of the donated pieces. But one by one the other members of the Ancient Civilization Superpowers—Shani, Doli, and Lin—gravitated toward me. "You guys notice anything missing here?" Shani asked as she looked around the room.

Though I knew it probably wasn't what she meant, I wanted to say *Jason*. Since he didn't want to have anything to do with Dr. Logan or his exhibit, he'd told me he would give his mother some excuse about homework to get out of coming. So far, Dr. Logan was a no-show anyway.

"Our families' donations aren't here," Doli pointed out.

"Bingo," said Shani. "After all that orb mumbo jumbo, this exhibit is still one sphinx, one golden fan, one blanket, and one vase shy. Why is that?"

It was a good question. It sounded like my aunt and uncle had gone through quite a bit of trouble to make sure that vase got here safely. But why did they bother if the only eyes that would ever see it belonged to the spiders that lived in the basement? It annoyed me to think that Ms. Benitez was keeping our families' treasures hidden away in the safe so that she could be the only one to enjoy them. What kind of museum curator was she?

"I'm actually *glad* the fan isn't on display," Lin said, making us all turn in her direction. "Just look at some of the people here. We might as well be in Walmart! And their kids—*yuck*. That fan is worth far too much money to let them near it with their grubby little hands."

Ugh . . . there she went again. Lin was always so determined to remind everyone that her family was rich that she forgot when she was standing with someone who wasn't.

She wandered away and Doli stared after her, glaring a hole in her back. "That little—"

I jumped as the screeching of the museum's fire alarm cut off the rest of her sentence. We all looked at one another in alarm as the light in one of the hallways flickered and went out for good.

The guests, who had been milling around, enjoying the artwork, began to chatter. Children started to wail, and rain battered against the windows. But even with that riot of noise, I could hear Principal Ferris talking to one of the other staff members. "This may just be a false alarm triggered by the storm," said a woman whom I recognized from around school.

"That may be," said Principal Ferris, "but I'm afraid we'll have to evacuate the museum to be on the safe side." She gave the staff members marching orders and asked that the student volunteers help usher everyone to safety. Once outside, they would be led to the closest dorm to take shelter from the rain.

As Doli, Shani, and I waved the last of the guests through the exit, we followed them out, relieved to see the rain letting up enough to allow people to get home safely. But before we'd reached the outside gate, something stopped me. One of the Superpowers was missing. "Where's Lin?" I cried.

"I don't know," said Shani. "I haven't seen her since the alarm went off."

"Good riddance," mumbled Doli. "She probably just took off early because she was bored."

I had to agree that did sound like something Lin would do, but somehow I had a strong feeling that wasn't the case. "Guys, there might really be a fire somewhere in the museum. What if she's trapped and can't get out? What if she needs our help? We have to find her and make sure."

Doli and Shani shared a look, then nodded in unison. "You're right, Ana," Doli said. "Let's go."

Together the three of us flew back into the now empty museum building.

"Where do we start?" Shani said. "There are so many rooms. . . ."

I closed my eyes and blocked all the sights and sounds around me. "Shhh," I said. "Just stop . . . and listen."

They did stop, and in the stillness, we all heard it: a voice crying out in fear from the basement. *Lin?* We dashed off toward the sound of the voice.

chapter 13

BEFORE WE EVEN GOT TO THE STAIRS TO THE BASEMENT, we heard the screaming.

"Is that Lin?" Doli asked, looking at both of us with wide eyes.

My heart was pounding in my chest. "It has to be," I whispered. "We have to help her, guys."

Shani nodded. "Knowing Lin, she might be screaming because someone has a knockoff purse," she said. But the joke fell flat. Even if none of us was *friends* with Lin, exactly, we were all still too worried about her to laugh.

Going down the stairs was like walking into a nightmare. The space beyond the freight elevator was darker than I remembered, and I couldn't see a thing at first, not even my hands as they stretched out ahead of me, groping for the walls. The only thing that comforted me was knowing that Doli and Shani were behind me.

We followed the voice through the hallways and around the corner, where a faint light illuminated the door to the safe.

The door hung wide open.

"This is a bad sign," I said immediately. "Ms. Benitez would never leave the safe unlocked."

We carefully made our way through the small room, barely glancing at the donated pieces from our families, and sped into the larger space, where Ms. Benitez had made us pass around the orb. There in the center of the room were Ms. Benitez and . . . *Dr. Logan?* What was he doing down here, and how did he get in without us seeing him? When Ms. Benitez shifted to the side, I realized that they were fighting over something . . . and when I got closer I saw it was the Mayan vase she'd told me my aunt and uncle had donated! She seemed to be trying to keep it from Dr. Logan, who was doing his best to tear it from her hands. Each time she wrested it away from him, she let out a scream that only seemed to give her power. I realized with a start that the voice we'd heard crying out had been hers. *So where is Lin?*

"What the . . . ?" Shani muttered, her blue hank of hair falling over her left eye. Suddenly Doli's hands closed around my arm and Shani's, and she yanked us back behind a large cabinet.

"What are you doing? We have to help Ms. Benitez!" I hissed, trying to break free. But Doli latched on to me and held me in place.

"Ana, *listen to them.* Something really strange is going on here."

I forced myself to stop moving and open my ears.

"Let it go, Anubis!" Ms. Benitez commanded. "It will never be yours!"

"You underestimate me, Ixchel. I will have what I came for."

"Never," replied Ms. Benitez—*Ixchel*—her voice strangely magnified, as if it were being broadcast in surround sound. "For years I have awaited your return, and ever since the earthquakes and thunderstorms began to plague us, I knew that you walked the Earth once more. It was only a matter of time before you revealed your true nature. But I have made preparations and they are complete at last. Go now or face your doom!"

As I listened to them argue, the air suddenly felt thin and cold, as if I were on a mountaintop, and my head swirled with images. The earthquakes, the storms, the Roman coin in Dr. Logan's hand, Lin's phone going black, the frightening dreams that were beginning to linger into the daylight, Ms. Benitez handing us the glowing orb, and her words: *Your ancestry makes you powerful.* It was all coming together now, but in a way that might mean I was crazy.

I turned to the other girls. "You guys," I started breathlessly, "that name. I've heard that word before. I know I have. Ixchel . . ." I rolled the name around in my mouth, the meaning tugging at the corners of my memory. And then it hit me and my eyes went wide. "Ixchel is the Mayan goddess of war—one of the most powerful there is. I might be losing my mind, but I think . . . Ms. Benitez . . ." I couldn't even finish the sentence. My mouth had gone dry.

Shani looked at us in alarm. I'd never seen such deep fear on her face. "If you're crazy, so am I. Anubis is the Egyptian god of death," she hissed. "He can assume many forms, but in his true demon form, h-he l-looks like—"

BOOM!

A sudden explosion rocked the whole basement, sparks flying in every direction, the whoosh of power sending us reeling to the floor. Our heads poked out from behind the cabinet just in time to see Dr. Logan shed his human skin and transform into a terrible creature. My heart froze in my chest as I recognized the demon I'd seen in my dream—a creature with a jackal's head and an almost human body, dressed in tattered strips of gauze like a mummy. A putrid stench like rotten flesh filled the air. Anubis held up a striped stick with three strands hanging from one end. I think it was called a flail. He reeled back, turned his demonic face to the ceiling, and laughed.

I turned to my teacher, fighting my instinct to save her, but she, too, was transforming. There was a cloud of smoke and ash, and when it cleared, Ms. Benitez was gone. In her place was the figure I'd always recognized as Ixchel, a warrior woman with a writhing green snake on her head and a heavy beaded chain around her neck. She wore a green leather tunic with a sash of feathers slung across her chest. She twirled a heavy two-headed ax as if it were as light as the feathers on her sash, and her hair rippled behind her like a black river.

"This isn't happening, right?" I heard Shani say. "I'm not seeing this."

"This is getting weird. Like, *Twilight Zone* weird. Are we dreaming? Someone pinch me," said Doli.

Shani and I both reached out and pinched her arm as hard as we could. Maybe if she could wake up, she could wake us, too. And I wanted more than anything to wake up. But she winced and rubbed her arm. *This is real.*

Turning back to the battle of the two gods, I saw Anubis aim the flail at Ixchel, firing off a bolt of light that crackled in the air. Ixchel returned fire with her ax, and soon the basement was ablaze with fire and magic. My brain felt like it might explode. *How can this be happening? These are just stories. These gods aren't real. Magic isn't real. And yet . . .*

A crack like thunder echoed against the walls, and the cabinet we'd been hiding behind exploded. Each of us dived in a different direction, taking cover behind the nearest statue and doing our best to stay out of sight.

"It won't be long now, Ixchel. My Chaos Spirits will be set free and the Brotherhood of Chaos will finish the work we started so very long ago." Anubis's voice was chilling. Icy and calculated, yet laced with malice and amplified, as if many demons spoke through him.

In answer, Ixchel raised her ax. I heard a scuffling noise and glanced to the other side of the room. There, in the doorway, stood Lin. When she laid eyes on the scene before us, her jaw went slack. So much had happened in the past few minutes that I'd almost forgotten we'd come looking for her. And now she stood between the two gods, though neither had noticed her yet. While I was watching Lin, Ixchel threw another bolt of magic at Anubis, who blocked it with his flail, sending it crashing into the support beam above Lin's head.

If she didn't move, she would be crushed by the falling masonry. But she seemed frozen with fear. Just like when I had swiped at Nicole, I didn't think. I leaped to my feet and dashed across the dark expanse behind Ixchel, driven by instinct. I saw the beam above Lin break apart, the pieces falling from the high ceiling. Lin looked up and screamed, but the sound was lost amid the thunderous sounds of the battle. I reached her just in time and tackled her to the ground, out of harm's way.

"What on earth is going on?" she cried out, staring at Ixchel and Anubis in shock as I helped her to her feet.

"No time to explain. We've got to get out of here!"

As I turned to lead Lin back to the other side of the room near the exit, I saw Ixchel's head swivel in my direction. She'd seen us, and for a second she lowered her ax and her timeless face glowed with supernatural light. She breathed out in what I think was relief.

But in that brief moment of distraction, Anubis, his back

to us, released a magical blast that struck the Mayan vase, which Ixchel had cradled in her arm. I gasped. "NO!" At the same time, Ixchel let out a bloodcurdling cry that tore at my soul. She released the vase as lightning rippled across its surface, illuminating the deep grooves on every side. There was a hush, and then the vase exploded into thousands of glittering shards, raining down like sand. Taking advantage of the cover provided by this cloud of debris, I grabbed Lin's hand and ran across the back of the room. We huddled behind the ornate bench where Shani and Doli were now hiding. But I had to see what was happening. I peeked around the edge of the bench and almost wished I hadn't.

As the shards settled into mounds on the floor, they began to writhe. I crawled forward a few inches on my hands and knees and watched in horror as four plumes of smoke arose from the ashes. The first to form was an eagle. The next cloud of smoke coiled itself into a snake. Then came a monkey, and finally a bat, spreading its leathery wings. I wasn't sure which to fear most, but I knew that in Mayan culture the bat represented the guardian of the underworld. Watching the bat form from the dust of the vase was like seeing death personified.

These must be the Chaos Spirits Anubis had mentioned— the ones he was determined to set free. The four of us looked on in awe as they blasted through the ceiling of the basement, leaving a scorched hole in their wake. Moments later I heard breaking glass followed by a howl of wind. That must have been the evil creatures smashing their way out of the museum windows and into the night sky.

Anubis once more lifted his clawed hands toward the ruined ceiling and let out a triumphant cackle that sickened me. Ixchel sank to her knees.

"Is it over?" asked Lin, her eyes squeezed shut.

Just then debris from the broken ceiling began to fall. With a sickening crack, a heavy piece of concrete and marble dislodged itself and tumbled down, crashing into the bench we were hiding behind. Splinters and bits of wood flew everywhere, stinging our skin. But we had bigger problems: Our cover was literally blown. Anubis turned his malevolent red eyes to us, seeing us for the first time.

"No," I whispered. "It isn't over."

chapter 14

The triumphant smile faded from Anubis's face.

Ixchel grinned. "Yes, Anubis," she intoned in her ethereal voice. "As I said, preparations have been made. I have assembled the Wildcats, and they will put an end to the Brotherhood of Chaos."

Doli, Shani, Lin, and I looked at one another. Wildcats? What was she talking about? And why did the sight of us seem to scare the god of death?

Ixchel chanted something in an ancient Mayan dialect and raised her arms. Soon the dust surrounding the remains of the once-beautiful vase swirled into life, and the shapes of the four cats that had been pressed into each side rose into the air. Gliding like apparitions, the tiger moved into position in front of Lin, the puma aimed itself at Doli, the lion faced Shani, and the jaguar squared off in front of me. They had a filmy ghost-like quality, as if they had been sketched in pencil on a bolt of silk. But as we watched, their soft gray outlines took shape and they became living, breathing animals, with brilliantly colored fur and rippling, muscular bodies. The lion let out a roar that rattled my rib cage, and my stomach dropped into my shoes. I'd seen all of these animals before in the zoo, but there had always been a deep pit and thick glass walls separating us. Now there was nothing. I couldn't remember the last time I'd been so scared.

"They're going to eat us," Lin said, her voice quivering.

"Run!" Shani cried.

But I couldn't move. None of us could. The jaguar had me locked in its gaze and I felt paralyzed. It huffed once, twice, then came charging toward me at full speed. Part of me wanted to pull back, to run, but a deeper part felt pulled toward the jaguar. *This is meant to happen.* I don't know where the thought came from, and I couldn't tell you how I knew it was true. But I did.

Crazy as it sounds, I spread my arms open wide and welcomed the cat as if it were a long-lost pet. The jaguar slammed into me like a freight train, knocking me off my feet.

"Oof!" I fell, my back slamming into the floor. But the pain never came. Instead an intense tingling sensation vibrated up the length of my spine, as if it were a plucked violin string.

For one horrifying moment all I could see was a blinding white light, and I thought maybe I'd died and had entered a tunnel to the afterlife. But within seconds my vision returned, the world around me slowly coming back into view. I was once again in the dark basement—only it wasn't dark anymore. Now everything was as clear as day, as if I were wearing night-vision goggles. I looked around me to see where the jaguar had gone, but my own personal spirit animal was nowhere to be found. Had it run away? Slowly I moved to stand on my two feet, but when I glanced down, I realized I didn't *have* feet anymore. Instead I had four paws and a long thick tail covered in blond fur and black spots. I ran my tongue across my teeth and felt two impossibly long fangs on top and a matching set on bottom.

Oh my God! I thought. *I* am *the jaguar.*

I craned my neck to find my friends—but they were gone. In their place stood a lion, a puma, and a tiger. I met the puma's gaze and could almost see Doli staring out at me. She batted her tail against the ground as if to say *What the heck just happened to us?* Shani tried to speak, but all that came out was another bone-rattling lion roar. And Lin kept shaking her whole body as if she could shrug the tiger's skin loose like an unwanted fur coat and be human again. But there was no going back now. We were Wildcats.

Before I could even figure out what that meant, Anubis, who I'd almost forgotten was still standing across from us, cried out and his face twisted with fear. He turned on his clawed feet and ran.

Ixchel stood up and faced us, the serpent on her head hissing and flicking its tongue. When Ixchel spoke, her mouth did not move. Her voice sounded in my ears, filling every corner of my mind. *Wildcats,* she said. *Together you are more powerful than Anubis could ever be. Go after him! You are the only hope.*

I was still so confused, but somehow I knew she was right. The dreams I'd had of the jungle flashed across my mind, and I knew what I had to do. When I shouted to the others to follow me, it came out as a low roar, rumbling in my chest. *Great,* I thought. *How am I supposed to make them understand?* But when I took off running, they did too. Together we sprinted, side by side.

I ran through the halls of the empty museum, feeling a little clumsy at first. It was weird to run with four legs. And every time I turned a corner, my claws slid comically against the smooth basement tile. But once I stopped thinking about it, the claws retracted and my legs fell into a natural gallop. The rubbery pads of my paws gripped the floor as my powerful leg muscles pushed me up the stairs and onto the main level. As I twitched my whiskers, feeling them shiver in the breeze, I somehow knew that they were more than decoration; they told me how far away I was from my prey. He had a big lead on us, but we were rapidly closing the distance. Preparing for the hunt, I inhaled the rank odor of Anubis, realizing with astonishment that I wasn't *learning* how to do this—I was *remembering*. The dreams I'd had were so vivid, they'd felt more like memories. Maybe they were.

I thought about the night I'd touched the orb and how my senses had changed afterward. I'd been able to smell things that would have been impossible to detect with my human nose; I'd heard sounds that only an animal could hear. And that first night . . . I'd attacked Nicole like a predator in the wild! Like a cat. I knew now that touching that orb had awakened an ancient power in me—in all of us—that we hadn't even known existed. And now that power was a million times more intense. It felt like I'd always been meant to be a jaguar, and even as my human mind struggled to understand what was happening to me, my cat self wanted nothing but to hunt Anubis.

I lifted my head and breathed in the foul scent of evil. It seemed to hang in the air all around me like raw meat. *Destroy it. Destroy it.* The thought pulsed in my mind, the need in me growing by the second. I looked at the other cats and saw the same consuming hunger in their eyes. I'd felt this way before. . . . Suddenly I remembered the hyena in the dream, and how I had longed to sink my teeth into its throat. The morning after I'd had that dream, I'd felt sick to my stomach, but now, in my jaguar state, the bloodlust returned. With me leading the way, we galloped out of the museum and around the corner of the building, following Anubis's stench.

At last I caught sight of him leaping through one of the windows that the Chaos Spirits had shattered on their way out. One of the jagged shards of glass from the broken window cut into my paw as I passed, but I kept going. Lin, Shani, and Doli matched my pace. Anubis turned back and saw that we were closing in. He stopped to lift a large potted plant off the lawn and heave it at us. Lin, Shani, and I dived out of the way, while Doli easily jumped over the clay pot, landing lightly on her paws and emitting an almost playful growl, as if to say, *Is that all you've got?* The jackal took off again, bounding over benches and around buildings, doing his best to lose us. But his horrible smell, now tinged with fear, plus the wet slapping sound of his taloned feet against the grass, gave away his presence, even when we briefly lost sight of him. He couldn't hide from us!

Finally we trapped him against the gate of a fence that enclosed the school grounds near the museum. *Gotcha!* But just as Shani bared her teeth and took a step toward Anubis, he bent his knees and leaped, vaulting over the barrier with amazing ease.

Doli roared and swiped at the gate, rattling it with her paws, but it was no use. The gate was locked. Why? It was usually left open. But that wouldn't stop me. I sensed that Anubis was not the only creature who had the power to vault over the gate. I backed up a few feet, feeling the tension in my paws, and then sprang forward. I ran and jumped, stretching my front paws ahead of me, sailing through the air. On the other side of the gate, I landed gracefully on all four paws. I wanted to jump for joy. I was really a jaguar! I still couldn't believe it. Was that why Aunt Teppy had given me the necklace? Had she known all along that this would happen? But I couldn't think about that now. Anubis was getting away.

One by one, the others ran and jumped over the gate too. I looked into each of their eyes, seeing both the cat and the girl inside. We were the Wildcats Ixchel had warned Anubis about. And, together, we couldn't fail.

I 'd landed on the dirt road near the front entrance of the school. I swung my head to the left and to the right. I couldn't see the jackal. But Lin chuffed and swung her head toward the mountains in the distance. Finally I saw what she did: the small puffs of dust kicking up from the ground as Anubis came out of his hiding place behind the fountain and ran for the red cliffs. If he made it, we'd never find him—he'd have too many places to hide. I growled and took off so quickly, I felt the wind whistle through my whiskers and ripple over my fur. In a flash he was almost in our grasp. Two more seconds and I'd be close enough to pounce on his back.

But just when we were about to overtake him, he whirled and aimed the flail in our direction. He fired a magical blast, which streamed through the air like the tail of a comet. Shimmering red and gold fire hit all of us at once. It felt like being struck by lightning.

I screamed and collapsed to the ground, feeling my body shift violently. I landed facedown, breathing into the grass. Craning my neck, I saw my human arms and my own black hair blocking my sight, and shuddered. What had he done to me? I moved my hair out of the way and saw Lin and Shani collapsed a few feet away. Doli lay on my other side, taking shallow breaths. We were all human again.

"Just as I thought," said Anubis, his stench intensifying as he dared to come closer. "You are new cats. You lack the strength to control your powers. You are no threat to the Brotherhood of Chaos." He aimed his flail. "And now I will obliterate the Wildcats forever."

I winced, preparing for the blow. But as the magic blasted from his weapon once more, a figure ran out from behind the low scrub brush that flanked the road. *Ixchel!* The full force of Anubis's attack struck the goddess's chest and she wailed, collapsing to the ground in a heap. I watched as the supernatural light that had radiated from her skin faded and disappeared. The Mayan goddess of war slowly faded, and in seconds she was Ms. Benitez again. But she wasn't moving.

I glared at Anubis. If Ms. Benitez had died protecting us, I would have my revenge.

In the distance I began to hear voices—the crowd of people we'd evacuated earlier were leaving the dorm and heading back to the museum, probably to check out the damage and see if they could recover their belongings. Soon they'd be close enough to see us outside the gates.

"This isn't over, Wildcats," Anubis said with a growl. "The Chaos Spirits are free, and the Brotherhood of Chaos will rise again!" With that, he loped away, disappearing into the darkness.

"This didn't happen. This didn't happen. This isn't real." Shani slowly got to her feet and paced back and forth, looking down at Ms. Benitez and shaking her head. Lin still sat in the dirt, staring at her own hands as if she didn't recognize them.

"Is she okay?" Doli asked, sounding as if she might cry. She gestured to where Ms. Benitez was slumped on the ground. "Tell me she's okay."

"I don't know." I struggled to my feet and went to her, calling out, "Ms. Benitez!" No response. I pressed my hand to her neck, feeling for a pulse. It was weak, but it was there. "She's alive," I breathed to my friends.

At last her eyes fluttered open and slid over to my face. "Ana," she croaked. "You know what you are now. These powers have been part of your families for centuries. I'm sorry I couldn't tell you before. You would not have believed me. But now that the mantles have been passed to the four of you, you *must* continue the fight."

"But how?" I cried. "How are we supposed to win against a *god*?"

I mean, could she hear how crazy that sounded? Three weeks ago my biggest concern was that some of the private-school girls might be mean, or that I wouldn't be able to keep up in my classes. Now I find out I'm part jaguar, my teacher is an ancient Mayan goddess, and my shape-shifting friends and I have to take on the demon king of the underworld and his minions—who want to kill us. Where had all *that* been in the Temple Academy welcome packet?

As if she could read my mind, Ms. Benitez reached out and touched my cheek, quieting my thoughts. "Ana, this is your destiny. Anubis is not as strong as the four of you are together. Can't you feel how strong you are? He was afraid of you."

Huh, I thought. *She's right.* I *had* felt strong in my jaguar body. Stronger than I'd ever felt before. As for Anubis, he was supposedly the big bad god, but he's the one who had run away from us. I recalled the nervous glint in his eyes when he spied us behind the destroyed bench, and I smiled. "Maybe we *can* beat him."

"Yes," Ms. Benitez said with a nod that seemed to take effort. "But don't underestimate him. Now that the Chaos Spirits have been released, he will use them to wreak havoc and dole out death and destruction."

Her voice was getting weaker. She pulled me closer to her and whispered, "Have faith in your powers." Then her eyes drifted closed and she went limp.

Doli shot to her feet. "Look! There's Jason!" she said, pointing to the walking path just beyond the gate, which led to the museum. *What is he doing here?* I wondered. I thought he hadn't wanted to be anywhere near the museum tonight. Had his mother made him come after all?

Doli started jumping up and down and waving her arms. "Jason!" she called. "Here! Over here! We need you!"

Jason turned to us and jogged over to the gate. "Hey, guys," he said. "What's going—" When he saw the rest of us, dirty and out of breath, and Ms. Benitez lying unconscious on the ground, he abruptly stopped talking and his eyes widened. "I'll go call for help!"

I had no trouble believing that Chaos Spirits were on the loose, because the next several minutes were definitely chaotic. Jason had called the paramedics, but before they got there, the crowd of people who'd been at the exhibit started streaming out of the campus, heading home. When some of them stopped to ask if everything was all right, we assured them that help was on the way, but the Navajo woman I'd met earlier, whose name was Aponi, stayed with us until the ambulance arrived, cradling Ms. Benitez in her arms and praying softly over her in Navajo. After what felt like hours but was really only minutes, the ambulance arrived, flashing its red and white lights. The EMTs checked Ms. Benitez's vitals then lifted her onto a gurney and into the ambulance, the sirens wailing as they sped to a nearby hospital. Firemen swarmed the museum to assess the damage to the building. And more EMTs examined the four of us at the scene.

Doli didn't have a scratch on her, so the EMTs let her go quickly. She went over to Aponi to thank her for sticking around and helping. I wasn't quite so lucky. My foot was bleeding—I guess from where the glass had torn into my paw when I jumped through the window. But the wound wasn't deep. Wanting more than anything to go home, I tried telling the EMTs that it was nothing, just a minor scrape. But they insisted on checking me over and bandaging me up.

"You think they can put a bandage on my brain?" Shani said quietly after the EMTs finished with us and moved on to Lin. "That's pretty much the only way I'll ever get over the fact that half an hour ago I turned into a real-life Simba. Or wait... Nala was the girl in *The Lion King,* right? Yeah, I was Nala!"

"Shhh . . . ," I said. "Lower your voice. He'll hear you." I nodded toward the EMT who was taking Lin's pulse. He told her repeatedly to stay still, but she kept staring at her hands, turning them back and forth, and saying, "Do I look a little... orange to you?"

Shani shook her head. "Who cares if he hears me? It's not like he would believe me anyway. I'm not sure *I* believe me. And I *saw* all of us turn into cats I've only ever seen on Animal Planet."

I knew I should have been a basket case too. I should have told the EMTs to cart me off to the nearest loony bin. That was clearly how Lin and Shani were feeling. But I felt strangely calm. I may not have understood what had happened to us, but after my conversation with Ms. Benitez, everything was starting to make a weird kind of sense.

It was no coincidence that Aunt Teppy had given me a jaguar necklace and Doli's parents had given her one with a puma on it. It wasn't dumb luck that I'd been placed in the same dorm as Doli, Shani, and Lin. The dreams I'd had since before I even got to Temple about the four of us as cats in the jungle . . . maybe Ixchel had caused those, to prepare me for what was to come. The truth was, we'd been changing ever since that first night in the museum basement. It was only after we touched the glowing orb that my senses started working overtime. That was also the night I took a swipe at Nicole—the way an angry cat would. For all I knew, Ms. Benitez was behind all of us ending up at Temple in the first place—so that we would all be here when we were needed.

I'd wasted so much time in the beginning wondering if I belonged at Temple Academy. Now that I knew about the mission, I felt that I not only fit in here, but I was destined to be here.

"How can you be so chill?" Shani asked, pushing her tattooed hand through her hair. "Aren't you freaked at all?"

I smiled evenly, glancing at Doli, then at Lin, and back to Shani. "I am," I said. "Totally. But at least we're in this together. And I have it on good authority that together we're not to be messed with."

The panic in her eyes faded, and a rebellious smile that

matched her pierced ears and blue hair spread over her face. "Yeah, all right. When you put it that way . . ."

Just then Jason came running up.

"Jason!" Lin said, noticing him first. "You came back." For the first time that day, Lin's face lit up. She quickly smoothed her hair down with her hand. "Where did you run off to?"

"Sorry," he said to all of us, scooting around the EMT who was cleaning a small cut on Lin's leg. "After I called for the ambulance, I had to go to the museum with my mom to help lock up once the police left. It's a total wreck inside! What happened in there, anyway?"

Lin flashed a look at us then turned back to Jason. "It's a long story. I hurt my arm, but I think I'll recover. It's so sweet of you to check on me, though."

"Yeah, sure. No problem," Jason interrupted, shifting on his feet kind of uncomfortably. "I'm glad you're okay." He chucked her on her arm the way you would a teammate.

Lin stopped smiling abruptly, but Jason didn't seem to notice. He hurried over to the bench and took a seat beside me. He pulled me into a quick hug and then leaned back, resting his hands on my shoulders. "I was so worried about you," he said. He looked down at my foot, noticing the small bandage. "Are you all right?"

I glanced at Lin and saw something I'd never seen on her face before: disappointment. She may not have been bleeding, but she was definitely hurt. And there was no bandage for the way she must have felt when Jason lifted a hand to tuck my hair behind my ear.

"Get off me. I'm fine," she snapped at the EMT, who had been checking her other leg for cuts. She slapped his hand away and announced, "I'm going back to my room," then stomped off toward the dorm without saying good-bye to any of us.

I felt a bunch of mingled emotions as I watched her leave. We'd just been through so much together. We shared a destiny—and a pretty huge secret that only four of us knew about. Maybe we weren't best friends, but we were something more than that now. She was my fellow Wildcat, and I hated seeing her look so heartbroken.

But at the same time, when I looked into Jason's beautiful eyes, I couldn't help feeling over-the-moon happy that he seemed to like me. I really liked him too, so why should I feel bad about that?

"Argh," Shani groaned, standing up. "I can't believe I'm saying this, but I'd better go check on her. Make sure she doesn't kick any puppies on her way home. See you back at the dorm, Ana?"

I nodded. "I'll be right behind you."

"Take your time," she said, winking before she walked off after Lin.

chapter 15

THAT NIGHT WHEN I'D GOTTEN BACK TO THE ROOM, I'D wanted to go over every detail of the night with the only people I *could* talk to about it: my new roommates. But Shani and Doli had both been so exhausted that they'd just wanted to go to sleep. I relented and climbed into my sleeping bag on the floor, wondering how I'd ever sleep again with so much going on in my head. But apparently fighting off rogue demon gods and shape-shifting into a giant cat really takes it out of you. Nodding off was easier than I'd thought it would be.

The next morning I asked if we should invite Lin to the dining hall with us for breakfast, but Shani shook her head. "I think we ought to give her a little time to herself. She was kind of upset last night—and not about the monster stuff." She gave me a pointed look.

"Right," I said with a sigh. *Jason.* "I'll go talk to her later and make sure she's okay."

We got dressed and headed to the dining hall for a breakfast of eggs Florentine and *crespelle*, which were Italian-style crepes. I pushed the food around on my plate, too preoccupied with everything that had happened the night before to eat. I couldn't stop worrying about what the fallout would be. How would the school possibly explain the damage to the museum, and what had happened to Ms. Benitez? The four of us had somehow gotten away from the scene without being asked any questions, but I figured they must be coming. And I had no idea what we'd say. I had a feeling that, *We turned into wildcats and fought off the Egyptian god of death,* would land us in permanent detention, if not the nearest asylum.

Jason texted me while we were at breakfast. According to his mom, our teacher was still unconscious in the hospital, but that's all she would say. "I wish we knew how Ms. Benitez was doing," I said, after giving my friends the news.

"Me too," said Doli. "She looked pretty messed up last night. But she'll be fine . . . right?"

"I hope so," said Shani. "Otherwise, we all might end up in the slammer."

I jerked my head back. "What do you mean? Why would we get in trouble for what happened to her?"

Shani leaned toward me and lowered her voice to a whisper. "Think about it. A teacher is hurt on campus and the four of us were the only ones nearby. We were also the last students in the building when the museum was wrecked. The

157

only other witness to what really happened is unconscious and might not recover. Put all that together, and it looks pretty bad for us."

I pushed my plate of food away, my appetite completely ruined.

"Oh, God, you're right," Doli said, frowning. "It's not like we can tell people what really happened."

"To be honest though," I murmured, glancing around to make sure no one was listening, "I'm dying to tell someone! Aren't you? Turning into a jaguar was scary, but incredible. I remember when I learned how to ride a bike—I went around telling everybody. Now I find out I can do something infinitely cooler, and I can't tell a soul?"

Shani shot me a skeptical look. "Who would you tell?" she asked.

Jason, I thought immediately. But I knew that was impossible. *Or my aunt Teppy and my uncle Mec.* I actually really wished I could talk to them about what was going on. . . . If only they would respond to my e-mails or Skype invitations.

"I don't know," I said out loud, forcing a piece of *crespelle* into my mouth.

"Anyway," Doli said in a sharp voice, "you can't. Not unless you want to be shipped off to a funny farm, that is. Navajo folklore is full of stories about shape-shifters, but I'm not even sure the people on the reservation would believe me. Besides, we don't really know enough about our powers yet. I felt amazing as a puma. But I also felt . . . out of control."

"Me too," Shani said. "Until we can figure out what the deal is, I vote we keep a lid on it."

I was disappointed, but I knew what they said made sense. "All right, fine. I'll keep my mouth shut," I said. "What should we do if someone asks us how we ended up outside with Ms. Benitez, though?"

Shani grunted. "The only thing we can do: claim that we have total amnesia and don't remember a thing. Deny, deny, deny."

It was as good a plan as any. But I hoped it wouldn't come to that.

During my next two classes all anyone could talk about was the damage to the museum and the fact that Dr. Logan had gone missing. "He didn't even show up to the exhibition," Jessica complained. "What's up with that?"

I felt like any second she would turn to me and ask, "And where were *you*?" But she never did.

All day I waited for the other shoe to drop. As morning turned into afternoon and nothing happened, I almost started to feel like it had been silly of me to be so on edge. There was no other shoe. But then during biology class, a voice sounded over the loudspeaker, summoning me to the principal's office.

My heart leaped into my throat. *What do I say?*

When I got to the office, my stomach sank as I made eye contact with my fellow Wildcats, already seated inside: Lin,

Shani, and Doli. I saw the same fear on their faces that must have been on mine. Principal Ferris couldn't possibly know the truth, could she? Or was she about to reveal that she was some sort of ancient god too? That would have sounded laughable a few weeks ago. But last night I'd seen Dr. Logan turn into a jackal-headed demon. Now anything seemed possible.

We sat silently in soft sky-blue chairs in front of the principal's desk while she slapped her hands together and brought them to rest over her face, as if she were praying. Finally she said, "Ladies, do you know why you're here?"

I craned my neck at the other girls. Of course we did. But did she really expect us to say it? I wasn't even sure where I would begin if I tried. We all remained quiet, my foot nervously tapping against the floor until Doli gave me a look that said, *Cut it out!*

Principal Ferris sighed. "I thought as much. Well, I know what you girls were up to last night," she said.

"You do?" Doli replied, her voice shaky. I shot Shani a frightened look. This was it! We were about to be expelled—or worse.

"I do." The principal smiled. "I know everything that goes on in my school. And what I know right now is that the four of you disobeyed orders to evacuate the museum and put yourselves in a very dangerous position."

Suddenly it struck me that I could tell Principal Ferris the truth. Part of it, anyway. "We only went back inside because we were looking for Lin." I glanced at Lin, hoping she could see that I meant what I was about to say. "I was worried about her."

Lin's eyes softened for a fraction of a second, but she quickly looked away and crossed her arms. "What for? I'd just gone downstairs to find a bathroom that wasn't swarming with women changing gross dirty diapers. But then the lights went out and I got a little lost, that's all."

Of course that hadn't been all. Her trip to the bathroom had nearly gotten us killed. But Principal Ferris didn't need to know that. "Anyway," I continued, "when we got to the basement, that's when we found Ms. Benitez and Lin." I hesitated, feeling guilty that I was about to fudge the truth a bit. "The ceiling was broken when we got there and we could tell Ms. Benitez was hurt. We thought maybe she'd been hit by some falling plaster. So we led her outside where she'd be safe."

Principal Ferris sighed. "Well, it's commendable that you were trying to help Ms. Benitez and locate your friend. But in the future, leave that to the professionals. No one could have foreseen the building getting struck by lightning and suffering severe damage, but that's what evacuations are for. By disobeying our instructions, you could have been seriously hurt or even killed."

I breathed out a sigh. She didn't know what I thought she knew. She was right that we hadn't evacuated the building along with everyone else, though. Who had told her? Had

Jason said something? Or was she a part of this somehow?

"How is Ms. Benitez?" I asked.

Principal Ferris sighed and she lowered her blue eyes to the floor. "I'm afraid she's in a coma," she replied. "The doctors are still running tests, but they noticed her heart was beating irregularly and there was significant bruising on her chest. They think she had a heart attack. If what you say is true, perhaps she was hit by a piece of falling debris, and the stress brought on by the lightning strike and then fleeing the building in her weakened state was simply too much for her. The doctors are hopeful for a full recovery, but for now we'll have to wait and see. I'm just grateful that you all left the building when you did. Otherwise, all four of you could have found yourselves in hospital beds alongside Ms. Benitez."

We nodded in unison. "We're sorry for worrying you, Principal Ferris," I said. "It won't happen again."

She gave us as stern a look as she could manage, though beneath that I could see her relief that we were all right. "See that it doesn't," she said. She stood and gestured toward the door. "Since this period is almost over, you may report to study hall until the bell rings. Please use that time to think about your actions. Remember, ladies: safety first."

"'Think about your actions,'" Shani mimicked later as we sat in the study-hall section of the library. "If only she knew! Pretty much all I'll ever be able to think about again is the fact that I transformed into a giant man-eating lion last night. Can you even believe that?"

"Um, yes," I said. "I was there, remember? We all turned into man-eating cats last night."

"Yeah," Shani said. "But I'm a vegetarian!"

There was a pause and then we all burst out laughing. Everyone but Lin. A girl at a nearby table shushed us, but I didn't care. It felt good to laugh after the strangeness of the past couple of days. We couldn't hold back our giggles.

"What do they call a vegetarian who eats men, anyway?" Doli asked.

"A humanitarian?" I offered. We started laughing again, earning more shushes from the next table and the librarian.

"Could you guys keep it down?" Lin hissed. "We don't need everyone hearing you talk about something so crazy."

"All right, yes, it was crazy," I said once I'd stopped laughing. I leaned over the table. "But wasn't it also *amazing*? I've never felt that powerful before, like nothing could hurt me."

"That must be nice," Lin said, shooting daggers at me with her eyes. I knew she was talking about Jason again. I hadn't had a chance to speak to her alone yet, and she was still clearly carrying the hurt she felt over Jason as if it were one of her designer purses. We would have to talk about it eventually, but I didn't want to make things any more awkward than they already were for Shani and Doli.

"Come on," I said, gently steering the conversation back to

the one thing that still bonded us. "Didn't you feel powerful while you were a tiger?"

"I don't know what you're talking about," Lin snapped. "Daughters of diplomats and movie stars don't turn into tigers. It's impossible."

Shani reared back in her chair and made a screeching sound as if she were in a car and had just slammed on the brakes. "What was that, Yang? I *know* you're not saying the whole thing never happened."

Lin straightened her spine. "Maybe it didn't. How do you know? Maybe we just imagined it."

"Really?" Doli regarded her with raised eyebrows. "Did we also imagine the hole in the basement ceiling of the museum? And is Ms. Benitez faking her coma?"

Lin had no response. She stared down at her hands. For a moment I thought she would start rotating them again, checking for orange fur and black stripes. "I just want to forget about it," she mumbled.

Doli gave her a sympathetic look. "I hear you. Trust me, I'd love to just go back to running track and taking classes, and pretend none of this ever happened. But it's too late for that now. What we saw was real. Anubis is still out there. You heard Ms. Benitez: We're the only ones standing between our world and total destruction."

"Not to mention those annoying Chaos Spirits," added Shani with a weak smile.

Doli laughed again, but in a nervous way that told me she was trying hard to hold on to her sanity. I guess we all were. "*Right.* Can't forget those," she said. "And they know who we are now, which means none of us will be safe until we find a way to capture them again. But where do we start?"

I tapped my pencil against my chin. "I think first we need to know why Mayan and Egyptian gods would be warring with each other in the first place, and why here?"

"Is it because of the temple?" Doli asked.

I shrugged. "Could be."

There was a pause, then Lin said, "I'm not saying there really was a jackal freak who tried to kill us, but *hypothetically*, if there had been, I might remember him saying, 'The Brotherhood of Chaos will rise again.' Maybe there's something on the Internet about—"

"Way ahead of you," said Shani, opening her laptop. "I'm going to Google that now. Ugh, the server is running kind of slow." While we waited for the Wi-Fi to connect, Shani looked at us somberly. "I just hope that whatever we have to do, we can do it quickly and it won't mess up our future life plans, you know? I mean, I've heard of computer programmers who are so good that people say they're like beasts, but none who actually *is* a beast."

We all chuckled quietly, not wanting to draw the librarian's attention.

"Finally! Here it is," said Shani. "Okay, this is odd. That

search term led to only one result—a research paper titled 'The Brotherhood of Chaos: The Secret History and Destructive Global Impact of the Ancient Mystical Order.' Boy, that's a mouthful. OMG! Guess who wrote it?" She turned the laptop toward us so we could see. *Yvette Benitez.*

"Click on it," I said. "Since we can't ask Ms. Benitez anything right now, this could be the next best thing."

But when Shani tried clicking on the link, she received an error message. "Foiled again." She sighed. "Says here the paper was removed from the history journal."

"Does it say why?" I asked.

Shani tapped a few more keys and scanned the screen. "Ah, right here. It's a retraction posted by the journal that published her paper. Let's see . . . blah blah blah 'research challenged,' yada yada yada 'paper is widely believed to be a hoax.' Ouch."

"In other words, no one believed her," I said.

"Whatever she wrote in that paper must have been pretty out there," Doli added.

"Let's see," Shani said, typing in more codes, her fingers flying across the keyboard. "Here we go," she said. "Page one. Saved forever in the Google cache."

I leaned over to read the screen:

It has long been held by scholars and archaeologists that ancient civilizations on various continents had no interaction due to geographical constrictions and language barriers. But that theory fails to explain the existence of the mystical order the Brotherhood of Chaos. Symbolized by a stylized cat, the order is mentioned in every major ancient civilization, from the Egyptians and Anasazi to the Mayans and Chinese. It is perhaps an overlooked area of scholarly research because the sole purpose of the Brotherhood was a dark one. They sought to . . .

That was it. The page cut off.

"Aw, come on!" Shani cried, clearly frustrated. "They can't leave us on a cliff-hanger like that." She furiously typed in more codes, but no matter what she tried, nothing came up. "Huh. Anubis must have a pretty genius tech guy on his team, because someone went to a lot of trouble to make sure that article never saw the light of day again."

I rested my elbows on the table and raked my fingers through my hair. I felt I was missing something that was right in front of my face. I reread the paragraph and froze when I got to the mention of the stylized cat. "Oh my God," I said.

"What?" said Doli.

"It says the Brotherhood of Chaos was symbolized by a stylized cat. I actually saw a symbol like that on one of the vases at the temple site. Dr. Logan gave me some song and dance about how the Anasazi worshipped cats. But now that we know who Dr. Logan really was, maybe he was just covering up." I told them about the Roman coin that Jason had found and how quickly Dr. Logan had snatched it away from us. "He claimed the coin was his, and he dropped it there. But he was clearly lying. What if the temple isn't Anasazi after all—or at least not *just* Anasazi? Then we'd know that the temple was really part of the Brotherhood of Chaos!"

"So the earthquake that exposed it is what started all this?" Lin asked.

"Maybe," Doli answered. "And that must be why Ms. Benitez invited us all to the museum that night. She must have felt that she had to assemble the Wildcats right away."

"It happened during that orb ceremony we did in the basement, didn't it?" Shani said. "Did you all feel a tingle go up your arm when you touched your territory?"

We all nodded. "That was the beginning," I stated matter-of-factly. "That's when we began to change."

"Fine. Whatever," Lin whispered. "We know what we are now and that the Brotherhood of Chaos is bad news. The question is, what are *we* supposed to do about it? We can't even control our powers yet."

"Maybe it's less about making ourselves stronger than it is about making Anubis weaker," I offered. "Ms. Benitez— Ixchel—told me that he would use the Chaos Spirits to bring death and destruction. But they were trapped by that Mayan vase. That's why he wanted it so badly."

"Don't forget the cats that were etched into the sides," Doli said. "This might sound crazy, but maybe they helped to keep the Chaos Spirits contained. Anubis figured if he destroyed the vase, he would destroy the Wildcats, too. But he didn't count on all of us being there so the cats had real bodies to jump into."

Doli grew quiet, and nobody else seemed to know what to say.

"That doesn't sound crazy," I said after a moment. "In fact, it sounds . . . right on."

Lin and Shani nodded. After a pause, Doli said, "I'm glad it happened that way, and not how the Navajo legends say people usually become shape-shifters."

"How's that?" I asked.

She twisted her lips to the side. "They perform all kinds of evil rites to get the power. I'm talking witchcraft and murder. Shape-shifters aren't quite as bad as skin walkers—who can turn into other people—but they still end up banished by the tribe."

"Well, that seems harsh," Shani said. "Some shape-shifters"—she pointed to herself—"are perfectly nice people."

Doli grinned. "If I ever get up the nerve to confess to my parents, I'll tell them you said so. For now, we've got to figure out how to get the Chaos Spirits back in the vase."

"You mean the vase that Anubis turned into a pile of dust?" I reminded her.

Doli slumped. "Oh, right. I almost forgot."

"Who says it has to be the same vase?" Lin said. "If they were trapped once, they can be trapped again. We just have to find some other container." We all looked at Lin with shocked faces, surprised by her participation. "Hypothetically," she added, shrugging as if she couldn't care less.

I smiled. "You're right, Lin. That could do the trick. Although it would help to know what it was about the vase specifically that held them prisoner. If they could burst through a concrete-and-plaster ceiling, why couldn't they break out of the vase?"

"Hmm . . . ," Shani murmured. "Maybe if we knew more about the vase, that would help. Ana, the vase was donated by your family. Had you ever seen it before?"

I shook my head sadly. "I didn't even know my aunt and uncle owned anything like it. And now it's been destroyed. But hey—I know there's information about the museum collection on the Temple website. Maybe there's a listing for the vase?"

"If it's there, I'll find it," Shani said.

Within a few minutes we were looking at a picture of the vase that had started the battle. There wasn't a lot of information about it, other than that it was of Mayan origin, which we already knew. But as I studied the photos, something finally occurred to me. "See those gems in the corners?" I said, pointing them out. "Where did they go? They were real gemstones, and those aren't easy to destroy. I'd bet you anything they secured the Chaos Spirits inside the vase."

"But where did the Chaos Spirits come from in the first place?" Doli asked.

"I don't know," I replied. There was so much I didn't know. "But according to Ms. Benitez, powers can be used for both good and evil. So maybe we can use them to our advantage— once we figure out where the heck they are now, that is. And once we get them out of the way, we can handle Anubis."

"How do you know?" Lin said, only a slight hint of annoyance in her voice.

"Because . . ." I turned to Lin. "Before Ms. Benitez passed out, she told me that together we are stronger than he is, and that we should have faith in our power."

Suddenly I heard a clatter outside the room and the sound of heavy footsteps walking away. The girl who'd kept shushing us at the next table had left, and we'd thought the librarian was the only one in the library. But she always stepped lightly. Those footsteps belonged to someone else. I felt the back of my neck prickle and I shivered. Was there someone spying on us?

"Is your Spidey sense tingling too?" Shani asked.

"Something like that," I said. "My jaguar sense, anyway." Slowly I crept out of my chair, tiptoeing over to the open door. I looked behind me and saw that the others had followed me without making a sound. We really were becoming more like cats every day. When I got to the entryway, I jumped out, hoping to catch the eavesdropper by surprise. But no one was there. The hallway was empty, and the nearest person searching the stacks was way on the other side of the library.

"Whoever it was moved fast," I said.

"It could just be our new weirdo cat senses," Lin reasoned. "I've been hearing a lot of things that sound as if they're happening right next to me but turn out to be far away. We need to be more careful about where we talk about this, though. If someone was really there and overheard us, we'd sound crazy. Last thing we want is the whole school gossiping about how we think we're big cats."

"Agreed," the rest of us said at once.

I hadn't forgotten that Lin had texted Nicole after our first meeting with Ms. Benitez . . . and I still wondered how much she'd actually told her. But she was finally starting to thaw toward me, and I didn't want to ruin that. We headed back to our table.

"Okay, you guys," said Shani, packing up her laptop. "I don't know about you, but I've had my fill of our little *National Geographic* saga for one day. Besides, we should probably cool it on discussing all this until we're absolutely sure we're alone."

But even as she said it, my earlier paranoia began to seep back in. Were we ever alone? Or was someone keeping tabs on us, watching our every move and just waiting for the right time to pounce?

chapter 16

WITH THE MUSEUM OFF LIMITS AND MS. BENITEZ STILL IN the hospital, there wasn't much we could do. Six days later, at our Monday morning assembly, Principal Ferris stood at the podium looking less bubbly than usual. Her eyes seemed a bit glassy and flat, and she spoke in a monotone. Jason had said his mom had a crush on Dr. Logan, who'd now been gone for a whole week. I wondered if she would still miss him if she'd seen him in his true demon form. I also couldn't keep my eyes off the Egyptian-style necklace she now wore around her neck, which was gorgeous, but not exactly Principal Ferris–style. Was she taking fashion risks to lure her man? Or had the whole world just gone crazy on the night we'd turned into cats?

I had unofficially moved out of my dorm room, bunking with Doli and Shani every night and avoiding Nicole as much as I could. I had to see her in history class, of course, but the school had arranged for a sub to cover for Ms. Benitez, and she mostly had us work quietly by ourselves. I spotted Nicole now, sitting next to Lorna a few rows up to my left. As I watched, she spotted me too, leaned over and whispered something into Lorna's ear, and then giggled quietly, her shoulders shaking. I was sure she'd just said something horrible about me, but whereas a few days before it might have shattered me, now it just made me feel sorry for her. Aunt Teppy often told me that happy people don't need to make others unhappy. Nicole must have been miserable.

At the end of morning announcements, Principal Ferris took a deep breath and said, "Finally, I have something important to tell you, which may come as a shock." She paused and looked up, over the crowd. "I've been puzzling over the right way to say this."

"She's not a natural blonde," Shani joked beside me. "I knew it! No one's hair is that perfect."

I grinned at her, but little butterflies of worry were fluttering around my stomach. What was Principal Ferris talking about? It sounded big.

Principal Ferris took a deep breath. "Since lightning damaged the museum, Dr. Logan has decided to continue his work at the New Mexico State University lab. However, according to Dr. Logan, word of the Anasazi temple's discovery has reached far and wide. In fact, the top archaeologists in the field have deemed the discovery so historic that Dr. Logan has offered to finance the temporary relocation of our school to another campus so the entire area can be excavated."

She may as well have taken a grenade out of her pocket, pulled the pin, and tossed it into the crowd.

The whole room erupted in angry shouts of, "This is our school!" and, "Where are we supposed to go?" The teachers didn't look any happier about it. Our math teacher, Mr. Gerard, stood and pulled up his pants, which always drooped below his generous gut. "You can't be serious about this," he shouted. "The whole idea is ludicrous!"

Ms. Duveaux, the French teacher, shouted out as well. "I've taught at this school for twenty years, and never have we been forced to vacate the premises. It's outrageous!"

"And some of us live here on campus," another teacher shouted from the back of the room. "What about us?"

That earned a chorus of "yeahs" and shouts. Students turned in their seats, excitedly talking to their friends in nearby rows or taking cell-phone pictures of the building mayhem.

"This is crazy," Doli said to me. "I feel like there's going to be a riot."

But before the protests went any further, Principal Ferris tapped the microphone several times, urging everyone to calm down. "Nothing is certain," she said. "We are still in talks, but I wanted to let you know that it is a very real possibility, and if it should come to pass, we will make sure everyone is accommodated. Our top priority is education, and that will not be disrupted."

"This has Anubis written all over it," I whispered. "He just wants us gone so he can get to the temple without a problem."

"So let's fight this and give him a problem," Shani said with a wicked grin. She and Doli fist-bumped and I smiled.

After everyone finally calmed down, the teachers grumbling quietly to themselves, Principal Ferris went on. "In other news, I regret to say that the rash of thefts has continued. I'm getting more reports from students every day of stolen items. This behavior is utterly unacceptable," she said, raising her voice. "Any student with information about the thefts *must* come forward. If we find out later that you knew who the culprit was and remained silent, you, too, will be held accountable."

She finally called assembly to an end, and when the crowd separated me from Shani and Doli, I ended up walking next to Nicole. She turned to me and said loudly enough for everyone to hear, "Hey, Ana. My phone was the most recent thing stolen. Funny how all the thefts started when *you* showed up!"

I rolled my eyes at her. "You *must* be joking," I said.

"Not at all." She held up two fingers and pointed them at her eyes then swung them around at mine. "I'm watching you," she said, and sashayed down the hall ahead of me.

Irritating. I sighed. Nicole was the least of my problems. I had bigger issues to deal with now. Life-or-death issues.

I took my laptop to the computer lab and set myself up in a private room. It had now been more than two weeks since I'd heard anything from Aunt Teppy and Uncle Mec, and I was determined to reach them. I needed them more than ever. I knew that the Wildcats had all agreed not to tell anyone the truth, but I felt certain they'd make an exception in this case. I mean, maybe my aunt and uncle could help us. Since they'd donated the vase, it was possible that they knew about the Chaos Spirits. Or the Wildcats! Or my connection to all of it . . . whatever that was.

Since my aunt and uncle hadn't responded to my Skype invitations, I used the program to call their home phone, instead. It rang three times and then a man answered. "Hello, Navarro residence."

"Finally!" I cried, relieved to have gotten through to my uncle at last. "Where have you guys been? And why did you answer the phone like that?"

There was a pause on the other end of the line. "I'm sorry," he said. "But you must be looking for Mec and Tepin Navarro. They seem to be away."

I felt like I'd been doused with ice water. *It's not Uncle Mec?* Only then did I realize the man's voice was thinner and higher than my uncle's. "Who is this?" I demanded.

"Who is this?" he shot back. "You called this number."

"Ana Cetzal," I said. "I *live* there."

The man's tone immediately warmed up. "Ana, I'm glad to hear from you. This is Steven Waterman. I used to be your parents' lawyer, and I've been managing their estate for many years."

I searched my mind. I knew I had heard his name before, though I'd never met him in person. When my aunt and uncle had started the process of accessing my funds to pay my tuition, Mr. Waterman had been the lawyer who arranged everything.

"Yes, I remember. I'm sorry for the way I spoke to you, Mr. Waterman. It's just been a hard week and I really need to speak to my aunt and uncle. Can you put them on?"

"I wish I could," he answered. "I've actually been trying to get in touch with them for several days now. I finally decided to come over to the house in person today to check on them. But they aren't here. I haven't been here long, but I don't see any sign of them."

I felt my hands begin to shake. If they'd been out of touch for so long that even their lawyer was worried, their silence had not been some tough-love strategy to let me thrive on my own, as Ms. Benitez had suggested. My stomach began to roil. "Well, where are they?" I cried, trying not to panic.

Mr. Waterman hesitated before he said, "That's the part that concerns me. I don't *know* where they are. They never mentioned travel plans to me, and they knew there would be some final paperwork to sign this week. The house seems to be in order, but when I showed up, the door was unlocked, which is strange."

"Strange" was an understatement! My aunt never left any door unlocked. She was paranoid about that. If we left the house and she wasn't absolutely sure we'd locked the door, she would drive home to check, even if we were already several blocks away.

Mr. Waterman continued. "I did notice some drawers open, some clothing seemingly missing. I'd hoped perhaps they had gone to visit you, but apparently that isn't the case. Is it possible they went on an unplanned vacation?"

"No," I said immediately. "They wouldn't do that. They wouldn't go on a trip somewhere and not tell me." Aunt Teppy thought it was really important that I never felt abandoned, which I guess a therapist friend had once told her is a common feeling for orphans. She wouldn't even leave for the grocery store without telling me.

"Let me ask you: Is this the first time you've called since you've been away at school?"

There was no judgment in his tone, but I felt guilty all the same. "Well, yes. I mean, no. I did e-mail them, and I tried to Skype them a few times, but the connection out here—"

"Ana, please don't misunderstand. I'm not accusing you of anything. I'm merely pointing out that since you've been away at school, you haven't been in day-to-day touch with them. Something may have occurred that prompted a last-minute trip."

"Something like what?" I urged.

"Maybe there was an unexpected death in the family. Perhaps a work trip? It's possible they took a little vacation to console themselves over your absence. I know how much they love you. In any case, I assure you I will do everything in my power to locate them. In the meantime, I don't want you to worry. From everything I've heard, Temple Academy is a fine school. So you should focus on your schoolwork and enjoy yourself. I'll be in touch if there's any news to share."

I was about to yell that I couldn't enjoy myself until I knew for sure that they were okay. But as I was about to say the words, the overhead lights began to flicker, just as they had done in the museum the night of the exhibition. I glanced around the main room and watched as one by one the computers shut down, their screens going black. I turned back to my computer to tell Mr. Waterman what was happening, but the call had been disconnected. Mr. Waterman was gone. When I tried to reconnect, I got an error message telling me that the network was unavailable. The Internet was down. *Arrrgh!* I couldn't take any more of these power outages. They always seemed to happen at the worst possible time. I wanted to throw my laptop across the room, but I was fairly sure Shani would kill me if I did.

So instead I gathered my things and walked back to Radcliff Hall, hoping that maybe it was a rolling blackout that had yet to reach my dorm and I could get online there. When I arrived, the dorm was totally dark except for the sunlight streaming through the windows. Several girls—including

Doli, Shani, and Lin—were all packed into the common room, chattering loudly, their arms crossed.

"What's going on?" I asked Doli. "Did the power surge here, too?"

"It's worse than that. Mrs. O'Grady said she got word from Principal Ferris that the entire computer network crashed. Plus, we have no electricity," Doli replied. "Shani is devastated."

"You joke," Shani said, "but I am. Mrs. O'Grady is checking to see why the generators haven't switched on yet, but for now we're in the dark."

Doli motioned for Lin, Shani, and me to follow her to the kitchen, where we wouldn't be overheard. "I've been thinking," she said. "Ana, you know how you said Lin accused you of causing the earthquakes and storms because they started when you arrived?"

I gave Lin a baleful look, and she had the grace to blush. "Yeah."

"Well, you weren't the only one who arrived right around that time."

It took me a moment to catch on. "Dr. Logan!"

She nodded. "And when we were in the basement, Ixchel said that she knew he was walking the Earth again when the strange weather started up."

"So what does that mean?" Shani said.

Doli took a deep breath. "I think that whenever there's a

power surge, or an earthquake, or a thunderstorm that comes out of nowhere, it's because Anubis is nearby."

Suddenly I felt the blood drain from my face. "Oh, God," I said. "The night before I left Ohio, there was a huge storm. It raged all night. And now I just talked to my family's lawyer and he says my aunt and uncle have gone missing. What if . . . what if Anubis was there in Ohio, plotting to get rid of me and my family? They're the ones who sent the vase. What if they knew something about how to capture the Chaos Spirits, so he did something to them before they could tell me? Or maybe he was there to try to stop me from coming to Temple so that the Wildcats would never meet." Every possibility made me shiver to the bone. "What if he has them?" I whispered, dread washing over me.

"You can't think that way," said Doli. "Your aunt and uncle sound pretty smart. And if they sent the vase, they probably aren't completely in the dark about all this either. Besides, if Anubis had them, don't you think he would have used them against you by now?"

She had a point there. I held on to that kernel of hope as if it were gold.

Shani gave us a mischievous smile. "There is one silver lining about the whole grid being down," she said. "No lights means no problem sneaking out to the woods tonight to practice shape-shifting into Wildcats."

Lin let out a disgusted grunt. "Ugh, you mean you want

me to trek through the muddy athletic field in the dark so we can run around in the woods? No way. It'll ruin my clothes, and the only shoes I own are designer."

"I'll lend you something more casual to wear," I promised.

"But—"

"Lin, learning how to use our powers might be the only way to stop Anubis. If he shows up again, Ms. Benitez won't be around to save our skins," I said. "We need to be able to defend ourselves. But we've got to do it together. We're a team, right?" I stuck my hand out, palm down, and Shani and Doli piled theirs on top. We all gazed at Lin expectantly.

Finally she added her dainty hand, so different from her tiger paw, on top and said, "Right. We're a team."

chapter 17

"AHHH, WHY CAN'T I GET THIS!" DOLI GROANED.

I'd never seen her this upset. She was usually so laid back. But Doli was also used to winning. And at that moment we were all failing miserably at transforming into the Wildcats.

We'd waited until eleven o'clock, when we were sure Mrs. O'Grady had gone to bed, then we sneaked out of the dorm. We trekked through the muddy athletic field in the dark, just as Lin had feared, stopping only when we found a clearing in the woods near an old hiking trail where we could practice transforming. The problem was, we had no idea how we'd done it the first time, so we had no clue how to do it again.

We tried chanting out loud using Navajo words that Doli taught us. We tried spinning in a circle like Wonder Woman. Lin even tried scaring us into transforming, as if she were trying to cure a bad case of hiccups, but she was wearing my Cookie Monster T-shirt and an old pair of my Keds, so how scary could she be? It was now well past midnight and not a single one of us had managed so much as a whisker.

"Maybe it only works in creepy museum basements," Shani suggested.

"If that's the case, I'm going home," said Lin. "I need my—"

"Beauty sleep," we all said in unison. It was the fourth time she'd said it, and we were all sick to death of hearing the same old thing.

Lin looked at us, pouting. "Well, I do."

"Guys," I said finally, "maybe we're trying too hard. I mean, these cats are a part of us now. Maybe instead of thinking, 'Turn into a jaguar, turn into a jaguar,' over and over, we need to just think like an animal. You know, let go and let the cat take over."

"Sounds a little New Agey to me," Shani said, "but let's give it a try."

I closed my eyes. First, I tried to clear my mind. I thought of nothing but the cool night air on my skin and the sound of lizards scurrying through the leaves. I could hear their three-pronged feet scratching into the dirt as they ran. I sniffed the air and smelled chlorine and dead leaves coming from the pool. When my breath was nice and even, I tried to recall the way I'd felt as a cat. I pictured my lean, muscular body walking on four legs, and balancing the weight of it with my tail. I saw myself moving through the woods on padded feet, finding the wind's direction with a shake of my whiskers. I imagined my teeth growing long and sharp in my mouth. . . .

Slowly, tingles traveled up my spine and down into my hands. I detected the musty aroma of fear as the horses in the stables picked up my scent. I felt loose and strong. When I opened my mouth to say, "I think it's working," what came out was a quiet roar, followed by a loud scream.

I opened my eyes to find Shani and Doli staring down at me with fascinated expressions on their faces. Lin was hiding behind Doli, her eyes just peeking over her shoulder.

"That. Was. Awesome!" Shani exclaimed.

"I think you traumatized Lin for life," Doli said with a touch of pleasure in her voice. She raised her fist in front of her and gave me a secret thumbs-up.

"Did not," Lin said, emerging from her hiding place. "I just . . . don't want to get any of her cat saliva on me. Gross."

I licked my paw and shook out my fur, settling into my jaguar skin, and let out a low growl full of warning.

Lin jumped back behind Doli, and Shani burst out laughing. "Guess we know who the alpha cat is. I'm so going next," she said.

Her transformation was slow but amazing. At one point she opened her eyes in time to see her hands turn into lion paws so heavy that her human arms were almost too weak to lift them. Lin, probably eager not to be the last human standing among a pack of dangerous—and possibly hungry—wild animals, took only ten seconds to change. Doli, ever the competitor, transformed almost instantly.

We did it! We had become the Wildcats, on purpose this time.

When the transformations were complete, the dogs in the kennel far from where we were began to howl and yelp. *They must sense that big cats are near*, I thought. I padded ahead to the hiking trails that led down into the valley, where we couldn't be seen from campus. As soon as we reached the valley floor, we took off running.

As a jaguar, I could see just as well in the dark as I could in the light of day, maybe even better. We'd managed to avoid human eyes, but here there were a thousand more. The night was alive! Blackbirds drinking from trickling streams took flight when we passed, and I could see every flap of their glistening wings against the moonlight. Raccoons scurried into their nests, and fat spiders hung from the ends of thin lines of silk, their webs quivering in the breeze. It was such a rush being one more creature in the night, feeling like I belonged here. It was the most fun I'd ever had in my life.

Even Lin looked like she was enjoying herself now. It didn't faze her when she galloped through clouds of buzzing mosquitoes. She just kept running, bounding over rocks and joyfully waving her striped orange tail.

We could have run all night, but the moon, which had been riding high when we first came out, had begun to sink behind the trees as if it were putting itself to bed. It was getting late. Eventually, Doli led us back to the clearing, and this time we focused on what it felt like to be human. I imagined walking upright, my fur replaced with smooth brown skin, my teeth small and even. Being a jaguar felt so natural to me that it was almost disappointing to open my eyes and find that I was a human being again.

When we'd all transformed into our usual bodies, it was Doli who spoke first. "That was incredible. I think we've got the hang of this now."

"I hope so," said Shani. "If Anubis comes back and hits us with magic again to turn us human, I want to be able to shift right back."

"Me too," Lin agreed. "But not tonight. I'm so tired."

"We should go back to the dorm one at a time," I suggested. "Everyone's probably asleep by now, but just in case. . . ."

Shani and Doli headed back first, leaving me and Lin on the athletic field. While we waited, Lin turned to me abruptly and blurted, "So Jason has been texting you?"

Taken by surprise, I furrowed my eyebrows. I vaguely remembering mentioning that in passing, but why was she bringing it up now? "Once in a while," I said. "Why?"

Lin tipped her chin up so she was looking down her nose at me. "He's like that with everybody at first, you know. He's just friendly. It doesn't mean he likes you. It doesn't mean anything."

"Okay," I said slowly. "So if it doesn't mean anything, why do you care?"

Her lips tightened into a hard line. "I don't," she snapped. But it was obvious that she did. Without another word she slipped down the path that led back to the dorm, leaving me speechless. *This is going to be a problem,* I thought.

I knew I should follow Lin back to Radcliff, but something about the early dawn air was intoxicating. No one was going to be up for another hour or so—did it really matter whether I lingered a few more minutes? I looked around and didn't see anyone. *No one will see,* I thought. So I cleared my mind, focused my cat senses, and changed back into my jaguar self once more. For a moment I wondered what would happen if I went into the dorm this way. If Nicole found me scary as a human, how would she react if she woke up and found a massive jaguar waiting outside her room? The image was almost too good to resist. But in the end, I did the right thing. I looked up at the full moon and changed back into my human form, like a werewolf in reverse. But when I turned to face the dorm, I found that I wasn't alone after all.

Jason stood on the running track in his sweats—and he was staring right at me. I felt my heart jump into my throat. *He must be out for an early jog. . . .*

Had he seen? The lights were low across the campus, but the stars were so bright. . . .

"Hi, Jason," I tested. "What are you doing h—"

Jason's eyes rounded in horror and he backed away, holding his hands out in front of him. "Don't . . . don't come any closer," he said.

My heart sank. He'd seen, all right. I took another step

toward him. "Jason, calm down. It's okay. I can explain," I pleaded—even though I had no idea how I could possibly explain.

"I mean it—*get back*!" He was terrified, I realized. Of me. With my jaguar senses, I could smell his fear. But even without that, it was written all over his face.

"Don't freak out," I said. "It's just me."

"Don't freak out?" He shook his head. "*You're not even human*!" he shouted. "I don't know *what* you are, but I want you to stay away from me."

He turned and ran, disappearing down the pathway. The exhilaration I'd felt earlier in the night crumbled, and I felt my heart shatter like glass.

chapter 18

Exhausted as I was, I spent the whole school day pumped up on adrenaline, panicked that Principal Ferris was going to call me into her office any minute. And what would I say? *Sorry, Principal Ferris, it's just that me and my Ancient Civilization Superpowers figured out that we can transform into Wildcats. No biggie! Sorry I freaked out your son. . . .*

I dragged my way through biology lab, then world history, then English. I kept expecting an office aide to come in and call me out of class, but the worst thing that happened all day was when Mr. Harper chided me for not participating in our class discussion of *Oliver Twist*. I'd actually read the chapters he'd assigned the night before. . . . I was just too jittery to form a coherent thought.

"You don't have *anything* to add about the story, Ms. Cetzal?" Mr. Harper asked, crossing his arms and looking down at me in disapproval.

Gulp. I tried to force my brain to produce something. "I think it's . . . really depressing," I managed after a few seconds. I heard a wave of titters go through the class, and when I looked up at Mr. Harper's scowl, I could tell I'd said the wrong thing.

He sniffed and pinched my shoulder before walking away. "Do try to have something more significant to add tomorrow," he muttered. I felt a wave of relief as he called on Nicole, who was smirking and waving her hand in the air. *Got a reprieve!*

After class, Lin and Shani came running up to me as I trudged along the path back to the dorm.

"Ana!" Lin cried, grabbing my arm. "Seriously, if we're going to practice our *special skills* at night, you have *got* to get better at hiding how tired you are the next day."

I turned to look at my friends. They both looked bright and alert, though when I looked closer, I could see the bags under their eyes. I hadn't told them about Jason spotting me in my jaguar guise last night. I wasn't trying to hide it from them, exactly—I just felt like it was my problem. And until I knew it involved them, I didn't want to freak them out.

"How are you two looking so perky?" I asked, avoiding the subject.

Shani chuckled. "Caffeine, and lots of it!" she said.

Lin nodded vigorously. "It's days like today when I really appreciate the espresso bar in the cafeteria."

Noting the slightly manic expression in her eyes, I couldn't help chuckling too. But then I spotted the person I'd been secretly searching for all day: Jason. He was striding toward us, a few yards away, walking with his head down. In a few seconds he'd cross our path. My heart leaped into my throat, and I stared at him, waiting for him to notice me.

Lin seemed to notice my sudden silence and followed my gaze to Jason. "Ooh," she murmured, and pasted on an even more manic smile as he came closer.

But her effort was wasted. Jason glanced up at us only briefly as he passed us. As soon as he saw me, he quickly focused his gaze back on the pathway and picked up his pace, practically jogging away.

Lin's head swiveled to watch him run off. "Wow," she breathed, turning back to me with a satisfied expression. "Guess the honeymoon's over, huh?"

I sighed. "Drop it, Lin," I huffed, and ran ahead to go back to the dorm alone.

I didn't feel like talking to anyone. I just wanted to crawl back into bed and hope things would feel more normal when I woke up.

I entered the dorm feeling like a deflated balloon. Despite all my worrying, it didn't look like Jason had any plans to tell anyone what he'd seen—who would believe him, anyway? But the way he had looked at me in that brief moment when he passed us, like I was a monster, broke my heart.

On my way to Doli and Shani's room, I ran right into Mrs. O'Grady, the dorm mother. She was holding a cup of tea and when she saw me, she took on a pinched expression. "Ana," she said in a reedy voice, "just the person I've been looking for. We need to talk."

For a second I thought she knew that I'd sneaked out the night before. I tried to figure out what I would say.

"Is it true that you've been sleeping in Doli and Shani's room?" she asked, surprising me.

I lowered my eyes. How had she found out? "Yes, it's true."

"I'm sure you know that's against dorm rules. If you want to switch rooms, that's fine. But you have to do it through the proper channels. Otherwise, you'll have to remain in your assigned room. Do you understand?"

I nodded. "What are the proper channels?"

"There are change-of-room request forms in the main building," she answered. "You can only put in for one room change per semester, though, so you'd better be sure it's what you want before you fill out the paperwork."

"Oh, I'm sure. I'll do it first thing tomorrow, okay, Mrs. O'Grady? Sorry for the delay." I started heading up the stairs to Doli's room, but Mrs. O'Grady grabbed my hand.

"I'm sorry, but until your request is granted, you need to sleep in your own room," she said. "Starting tonight."

I sighed miserably. *Just what I need to make this day even harder: face time with Nicole.* "Fine. I need to get my blanket and pillow from their room, though."

Mrs. O'Grady nodded. "We'll go together."

Upstairs I opened the door to find the room empty. Shani must have stopped in the common room or to chat more with Lin; Doli was probably taking her time walking back from Spanish class. Quickly I gathered my things, wrote a quick note, and rejoined Mrs. O'Grady in the hallway, sticking the note to the door behind me. Mrs. O'Grady nodded and walked me back downstairs to my old room.

After she left, I hesitated outside the door. I could hear music playing and smelled something like ammonia. I heard a giggle behind me, and turned around just in time to see the door across the hall slam shut. *Great.* Someone had already gotten wind of the Disgraced Roommate returning to the site of her shame. I might as well go in before the hallway filled with spies.

I turned the knob. At least the door was unlocked. I found Nicole inside, sitting on her bed and painting her nails. Bruno Mars blared from her iPod dock. Between the nail-polish fumes, the throbbing music, and the very sight of Nicole, I suddenly had a pounding headache.

She looked up at me, her face registering surprise and then contorting into a frown. "What are *you* doing here? I thought I told you to find somewhere else to sleep."

I sighed. "I did. But someone told Mrs. O'Grady, and she says I can't move out without filing a room-change request. I'll do that first chance I get, but for now, you're just going to have to deal."

"I don't *have* to do anything," Nicole snapped, slamming her magazine shut and tossing it to the floor. "And I don't want you in here if you're going to be growling at me and acting all insane."

The veins in my forehead pulsed and I felt the same tingling in my spine that I'd felt the first time I'd transformed. *Uh-oh.* "Be careful, Nicole," I warned. "I don't think you should make me angry right now. Back off, or . . . or . . ."

Her voice went up another octave. "Or what? You'll do something to me like you did to Ms. Benitez?"

This time I took a step back. Thanks to my new superhuman cat senses, I could hear the other girls on our floor gathering on the other side of the door to eavesdrop. They were whispering and jostling for space.

"What are you *talking* about?" I exclaimed.

"Don't play innocent. I know you were there the night Ms. Benitez was taken away in an ambulance. She tried to be nice to you and now she's in a coma."

I felt off balance, my legs shaky. "That wasn't my fault!" I insisted. "She—"

But I couldn't say, *She was protecting me.* If I did, I'd have to tell Nicole what Ms. Benitez had been protecting me from. "S-she got hurt when a piece of the museum ceiling fell on her," I tried. "I helped drag her out of the building."

Nicole shook her head. "You're such a liar. I know you know more than you're letting on. Something happened that night but you're covering it up. Miss Benitez was young and healthy. Why would a bump on the head send her into a coma?"

I wanted to tell her that Ms. Benitez was far from young. She was probably older than everyone in the dorm combined times a hundred. But I clamped my lips shut. That was one piece of gossip Nicole would not get her hands on.

"It's like you cast some evil spell on her or something," Nicole hissed. "You must be some kind of witch and you're out to destroy this school!"

I was furious. Here I was trying to fight the forces of evil, and she was accusing me of being a witch!

"I'm no witch," I cried, as much to all the girls I knew were listening from the hall as to Nicole. I balled my fists at my sides, aching to knock her to the floor. We'd be the talk of the campus for months, thanks to her. But after the first time I'd lashed out at Nicole, I'd checked the welcome packet again, and she was right about one thing: They weren't kidding about their zero-tolerance violence policy. It was mentioned at least three times. I knew that if I lost control with the jaguar so near my surface, there was no telling what would happen. But the tingling in my spine was getting stronger.

"Nicole, would you please just turn the music down?" I begged, dumping my blanket on the bed. "I'm exhausted. All I want is to take a nap."

But instead of lowering the volume, she rose from the bed, crossed over to the iPod on her desk, and turned it up. She started dancing around the room. "Puh-lease. Because we're running on generator power, they're only letting us use electricity for a couple of hours. I'm going to enjoy it while it lasts," she shouted over the music.

"Nicole, come on. . . ."

She cupped her hand behind her ear. "What? Sorry. Can't hear you." She kept dancing.

That was it; I was done being polite. I went over to her desk and turned the iPod off altogether. She whirled to face me, her eyes bulging. She stomped over to me and turned the music on again. I turned it off and ripped the iPod out of the docking station, glaring at her defiantly. But she came at me, her lips pulled back in a sneer. "Give it back—"

Acting on instinct, I bared my teeth and let out the same sound that had sent Lin scurrying behind Doli the night before.

Nicole pulled back with a grimace. "OMG, did you just *growl* at me? You're a freak!"

Last night's practice had gone well, but I knew I didn't have much control over the big cat inside me. I could feel it tugging at my insides, as if it were itching to be let out of its cage. "I don't want to hurt you, Nicole," I said in a low voice. "So please don't make me."

"What did you just say?" Nicole asked.

"I said don't make me hurt you!" I couldn't help shouting, and I felt the cat within preparing to pounce, to rip, to . . .

I gasped in horror at my own thoughts. I took a few deep breaths and backed away from Nicole, holding up my hands in surrender.

But Nicole just flashed an evil smile. "Get away from me," she said loudly, in a frightened voice that didn't match her expression at all. Then as I watched in disbelief, she raked at her face with her own freshly painted fingernails.

"What are you *doing*?" I breathed, barely able to form words. I knew she was evil, but surely she couldn't be evil enough to fake an attack on herself . . . could she?

"Ana, don't! No! HELP!" she screamed.

Nicole's scream was all it took to bring the girls from the hallway crashing into the room.

Jessica rushed to Nicole's side. "What's going on here?" she said.

They all looked from me, in my near-catatonic state, to Nicole, who was bleeding from her self-inflicted wounds.

Nicole pointed a shaky finger at me and cried, "She attacked me!"

That's when I spotted Shani, standing with Doli and peering through the doorway. Shani raised an eyebrow at me. *Did you?* When I shook my head, she shrugged as if to say, *Eh, too bad.*

Most of the other girls seemed to buy Nicole's story hook, line, and sinker. They fawned over her, sending me accusatory glares. Only a few girls hung back, regarding Nicole with wary glances. Lin stood in the middle of the room in her 7

For All Mankind jeans, seeming unsure whose side to take.

After a few seconds Doli spoke up. "Get real, Nicole. Ana never touched you. You're lying."

"What?" Nicole screeched. "That's insane."

"Yeah, why would you even say that, Doli?" Tanya asked.

Doli cast a bored glance in Nicole's direction. "For starters, there are smears of pink nail polish on her face. As far as I know, Ana doesn't even own a bottle of nail polish. And look at Nicole's hands. Either smeared polish is the new style, or she did this to herself."

Some of the girls backed away from Nicole then, uncertainty evident on their faces. Nicole, seeming to sense that she was losing them, started sobbing dramatically. There were no actual tears and it seemed clear to me that she was just putting on a show. But her friends thrived on drama. The girls who were already crowded around her moved even closer, making little clucking noises of pity.

Shani rolled her eyes at the obvious ploy. Then she gave me a smile and pulled out her phone. *Time for some distraction,* she mouthed to me. I watched as she dialed Nicole's number, waiting for the song about big butts to start playing from Nicole's purse. Only, when the song did start to play, the sound came out of Lin's back pocket.

Lin looked horrified, and I tried to work through my confusion. How had Nicole's phone ended up in Lin's pocket? Shani's own puzzled look told me that she hadn't expected this either. But her expression soon changed to one of shock as she realized the truth. "Lin, *you're* the thief?"

"What?" Lin screeched, a little too loudly. "That's crazy. *You're* crazy."

Someone gasped. "Hey! The night my ring went missing, Lin had been in my room."

"Get real," said Lin. "My father is a diplomat and my mother is a famous actress overseas. They'd buy me this whole *school* if I asked them to. What would I want with your stupid ring?"

If I hadn't gotten to know Lin better over the past few days, I might not have noticed the self-conscious shift of her eyes, or the way her bottom lip trembled. She was trying to hold on to that infamous Yang demeanor that had always kept the piranhas at bay, but I could see that it was slipping away from her.

"And my iPod disappeared after we shared a locker for gym class," said another girl, ignoring Lin's denials. Once the ball got rolling, it was impossible to stop. The girls began to pile on, shifting their attention away from Nicole and focusing it on Lin. It seemed that Lin had been nearby each time one of the stolen items went missing.

"Leave her alone," I tried in vain. I wanted to give Lin the benefit of the doubt. After all, I thought, glancing at Nicole's scratched-up cheeks, I had just found out what it felt like to be accused of something I absolutely didn't do. But the guilt-ridden, mortified look dawning on Lin's face told me that her presence at the scene of each crime was no coincidence.

Finally, avoiding everyone's eyes, Lin pushed her way past the girls and ran.

I stared after her in shock. I couldn't believe she was the thief. Why would the wealthy daughter of a movie star and a diplomat have to steal? There must have been a reason. At least, I hoped there was.

Nicole, meanwhile, had all but forgotten her little crying display. She rubbed her hands together as if she were about to dig in to a delicious meal. "I can't wait to tell Principal Ferris all this," she said, smiling cruelly.

"Why don't you start by telling me," said Mrs. O'Grady, suddenly materializing in the doorway, "what's going on here?"

Immediately, every girl in the room started talking at once. Mrs. O'Grady massaged her temples then said, "Enough! I can only listen to one of you at a time. Anyone who doesn't live in this room, please go. My guess is, this is no concern of yours." Some of the girls protested, but Mrs. O'Grady pointed to their rooms and sent them packing.

"Good luck," Doli whispered as she passed me on her way into the hall.

When it was finally just Nicole and me with Mrs. O'Grady, she asked again for us to tell her what happened.

"Mrs. O'Grady," Nicole began, batting her eyelashes—the picture of innocence. "I was just sitting here minding my own business when Ana barged into the room and started yelling at me. I asked her to leave me alone and told her that if she didn't stop, I'd go get help, but she just said, 'Don't make me hurt you!'"

I winced. If Mrs. O'Grady asked any of the girls in the hallway what they'd seen or heard, they could all confirm that I'd said those words. Out of context, it sounded all wrong.

"I tried to lighten the mood by playing some music, but she ripped my iPod out of the dock. When I asked her nicely to give it back, she growled at me like some kind of animal. And then she . . . she attacked me!" Nicole dropped her head as if she was tearing up, but I knew she was probably hiding a grin over her Academy Award–worthy performance.

Mrs. O'Grady turned to me, studying my reaction. "Is that what happened?" she asked.

"No!" I exclaimed. I countered with the truth about Nicole blaring her music and accusing me of being a witch. I laid out the same evidence Doli had mentioned, pointing out Nicole's smeared nails and my lack of polish. "She's trying to frame me!" I insisted.

"She *growled* at me," Nicole snapped, satisfied, I guess, that she could use that kernel of truth against me.

"She called me a freak."

"You *are* a freak!"

Mrs. O'Grady pursed her lips and let out a long, high-pitched whistle, silencing us instantly. She sighed wearily. "Well, it looks like you two will not be able to resolve this any time soon. So perhaps it is best that we see about getting you a new room assignment immediately, Ana. For tonight, although it is technically against the rules, you may sleep in Doli and Shani's room. As long as it's all right with them."

I breathed a sigh of relief and said, "Thank you, thank you. I really appreciate—"

"However," Mrs. O'Grady interrupted, "both you and Nicole will have to go to student court. Since assault is grounds for expulsion, there will be a peer trial over this incident to determine whether you really did attack Ms. Van Voorhies."

"A trial?" I repeated, stunned.

"I'm afraid so," she said.

"But I didn't do anything!" I cried.

"You'll have your chance to say that in court," said Mrs. O'Grady, giving me a stern look that told me she didn't want to hear another word about it.

"Fine, fine," I mumbled. I glanced at Nicole, waiting to see if she would bring up the fact that Lin was the thief. But to my relief, Nicole said nothing. For now, she seemed satisfied with having gotten me into trouble. But I wondered if any of the other girls would report Lin in the morning. If they did, there was a good chance that Lin and I would be leaving Temple Academy together.

At that point, I hated the sight of Nicole so much, I would have done anything to get out of that room and away from her. I grabbed my pillow and blanket and walked back to Doli and

Shani's room. They were sitting on Doli's bed talking, and they immediately perked up when I entered.

"What happened?" Doli asked.

"Did you get expelled?" Shani jumped in. "Did she? *Please* tell me Nicole got expelled."

"And what about Lin?" Doli sat up, hugging her pillow to her. "I went to her room to check on her, but she wasn't there or in the common room. Did Nicole report her to Mrs. O'Grady?"

"I don't want to talk about it right now," I grumbled, ignoring their questions. I didn't want to spend one more second thinking about Nicole. Without another word, I crawled into the sleeping bag, closed my eyes, and fell into a dead sleep.

chapter 19

CATS CIRCLED MY DREAMS. THE MANY BECAME ONE. THEN one insistent cat was meowing directly in my ear. Along with the sound of Shani snoring and the soft *tick tick tick* of Doli's alarm clock. Wait. No, this wasn't happening in my dreamless sleep. The sounds were real. The meowing continued, getting louder. I opened my eyes.

When I'd settled into Doli and Shani's room that night, I guess I'd succeeded in blocking out the world. It looked like they hadn't even woken me up for dinner, just letting me sleep through till bedtime. But now there was a cat calling to me somewhere in the night. I unraveled myself from the sleeping bag and tiptoed to the window. There, right below me, was the black cat with the brilliant green eyes that I'd seen near the temple. It let out another loud mewl when it saw me.

"Doli!" I whispered. "Wake up, wake up." She mumbled

something but kept her eyes closed. Finally I went to her bed and shook her awake.

"Ana? What's wrong?" She craned her neck to check her clock. "It's three in the morning."

"I know, sorry. But you have to see this." I shook Shani awake too and brought them both to the window. The cat was still there.

"Uh, you woke me up to look at a cat?" Shani grumbled. "I'm going back to bed."

I pulled her closer to the window. "Wait!" I urged. "I've seen this cat before. I think it's trying to get my attention."

Shani peeked down, one eye barely open. "Huh. It does seem to be looking right at us, doesn't it? You think it knows about . . . the Wildcats?"

"Maybe," I said. "Either way, I think it's trying to tell us something. It's been meowing for a while now. It woke me up."

We watched as the cat spun in frantic circles. It padded away from the building, then looked up at us and waited, its back turned.

"Looks like she wants us to follow her," Doli said.

I tilted my head. "She?"

"Just guessing."

"I don't get a bad vibe from her, but then what do I know?" I asked. "I went all these years not knowing I'm part jaguar. What if it's some kind of trap?"

Shani smiled and left the window to pull on her jeans and

sneakers. "We know how to use our powers now," she said. "Kind of. If it's a trap, I say bring it on."

Just like the night before, we sneaked out of the dorm one at a time, careful not to rouse Mrs. O'Grady, who'd already had an earful tonight. When the three of us reunited outside, we found the cat waiting patiently. I reached out to pet her, but she turned and ran down the pathway.

I grinned at my friends. "Time for our three a.m. workout." If Lin had been there, she would have griped about being forced to run when she wasn't even in gym class, or she'd complain that the cat had ruined her beauty sleep. But Lin wasn't there. It surprised me how sad that made me. I'd told her before that the four of us were a team. Going off to do something that might involve the Wildcats without her didn't feel right. But since we didn't know where Lin was—or if she wanted to see anyone right now—we had no choice.

Together we jogged behind the cat. She cut behind the academic building and through the athletic field, then disappeared into the woods. Finally she came to a stop when she reached the yellow cautionary tape that bordered the temple. The cat crossed beneath the tape and looked back at us.

"We've come this far," Doli said with a shrug. She ducked under the tape, and Shani and I did the same. The cat darted past the parts of the temple that had been fully excavated, coming instead to a pile of rubble around the side. It began to paw at the rocks, meowing plaintively.

"Let's help her," I said. I fell to my knees and started tossing aside pieces of heavy stone and clumps of dirt. Shani and Doli worked at the other side of the pile until finally we could see the bottom half of the wall that had been buried beneath. It was engraved with what looked like hieroglyphics of cats. But they were each exaggerated in some way, and no two were the same. I scanned the rows until I landed on one that stopped me cold. "That one," I said, pointing it out to the others. "It looks exactly like the jaguar on my necklace." I pulled the necklace out of my T-shirt so they could compare for themselves.

"Whoa, you're right," said Doli. "Look at the one right next to it. That's the same puma I have on my necklace. Shani, that's a lion next to the puma. Do you have anything with a lion on it?"

"You mean like this?" Shani held up her arm and pushed her sleeve back to reveal a thin bracelet, the image of a lion etched into the gold.

"I didn't know you had a bracelet like that," Doli said. "When did you get it?"

Shani caressed the bracelet lovingly. "My grandmother gave it to me before she passed away. She brought it all the way from Cairo. I never take it off."

"Sound familiar?" I said to Doli, who nodded. "This means something." I lifted my jaguar to the carving on the wall, but nothing happened. Doli and Shani did the same with their jewelry pieces, but the wall remained unchanged. I looked at the black cat. "What do we do now?"

But the cat was staring at another symbol to the left of the jaguar. It was an engraving of a tiger. "We need Lin!" I cried. "The tiger is her symbol."

"I told you," said Doli. "She wasn't in her room when I went to make sure she was okay. I think she's gone into hiding."

Shani looked at the tiger symbol as if it were Lin. "I don't blame her. She's probably embarrassed to the nth degree. Plus, I'll bet she thinks somebody turned her in to Mrs. O'Grady already." She glanced at me. "Did Nicole do the honors?"

I shook my head. "She was too busy making up lies about me," I said miserably. "Mrs. O'Grady told us we have to go to student court now."

"Whoa," Shani said. "That's serious. If Nicole would take it that far, it's only a matter of time before she tells on Lin."

I sank back onto my heels, disappointed—about Nicole's lies, about Lin's absence, and about our early morning mission coming to a halt. "Well, that's it then. I doubt we can do whatever this is without Lin."

Just then the cat slinked between us and sidled up to the wall. She lifted up onto her hind legs. She pressed her small paw against the tiger engraving and backed away. Seconds later the entire wall slid to the side like a pocket door. We were left staring into a dim hallway with lit torches nestled into sconces.

"Oh, uh-uh, no way no how," Shani blurted immediately. "Follow a teacher into a dark secret basement and pass around a glowing orb? Sure, sounds fun. Follow a black cat into the woods in the middle of the night? Why not? I love cats. But crawling into a creepy temple that somehow has lit torches inside even though supposedly no one's been here for hundreds of years? Now you're pushing it."

"What happened to 'If it's a trap, bring it on'?" Doli said, lifting one eyebrow.

Shani winced. "Aw, using my own words against me. Touché."

I held out my hand. "Shani, we have to find out what's in there. It might help us defeat Anubis. And Ms. Benitez said that we're stronger together. We're already missing one Wildcat. We need you."

She rolled her eyes and sighed. "Argh . . . fine. But you *so* owe me one." She took my hand and we ducked into the small opening followed by Doli and the black cat.

Inside, we found ourselves at the end of a long corridor lined with symbols and hieroglyphs. "These symbols are Mayan," I said, surprised to see some characters I recognized through my frequent museum trips with my aunt and uncle.

"The ones over here are Greek," Shani added. At my look of surprise she said, "One of my old schools was big on Greek history. I learned all the letters . . . before they kicked me out for hacking into their computer system."

"Um, guys," Doli said. "I'm having second thoughts. Have you guys noticed what all these pictures have in common?"

Scanning the wall, I felt like every ancient civilization since the beginning of time was represented. There were Egyptian symbols, Persian, Navajo, Tibetan, Japanese, Greek, even Norse—and some we couldn't recognize at all. But we didn't need to speak any of those languages to pick up the common thread. In every image carved into these walls, the figures were in pain. Horned demons stepped on the backs of people crying out in agony. Men stabbed one another through the chest with long spears. Hellish animals sat engulfed in flames while armies of skeletons danced around them. It was beyond creepy. It was a hallway dedicated to suffering.

And it was giving me serious regrets about entering the temple. Maybe Shani's instincts had been right. I considered fleeing back through the temple's secret door, but then I thought of Ms. Benitez and how she had sacrificed herself for us. When she woke up from the coma—*if* she woke up—I didn't want her to think it had been for nothing.

I steeled myself and continued down the hallway, willing myself to be brave. But when I turned the corner to enter the next room, I yelped. There stood a man with the head of a jackal adorned with a grand Egyptian headdress. He held a long thin staff and his lips were pulled back in a snarl. It was a statue, but it had been realistic enough to make me break into a cold sweat. Goose bumps rose on my arms.

Like the wall, the statue had multiple languages carved into the base beneath—most of which I couldn't read. I remember Aunt Teppy once showing me pictures of the Dead Sea Scrolls. Some of the letters I was looking at now reminded me of sections of the Scrolls that Aunt Teppy said were written in Hebrew or Aramaic. But some other words were inscribed in alphabets I actually knew. I got closer and saw three words in Latin that filled me with dread.

"What does it say?" Doli asked, joining me at the statue.

"*Fraternitas de Chao*," I whispered.

"Um, Fraternity of Cows?" Shani guessed. "That's not so scary."

I swallowed hard. "Brotherhood of Chaos. This is why Dr. Logan was so interested in this temple. He—I mean, Anubis—must be their leader."

"Can we get out of here now? Please? Pretty please with a cherry on top?" Shani shivered and rubbed her arms, even though the torches made the confined space uncomfortably hot.

I started to tell her that I agreed. We weren't ready for this yet. But just then the light flickered and the shadow of a figure appeared against the wall. We screamed and clung to one another. I squeezed my eyes shut, not wanting to see what horrible creature had manifested in the temple that we now knew was an ode to death.

"Ana?" a voice called out. I knew that voice. . . .

"Jason?" My eyes flew open to find Jason standing there in

his lacrosse jersey. "What on earth are you doing here?"

He opened his mouth to speak, but before he could utter a word, the chamber filled with a bloodcurdling shriek.

Suddenly a smoky creature appeared behind Jason. Just like the cats when they'd emerged from the ashes of the vase, the filmy form of an almost see-through bat wavered in the air. Then it began to solidify, its furry body taking on monstrous life. It spread its black leathery wings like a cloak and blocked out the light of the flames behind it. For a moment all I could see were its glowing red eyes, pulsing with menace. *One of the Chaos Spirits!*

I froze, looking at Jason with a growing sense of dread. Paranoia reared its ugly head again. Had he followed us here? *Has he been following us for weeks?* I thought of all the times he'd shown up unexpectedly when the Wildcats were together. I wondered about the time in the library when I'd been sure someone had been eavesdropping on us. Then there'd been the night Ms. Benitez was attacked, and the way he'd just happened to be near our dorm the night we'd come back from practicing our transformations. Now he was here again, only this time he seemed to have brought one of Anubis's minions with him. Could it be? Had Jason been spying on us for Anubis?

"Ana, look out!" Doli cried, pointing at the bat. It flapped its midnight-black wings, let out another terrible shriek, revealing its vampire fangs, and charged.

chapter 20

Just before the bat crashed into us, right before it seemed it would sink its terrible teeth into my neck, it exploded into hundreds of pieces that glowed red like the embers of a fire. Even after all the crazy things I'd seen since arriving at Temple, watching a bat blow itself up on purpose still shocked me to the core. "Oh my God!" I had time to scream, right before the force of the explosion blew us back and we ended up in a pile on the hard stone floor. I groaned, feeling red-hot pain sear through my arm, which was pinned beneath me. Shani's hip was jammed into my stomach, and for a few moments I couldn't breathe. Beneath me, I heard Doli moan.

"We need to get out of here!" Shani screamed, scrambling off of me and pulling the rest of us to our feet.

I couldn't have agreed more. I wasn't ready for this. My hands were shaking uncontrollably and I felt sick to my stomach. I thought I'd been scared when I'd first been faced with my jaguar, but it was nothing compared to how I felt now, trapped in a buried temple with a demon that clearly had enormous power. Ms. Benitez had been wrong. We were out of our league.

But there was no way out now. The pieces of the Chaos Spirit had flown into the creatures carved into the wall, and one by one they were coming to life! At first they seemed to be moving statues, pulling themselves out of the soot-covered stone like animated pieces of rock. But as they crept out of the wall, the stone fell away in clumps, revealing the flesh-and-blood creatures beneath. Poisonous rattlesnakes hissed and slithered down the walls, flicking their forked purple tongues. Black-widow spiders with fat bodies and hairy legs scuttled out of every crevice. Crows formed by the hundreds and gathered in ominous clouds above our heads, preparing to dive. Everywhere were the servants of death and destruction.

It was like no nightmare I'd ever had before. But it was real! I looked at Shani and Doli and saw the terror in their eyes. What hell had we walked into? I choked back a sob. In seconds the plague of snakes and spiders and birds would descend on us and that would be the end of us. I thought of Aunt Teppy and Uncle Mec and how destroyed they'd be if I never came home. Thinking of them gave me one last gasp of courage. There was still one chance for us to get out of this alive, and we had to take it now.

"Wildcats!" I yelled into the chaos. "We have to shift!"

But would it work this time? My heart pumped with so much fear and confusion, I couldn't clear my mind, couldn't let go as I'd done in the woods. But when I clamped hands with Doli and Shani, the magic sparked and crackled around us. I felt my eyes enlarge, and the dark room seemed to blaze with sunlight. I fell forward on heavy paws, and my muscles stretched beneath my spotted coat. Doli now stood beside me, her regal puma's body rippling with muscles. To my right Shani crouched in her golden lion's skin, her heavy paws scratching at the stone floor as she eyed the prey all around her. Doli nudged us with her nose so that we formed a tight circle, facing our foes. Shani lifted her head and gave a thunderous roar, and we ran toward our enemies.

Doli used her extra-long hind legs to bound onto a stone altar in one graceful leap. She positioned herself on the edge of the lip and jumped, landing directly on top of a huge snake that had been slithering across the floor toward me. Doli crushed its head and bit off its rattling tail. Meanwhile, Shani leaped onto her gold-colored back legs, swiping birds out of thin air with her powerful paws. Using my slightly smaller size, I crawled beneath a low stone bench and then rose to my full height, knocking the bench over and crushing dozens of venomous black spiders.

To my left I noticed flames waving side to side. Jason had pulled a torch from its sconce, wielding it like a lacrosse stick—just as he had shown me—and was using it to beat away a flock of crows. One bird's shiny onyx wings caught fire and soon its furious flapping spread the flames like a wildfire. In seconds the whole cloud was ablaze.

I felt a tiny pang of hope. Jason was fighting on our side and holding his own. *Was I wrong about him?*

I didn't have time to think about it now, though. Instead I fought by his side. A thick snake wrapped its body around Jason's leg, rearing its head back to strike. But I sliced through its flesh with my claws, knocking it away from Jason just in time. Then I used my jaws to shatter the snake's skull.

"Ana—I," Jason said, sparing a moment to eye the serpent as its headless body continued to writhe on the floor. But there were more where that one came from. From the other side of the corridor, an army of snakes crawled its way toward us, circling one another like an angry nest of bees. "I can't believe any of this is real!"

He lunged with the torch, slamming the diamond-shaped head of a snake hard into the floor. Not bad for someone who couldn't believe this was actually happening.

"I have an idea." He ran in the opposite direction, leaving me to face the poisonous snakes alone. I ran toward the oncoming serpents, swiping at the one closest to me. It rattled its tail and moved to bite down on my paw, but I leaped out of the way, letting its strike meet with hard stone. We went back and forth for a while until I felt a growing heat at my back. Jason had returned with five more torches pulled from their sconces. "I can't believe I'm playing defense with a giant cat!" he said, gesturing for me to get behind him. Quickly, he laid the torches side by side across the length of the hallway. The snakes would not cross the barrier of fire. They hissed and snapped, but the fire held them in place. Then he pulled one last torch from the wall and threw it directly into the middle of the pile of serpents.

The charred smell of burning snakes filled the chamber.

Eventually the room grew quiet and still. I turned my head to find Doli and Shani standing among a sea of corpses. We had destroyed the creatures that the Chaos Spirit had unleashed on us. But I felt too wary to be relieved. It couldn't be that easy!

In the calm, I checked on the only truly vulnerable being in the room—Jason. He had scratches on his face and hands, but other than that he seemed to be unharmed. Physically, at least. I could only imagine what was going on inside his head. I might have been a cat, but I wanted him to know that I was still me. Since I couldn't form human words, I nuzzled my head into his hand.

He crouched down as I sat on my haunches. "It's really you, isn't it, Ana?" He reached tentatively for the spotted fur of my cheek. "Can you understand me?"

I nudged his hand. *Yes, I understand.*

"I'm sorry about what I said the other day. It was just— seeing you change like that—I didn't know what to think. You have to admit this whole thing is crazy!" He looked around at the torch-lit walls and the other Wildcats. "But I think I'm starting to get it." He paused, holding my head in his hands and gazing into my large yellow cat eyes with his blue, clear-as-crystal human ones.

I had such a strong urge to hug him then that I feared I might turn back into a human, which wasn't safe to do just yet. So I licked his arm to let him know he was forgiven, then turned away.

Shani came over to stand beside us, waiting to catch my attention. She pawed at the air, staring at a hidden chamber that had been revealed when I'd overturned the stone bench. I struggled to see, but even with my enhanced eyesight, it was hard to make out anything inside the secret room. So I crept closer, sniffing the air for clues. Nothing I smelled made any sense to me. Finally I inched my way inside the smaller room and let my eyes adjust. But when they did, I squeezed them shut again, desperate to block out the nightmarish sight.

In the center of the room was an altar made of human skulls. Hard-shelled black beetles scuttled in and out of the eye and mouth holes. And around the base were strewn the bones of countless bodies. I screamed at the top of my lungs—which came out like a strangled roar. I started to back away, my claws scrambling for purchase on the dirty stone floor. *Let me* out *of here*, I thought frantically. But just before I could back all the way out into the other room, I caught a brief glimmer of light.

Hold on. . . . Was that . . . ? I scooted closer to the altar, my heart pounding.

I couldn't believe my eyes. Perched on top of the hideous altar was a glittering green jewel, the same color as the eyes of the black cat who had led us here. As I got closer I realized that it had to be one of the jewels from the Mayan vase! It must have disappeared the night of the battle in the museum, but there it was, gleaming and perfect. I didn't know how it got there but I somehow knew it was important. *This must be why the cat brought us here.*

I approached the altar, testing the skulls with my paw. Would it hold my weight? I began to slowly climb the pile of bones. Soon the jewel was within reach. I only had to stretch my neck and—

The bat, back to its original form, suddenly appeared behind the jewel, flapping its massive wings and eyeing me with evil glee. I met its stare, determined to prove I wasn't afraid of it—or its master, Anubis. As if it found that amusing, the bat spread its mouth into what looked almost like a smile, and without warning it descended on me. I felt its sharp claws sink into my head, and the terrible pain clouded my vision. Rearing on my hind legs with a growl, I lost my footing and went tumbling down the deathly altar. I felt the hardened skulls pounding into my back like hammer blows, raising large round welts under my fur. At last I hit the floor, whimpering in pain.

As a human, I'd never been in a fight. Not a real one. And now I knew why. This fight had just begun, and already my whole body was a throbbing ball of pain. Sensing my moment of weakness, the monstrous bat swooped in for the kill. I didn't have the strength to run. *This is it,* I thought.

But suddenly Doli was there, jumping in front of me and letting out a snarl. She leaped at the bat, sailing through the air at an unbelievable height that would have made Coach Connolly proud. But before she could reach the flying demon, it rushed into the wall. Immediately, arrows shot out of holes with lightning speed. Weighty stones loosened themselves from the ceiling and walls, crashing down around us. Trembling with fear, I rolled onto my stomach and flattened my body against the floor. I listened to the arrows whiz past my ears, dangerously close. They clattered against the far wall or smashed into the skulls, shattering them on impact. *That could have been my skull!* I thought. *I might die!* The idea seemed impossible, ridiculous. How could I die? I was just a kid. I imagined again how devastated Uncle Mec and Aunt Teppy would be if I never came home. I couldn't let that happen. Plus, I had to help protect Jason.

Gathering my courage, I rose to my feet, crouching low as if I were hunting through short grass. Doli followed my lead, and as the stones fell around us, we maneuvered through the room, using the larger boulders as cover from the murderous arrows.

Jason stood at the doorway, waving us toward him. "Come on, Ana!" he cried. "You've got to get out of there!"

What did he think I was trying to do?

I stayed put until the arrows finally petered out and the stonework ceased to move. Then Doli and I made a run for the outer chamber, panting with relief as we rejoined our friends. But the monster bat wasn't done with us yet. Enraged that we'd escaped its trap, the red-eyed demon rose in the air, opening its mouth and coughing out a plume of smoke. The cloud whirled near the ceiling like a tornado, and a dozen bats were born from the mouth of the funnel, each a miniature version of the Chaos Spirit. I knew I couldn't fight the bats if I was worried about protecting Jason. I grabbed his shirt with my teeth and dragged him behind a heavy stone pillar, pushing him as far back against the wall as I could with my head.

"I can help!" he yelled. But I growled at him until he retreated. I didn't want to scare him, but this was my fight and I needed him to be safe. I turned away, licked my muzzle, and prepared for battle. The cloud of flying demons sounded like a hundred squeaking mice trapped in a maze. That is, until their wings, flapping in unison, drowned out the squeaks and clicks, replacing them with the sound of distant helicopters getting closer and closer. The swarming mass had a black-hole effect, sucking all the light from the room with their leathery wings, which were spoked like black umbrellas. They flashed their ratlike teeth, and when they came near enough to bite, their rancid odor filled my nostrils and made me gag. I remembered reading once that bat caves tend to smell like corn tortillas, but clearly whoever did that research hadn't met an evil-spirit bat. Their scent was all rotting mushrooms and swamp water. Shani turned out to be the best at capturing them, and then she crushed their furry bodies between her jaws. I'm not sure how she stomached it. The first bat I bit into tasted like raw liver covered in slime. I made a vow then and there to forever cross bats off my menu. The bats we couldn't reach fled to a small ridge in the ceiling, from which they hung like blackened fruit. They saw what we could do and they wanted no part of it. *Good,* I thought. *They should be afraid.*

I looked around at the floor, now littered with crushed and mutilated bats. Finally the coast was clear. Once more I climbed the altar of skulls toward the glittering green jewel, but the re-formed bat swept into the room like a gust of air, swooping in between me and my prize. It was more terrible than ever, its crimson eyes bulging in their sockets. I realized then that those eyes were windows to the underworld. If I looked long enough, I would see true suffering and pain among the leaping flames.

But the bat wasn't here to look into my eyes as if we were some romantic TV-show couple. Defeat had made it angry, and now it wanted revenge. It reared back and breathed out a black flame as if it were a dragon. *Duck,* I told myself just in time. But still I felt the fire scorch the tips of my fur and inhaled the smell of barbecued jaguar mixed with rotten fungi. I yowled, imagining my back turning bright red like coals in a grill. The heat from the geyser of flame disintegrated an ancient support beam, bringing a whole section of the ceiling down in a pile of rubble. Fleeing the falling stones, we all joined Jason in the corner behind the pillar. For the time being, we were safe. But I quickly realized that we'd been herded into this corner like clueless sheep. The only way out of this spot was through the Chaos Spirit, which was approaching slowly, taking its time. I could tell by the spark in its evil eyes that it relished our fear. In fact, the more afraid we were, the larger the bat seemed to be, as if it were feeding on our terror. It was too much for us to take on in our exhausted state. The demon would destroy us now, and there was nothing we could do.

I'm sorry, Ixchel, I thought. *We failed you.*

But then a formidable roar sounded from behind the bat. The demon turned, and a huge tiger leaped for its throat. *Lin!*

Where had she come from? And how did she know that we needed her? I tried to puzzle it out, but there was no time.

The bat easily used its wings to brush Lin aside, but the distraction gave us the time we needed to get out of the corner and run back to the larger room, where the statue of Anubis glared down at us. As we ran for cover, Jason broke away and headed straight for the towering statue. I screeched to a stop. *What is he doing?* I wondered. If he was trying to escape, he was going the wrong way. But as I watched, Jason clamped his hand over Anubis's staff and pulled it free. He balanced the weight of it in his hands like a lacrosse stick and crouched into a fighting stance. Now I understood. *Good thinking!* I thought. *Now he has a weapon.*

Meanwhile, Lin was able to sneak past the bat and rejoin us. As soon as the four of us stood together, I felt a surge in our strength that overwhelmed me. Ixchel's words echoed in my mind: *Together you are more powerful than Anubis could ever be.* It was true. I realized that we should never have risked coming here without Lin. Our power lay in our unity.

Feeling bold, I crept forward enough to spy the giant bat in the other room. It had collapsed against the pyramid of skulls, its right wing torn and bleeding where Lin had swiped it with her claws. Thick drops of blood dripped from its back where she had managed to sink her teeth. It was clearly hurt, but I reminded myself that it was no ordinary bat. It had magical powers, and that included the ability to heal itself. With each tortured flap of its wings, it seemed to get stronger, the wounds closing up before my eyes as if they were being sewn shut with invisible thread. It was only a matter of time before it attacked again. And when that happened, even with our renewed strength, we would be no match for the bat. We needed to find its weakness. I angled my head, searching for any advantage. My eye landed on the green jewel, still safe on its altar in the other room. *That's it!* I thought. Ixchel had defeated the Chaos Spirits once by trapping them in the vase.

Confined, their powers ebbed. If we could trap it, even for a short while, maybe we could weaken it enough to vanquish it. How could I communicate with the others so they could help me with my plan, though?

I thought back to the battle between Ixchel and Anubis. She had spoken to me without using her voice. So maybe I could do the same. I looked at Lin, Doli, and Shani and focused all my energy on reaching their minds with my own. *Wildcats, can you hear me?*

Yes.

Yes.

Loud and clear, boss.

I breathed out in relief. *We need to trap the bat's wings under something heavy.*

Doli swung her head to the right. *The stone bench?*

It's too *heavy. We can't lift it.*

The statue! Shani circled behind the huge statue. *Let's push it over and drop it on him.*

Will it move? I asked, worried that the writing below the base might contain some sort of magical words to protect the statue.

Lin moved behind the statue with Shani. *We can do it together.*

I didn't want to put Jason in harm's way, but I needed him to draw the bat's attention away from us so it would fall into our trap. I didn't think the telepathy would work on him, though.

So I pulled him away from the statue and positioned him in front of the pillar. I nudged the hand with the spear so that he raised it in his defensive stance. When he spotted the other cats behind the Anubis statue, he said, "Got it. Good idea."

I left him there, joined my fellow Wildcats behind the statue, and waited.

It wasn't long before the bat came swooping into the room, hovering five feet above the floor like a ghost, even while barely flapping its wings. I wondered if it even needed to flap to fly or if that was all just part of the illusion. Its eyes, red as molten lava, swiveled in its head, searching for us. But the first thing it saw was Jason, wildly waving his spear and shouting, "Come get me, you filthy rodent!"

The bat screeched and charged at Jason, its talons dragging along the floor. Jason's eyes rounded like saucers and his mouth fell open, as if he hadn't really expected the bat to do as he said.

Come on, Jason, I thought. *You can do this.*

He couldn't possibly have heard me, but a look of determination came over his face, his blue-green eyes darkening like seawater as he lifted his spear. *Swoon.* He jabbed the bat with his spear, then dodged and turned, using all his lacrosse moves to attack the demon. Slowly he prodded the bat back and back, getting it into perfect position. And when he was just the right distance away, I shouted with my mind: *NOW!*

Together we leaned into the statue with our powerful

shoulders, pushing against the walls behind us with our legs. Slowly the statue teetered forward, then came crashing down onto the bat like a felled tree.

"She shoots and she scores!" Jason shouted, pumping his fist in the air.

The statue had fallen facedown across the bat so that its furry body and wings were flattened by Anubis's broad chest. The hand that had been holding the staff fit snugly against the bat's face, almost as if Anubis were punching it. Only when the arm cracked and snapped off did the demon have enough room to screech and moan. It struggled to free itself from Anubis's grip, wriggling and fighting for every inch. When it finally pulled itself loose, I saw that its wings were crushed where the statue had pinned them to the floor. It seemed diminished somehow, and it no longer pulsed with the supernatural strength that had scared me before.

While the others stood guard, I tugged Jason back by his shirt, pulling him toward the hallway of suffering. I nudged him toward the exit.

"What are you doing?" he demanded. "I'm not leaving. Not without you."

It was sweet that he wanted to protect me. But this was Wildcats business and I didn't want him to see what we were about to do. The jungle dreams raced through my mind, a savage bloodlust building in me. I could feel my thoughts becoming less human the closer I got to destroying my prey. The jaguar was almost completely in control. So with my last bit of humanity, I had to make sure Jason was safely out of the way and that he wouldn't see something that might give him nightmares about me for the rest of his life.

I lifted my head and roared, showing him the full length of my fangs. Jason trembled and backed away. "All right, all right," he said. "I get it. I'll wait outside. But roar if you need me."

I waited patiently until I was sure he was gone, and then I rejoined the Wildcats, ready to finish this.

Just like in the dream I'd had about the hyena, the four of us pounced on the weakened bat at once. Lin and Doli each pulled at a wing with their teeth until it ripped right off. Then Shani charged the bat, pouncing on its chest and biting until its tainted blood spilled black onto the temple floor. I held down its head with my paws and found its throat, piercing it in one powerful bite and snapping its neck. The small piece of me that was still just Ana from Ohio was completely grossed out. I had never even liked hamburgers that were too pink in the middle. And here I was biting into a live animal, its blood oozing down my face. But the hunter in me was in heaven. And I saw the same catlike bloodlust in the eyes of the others. For a moment I worried that the longer we stayed in our cat forms, the less human we would become. But all I knew right then was that we had a job to complete. Together we tore and ripped and clawed at the bat's mangled body until it was beyond all repair. From the pile of broken and wasted parts rose a puff of smoke that rose into the air and evaporated into the walls.

When it was over, I lay down away from the carnage, my energy spent. The others lay down next to me and rested.

We did it, I said wearily.

To think I used to like bats, Shani said.

Doli ruffled the tiger's fur with her nose. *We couldn't have done it without you, Lin. Thanks for coming. How did you know where to find us?*

I had this feeling you were in trouble and that you needed me. I couldn't let you fight alone. So I followed your scents. It must be one of our powers. She chuffed contentedly.

Something about Lin's answer made me uneasy, but I didn't know why. She'd saved us tonight, and for now that would be enough. *Guys, I miss being human*, I broke in. *Are we ready to go home?*

Yes.

Yes.

About time.

It wasn't hard to shift this time. I was too tired to over-think it. Within seconds we'd all changed back into our human selves. After we'd struggled to our feet, I groaned, feeling each injury the jaguar had suffered. I lifted my shirt and craned my neck, seeing the welts from my fall down the altar of skulls. I looked at Shani. "I should check you for wounds," I said.

Shani sighed. "Can we do it later? I reek of evil bat blood

and thousand-year-old dirt. I *need* to take a shower. Can we get out of here?"

"Not yet," I answered. "One last thing . . ."

I walked into the adjoining room, climbed the altar one last time, and took the emerald gem in my hands, hugging it to my chest. When I rejoined the group, I held up the jewel in victory. They all cheered and surrounded me in a group hug.

As we passed through the hallway of suffering, I noticed it didn't have the same effect on me as it had on our way in. The gruesome scenes no longer seemed as scary or depressing. Maybe it was because tonight it had been the side of evil that had done the suffering, which meant the good guys might actually stand a chance. Or maybe it was because I felt grateful to be alive, to be with my friends. Either way, there was no question that we'd won this battle. We'd saved the school, and I had a feeling we'd played a small part in a much greater story that we didn't yet understand.

chapter 21

BY THE TIME WE EXITED THE TEMPLE, IT WAS DAWN AND the night sky had given way to a soft heather-gray mist with traces of amber and magenta.

"Wait . . . so *you* followed a cat into the woods in the middle of the night too?" Shani was talking to Jason and sounded relieved. "Well, I guess that makes me feel a little better. Glad we're not the only ones."

"Following a cat into the woods doesn't come close to cracking the top-ten weirdest moments of my night," Jason said. He grasped my hand to help me out of the small temple door. "But, yeah, I was asleep but kept hearing this loud yowling sound. I tried to ignore it at first, but it got louder and louder until I finally went to my window to tell whatever it was to knock it off."

"Don't tell me: It was a black cat with green eyes, right?" I guessed.

"Right! You've seen it?"

"We wouldn't have been here tonight if she hadn't," said Doli, climbing out on her own. "It led us here too."

"Weeeird," Jason said. "I mean, not as weird as a giant demon bat and a chamber full of snakes, but . . . Well, you know what I mean."

I laughed at how ridiculous it sounded, but I knew *exactly* what he meant.

He reached down again and helped Lin out of the temple. I saw her gaze linger on his hand for a moment then flicker away. "Anyway," he continued, "I followed it straight to the temple, and when I saw the light coming from inside, I just had to check it out."

"Aren't you glad you did?" Lin said sarcastically. But I detected a hint of sadness beneath her words. I wondered if she was embarrassed that Jason had seen her as a tiger. Any girl would want to hide the weirdest things about herself from her crush. Usually that meant a big red pimple or an overlong toe. But she'd turned into a real-life tiger in front of him and sprouted whiskers and claws. Talk about letting the cat out of the bag.

But Jason gifted her with a smile that made her blush. "Actually, I am," he said enthusiastically. "If I hadn't come, I wouldn't have seen how amazing you guys are. You kicked major bad-guy butt back there."

Shani nodded. "We sure did. And you didn't do so bad yourself—for a boy." She winked.

Jason shrugged good-naturedly. "Thanks. But now that we're all out of that temple, somebody want to fill me in? What the heck is going on around here?"

As we walked away from the temple entrance and made our way through the excavation site, we gave Jason the lowdown on the Brotherhood of Chaos and Dr. Logan's real identity.

After a long pause, Jason shook his head. "My poor mom," he said. "She's going to be so disappointed. She thought she'd finally found a nice guy. Turns out he's the god of the underworld."

"Yeah, that's some bad dating karma on an epic scale," said Shani as she ducked under the yellow caution tape. "Dr. Logan did have pretty nice teeth as a human, though. I'll give him that."

"You mean, he *does*," I corrected her. "He's still out there somewhere."

"Don't remind me," Lin said. "I can't believe we have to do this three more times. Don't these evil Chaos whatevers even know who I am?"

"They do now," Doli said. "You're a Wildcat. And that beats pampered princess any day."

The old Lin would have bristled at that comment, but instead I saw pride on her face. It must have felt pretty great to be respected for something she *was* instead of something she had.

I had just crouched under the yellow tape, stepping on a plank of wood set up by the archaeologists—Did *they* know they were working for a demon god?—when I caught a flash of movement. A figure, silhouetted against the lightening sky, stumbled away from the site, running to hide behind a tree before we noticed her. But I'd know that golden-blond hair anywhere. "Nicole!" I shouted.

Catching my gaze, Doli took off running and caught up to Nicole easily, trapping her against the cliff wall. The three other Wildcats ran to catch up, Jason trailing behind. Soon we all surrounded her.

"What are you doing here?" I demanded.

Nicole sneered at me, narrowing her eyes. "What? A girl can't go for a run in the morning? You get three friends—"

"Four," Jason interrupted.

Nicole rolled her eyes. "Whatever. You get a few friends and suddenly you think you own the place."

Doli scoffed. "You can't seriously expect us to believe you went running in your jeans and those shoes."

We all looked down to take in her expensive Jimmy Choo ballet flats.

Nicole's eyes shifted nervously. She cleared her throat. "I don't give a flying fig what you believe," she said. "Besides, you're the ones who have been trespassing here, taking coins that don't even belong to you."

"Coins?" I said. "How could you possibly know about . . ." I trailed off, slowly putting the pieces together like a complicated jigsaw puzzle. I looked at the other Wildcats. "The last time I talked about the coin Jason found at the excavation site was when we were in the library—the day we thought we heard someone outside, eavesdropping on us. Remember? The only people who knew about it were the five of us and . . . Dr. Logan."

Understanding dawned on everyone's faces.

"It was you, wasn't it?" I said, shaking my head in wonder. "You're the one who's been spying on us for Anubis!" So many things made sense now. I'd thought Jason had led the demon bat to the temple, but I realized that Jason would never have done that. Nicole, on the other hand, had told me to stay away from Doli; she'd egged on fights between Lin and me; she'd tried to tease me out of meeting with Ms. Benitez. Maybe being assigned as her roommate had been no accident. She'd been a horrible roommate to Shani, too, I remembered, possibly hoping that Shani would give up and transfer to another school. It hadn't worked, but she tried the same tactic on me, beginning with spilling the mocha latte on my laptop. Anubis and his minions hadn't been able to stop us from coming to Temple, so they did what they could to keep us apart once we all got here. "How long have you known about us?" I demanded.

Nicole brushed her hair away from her face. "I don't know what you're talking about."

"Oh, sure you do," Shani offered. "And I'm betting we have you to thank for locking the school gate the night Anubis got away!"

Nicole's eyes widened. "You can't prove anything!"

"Can't I?" Shani asked with a slow grin. "You know there are security cameras all over this school, right? You roomed with me—do you doubt my ability to hack into that system?"

Nicole opened her mouth to answer, but no words seemed to come. They weren't needed, anyway. Her guilty expression was enough.

Lin gasped. "How could you, Nicole?"

"Oh, who are you to judge me?" Nicole spit out. She skewered Lin with a look, as if she were searching for a target to hit. "You used to be important around here, but now you're just a thief who hangs out with rejects."

Bull's-eye.

I watched Lin's face harden her into the take-no-prisoners mean girl I'd first met just more than two weeks ago. I thought she was about to give Nicole a verbal body slam, and I had to admit, that was something I desperately wanted to see. But Lin just leaned in, narrowed her eyes, and let out a deep, menacing growl from deep within her tiger self. Any self-respecting human would have peed her pants.

Any *human*.

But as it turned out, Nicole wasn't strictly human.

When Lin stepped closer to her, the acrid smell of fear filled the air around Nicole. If I hadn't seen it with my own eyes, I wouldn't have believed it. But as I watched, Nicole's sky-blue eyes receded into their sockets until they were hard little onyx marbles. Muddy brown fur grew like weeds until her peaches-and-cream skin was covered with it. Gone were the perfect cheekbones, the expertly tweezed eyebrows, and pert button nose. It their place was a wide, bulbous black nose, a high, sloping forehead, and sunken jowls. Before our eyes, Nicole's face, which I had thought was so beautiful, transformed into that of a beady-eyed scavenger—framed with gorgeous blond hair.

Marilyn Monroe was a hyena.

Just when I thought nothing else could surprise me. Were there *any* humans at this school? Temple Academy was turning out to be a much crazier place than I'd thought. I stumbled backward, unable to form a coherent sentence. "What? Huh? How did . . . ?"

"You took the words right out of my mouth," said Shani, gaping at Nicole in utter disbelief.

Lin, if possible, looked even more unnerved, her hand flying to her mouth. "Did I make that happen?" she asked guiltily.

Doli, the first to recover from her shock, approached Nicole calmly. "In a way," she said. "Nicole, you'll tell me if I'm wrong, but you're not a human who can turn into an animal, like us. You're an animal that can turn into a human, right?" At Nicole's silence, Doli nodded as if that had been all the confirmation she needed. "I'm guessing Anubis granted you that power, but it takes a little effort to maintain the illusion." Doli cast an appreciative glance at Lin. "You just scared some of the human right out of her," she said.

Lin let her hand fall to her side and gave Doli a slow smile. "Cool."

Nicole whimpered, emitting a noise that sounded like goofy laughter but was probably a cry for help.

"Relax, Nicole," Doli said. "We're not going to kill you when it's four against one—"

"Five," Jason chimed in.

Doli smiled. "Right. Make that five against one. That's just bad sportsmanship. We're going to set you free. But there is a saying among my people. It goes . . ." Then she said some beautiful-sounding words in her native Navajo language.

"Pretty," I said. "What's it mean?"

"'When you see a rattlesnake poised to strike, strike first.' In other words, you'd better not cause us any more trouble, because we *will* strike, and a scrawny hyena is no match for the Wildcats. Got it?"

With a voice that sounded like boots crunching on gravel, Nicole looked right at me and said, "You are fools."

I stepped closer until our faces were only inches apart. "What was that?"

"Did you think you're any match for a god?" she said. "You're so proud because you defeated the bat, but Anubis's plans are so far beyond you. The battle means nothing when Anubis has already won the war."

"What does that mean?" I demanded.

Nicole gave me the same infuriating smirk she often had

as a human. "You don't really think I'm the only hyena at this school, do you? That I am the only one in his service?"

I took a small step back and shuddered. "There are others?"

"Aww . . . ," Nicole said, reaching out with her still-human hand and stroking my cheek. "You're so cute. You don't know anything!"

In a flash, Jason stepped forward and batted Nicole's hand away from my face. Nicole emitted another whooping laugh, this time full of satisfaction. But we quickly closed in around her and joined in a chorus of warning growls.

Immediately, teacup-size hyena ears sprang up through Nicole's blond hair like the Mickey Mouse hats they sell at Disney World. The effect was so funny that despite the tension in the air, we collapsed into helpless giggles.

Nicole eyed us nervously, seeming to sense the shift of power. As my laughter died down, I felt my confidence return. "We may not know who the others are," I began, "*if* there are others. But we know you. And you won't be bothering us anymore. In fact, you're going to talk to Mrs. O'Grady tomorrow and tell her you lied about me attacking you and that you're *very* sorry, am I right?"

Nicole looked away, clearly resentful that, for once, I was the one in charge. Reluctantly, she nodded her head.

I leaned in. "And tell your boss we're coming for him."

I gestured for the other girls to back off, and as soon as they did, Nicole scurried away, her shoulders curving and ripping through her expensive blouse, wiry hair sprouting along her arms. I had never seen anything as hilarious as Hyena Nicole loping through the woods in True Religion jeans and ballet flats.

As we walked back toward the dorms, enjoying the cool night air, Jason asked all kinds of questions about what it was like to be a big cat. He said he'd had trouble accepting it at first, but now that he'd gotten used to the idea, he wanted to know everything.

"Is that why you were so good at lacrosse?" he asked. "I mean, some of the moves I taught you took me years to learn, but you picked them up like that." He snapped his fingers.

"I'm not sure," I answered honestly. "There's so much we don't know yet about our powers. If Ms. Benitez ever wakes up, maybe she can help us figure it all out. I have more questions about that temple, too."

"Oh, that's right! I never got a chance to tell you," Jason said.

"Tell her what?" Doli asked.

"You know the other night when I saw you change into a human?" he said.

"He *saw* you?" Lin stared at me.

"It was an accident," I explained. "We'll talk about it later. Promise. Go on, Jason."

"Well, the reason I was looking for you was to tell you that

I figured out the temple couldn't be Anasazi. Remember how I told you that all the Anasazi settlements were on the same meridian?"

I nodded. We'd had that conversation right after I'd seen the green-eyed cat for the first time. *Where is the cat, anyway?* We hadn't seen it again once we'd entered the temple.

"After I figured out what the meridian was, I mapped it out, and the temple is nowhere near the line. There's no way it is an Anasazi structure." He shrugged. "But I guess you figured that out already."

"Kind of," I agreed. "I think that's why Dr. Logan was so quick to take that Roman coin from you. He didn't want anyone to know that the temple wasn't Anasazi, because it was a great cover."

"Poor Mom," he said again. "She's got all these archaeologists all over the country talking about the Anasazi temple. What's going to happen when they start poking around and realize it's something else altogether?"

"Are you kidding?" said Shani. "They'll have found a real-life temple of evil from every civilization they've ever studied. They'll be stoked."

"Plus, at least they'll see that the Brotherhood of Chaos was real, and Ms. Benitez will be vindicated. Maybe they'll finally publish her paper!" said Doli.

"I don't know, you guys," I added. I turned to Jason. "Anubis was able to get your mom to agree to move the whole school to protect his secret. Who knows what other crazy plans he has in mind."

Jason took a deep breath. "As long as none of those plans involves my mom . . . ," he said.

"Tell her Dr. Logan was a jerk anyway," I offered. "She's better off."

Jason smiled. "Will do. Speaking of my mom, I'd better get home now. With any luck, she hasn't woken up yet to find out I'm not there. See you around, Wildcats." He smiled at each of us, lingering an extra second or two on me, then headed down the path toward his house.

Out of the side of my eye, I saw Lin gazing after him as he went. But when she noticed me watching him too, she huffed in frustration and turned away. I sighed. I could take on an evil demon god, but I had no clue how to fix Lin's broken heart. There had to be a way to have Jason in my life without hurting my friend.

We reached the circle of benches outside of Radcliff Hall a few minutes later. I noticed Lin looking at our dorm with worried eyes.

"What's wrong?" I asked.

Lin bit her lip. "I don't know if I can go in there. Everyone hates me."

"That's not true," I said. "We don't. Besides, Doli told me she went to check on you after what happened and you weren't in your room or in the common room, so you must have hidden out in someone's room, right?"

"No." Lin hesitated. "I stole Antonio's keys and hid in the jet."

No wonder Doli hadn't been able to find her! "He's really touchy about people going near the jet without permission," I said, remembering how he'd reacted to Nicole.

"I'm aware of that," Lin said miserably. "I just didn't know where else to go. Now that everyone knows I'm a thief, how can I even show my face?"

"You can start by telling us why you did it," Doli said evenly.

Shani sat down on the back of one of the benches, resting her arms on her legs. "Yeah, why would someone as loaded as you are turn into a klepto?"

Lin bowed her head and whispered, "I'm not rich."

We all looked at one another, completely confused. "Of course you are. Your dad's an ambassador; your mom's a famous actress . . . ," I said, repeating Lin's favorite speech.

"That was before," Lin cut in. "My dad's accountant turned out to be a con man who cheated him out of millions. And my mom got cut from her last movie so they could hire a younger actress. That Marchesa bag was their parting gift to her so she wouldn't talk about it in the press."

"But if all that is true, how can you afford to go to this school?" I wondered aloud.

Lin sighed. "Principal Ferris is an old family friend. She met my mom in college when she was studying abroad.

Anyway, she agreed to waive the tuition fees, provided I make a donation to the school someday, after I graduate."

Doli folded her arms and turned to Lin. "You mean to tell me all this time you've been on my case about being here on scholarship, you've been here on one too? You tortured me about that!"

Lin shifted her eyes away guiltily. "I know, and I'm sorry. But you don't know what it's like for me! I have always been rich. Everyone knows that. And you may not think so, but there's a lot of pressure that comes with having money. When I found out that we were . . . *poor*"—she contorted her face as though the word left a disgusting taste in her mouth—"I was so embarrassed. I figured the bigger deal I made about you not having money, the fewer questions people would ask me."

"And the stealing?" I prompted.

She sat heavily on the bench next to Shani's legs. "I've been collecting things that I could sell online so I'd have money to buy clothes and jewelry—keep up appearances. That was the plan, anyway. Stupid, right? You all must think I'm an idiot."

"No," Doli said.

"No." I shook my head.

"Totally," Shani said, nodding emphatically. When Doli and I glared at her, she lifted her hands and shrugged. "What? You thought no one would notice when all the stuff missing around school shows up for sale from the same eBay seller? Even she admits it was a dumb plan. But look." She climbed down from her perch atop the bench and sat down next to Lin, throwing her arm over her shoulders. "Who cares what those snooty girls think anyway? Half of them are only like that because they were trying to impress *you*. But now that you've got us, you can just be yourself—which happens to be pretty cool."

Lin gave her a grateful smile. "Thanks, Shani."

"But what about Nicole?" said Doli. "What if she reports Lin and tries to get her expelled?"

"I don't think she will," I replied. "Not after the scare we put into her tonight. But, Lin, it wouldn't hurt if you apologized to the girls you stole from."

"I will. And I promise I'll return everything I took, starting with Antonio's keys." She looked at each of us with genuine affection on her face. "Who needs designer clothes anyway when you've got the Wildcats as friends?"

"Hear, hear!" Shani said. "Now, if you don't mind"—she stood up and pulled her blue hair under her nose and sniffed at it—"I need to go wash the bat smell out of my hair."

We laughed and followed her toward the dorm. As we got closer, I noticed that the lights were on at full power. If I had to guess, I'd say the lights came back on at the same time that the Chaos Spirit's light went out.

Later that night I got a text from Jason.

Mom just got a call from the hospital. Ms. Benitez is awake.

chapter 22

TWO DAYS LATER SHANI, DOLI, LIN, AND I WERE SITTING in the uncomfortable chairs of the hospital's waiting room. I was jittery with impatience. Today was the first time since Ms. Benitez had woken up that she'd been allowed visitors, and I couldn't wait to see her. Even though I'd been told she was all right, so many things I'd been told lately had turned out to be lies, I wouldn't believe it until I could see for myself.

At last a young nurse in light blue scrubs entered. "You can all go see her now," she said.

I tore out of my chair, eagerly following the nurse down the hallway to room 218. When we got there, she gestured for us to go inside. But now that I was there, I hesitated. I was scared that I'd find Ms. Benitez still unconscious with wires and tubes crisscrossing her body. Slowly I took a step in, followed by the others.

A rush of relief coursed through me when I saw Ms. Benitez

sitting up in bed, bright eyed and smiling. She greeted each of us by name.

"I'm so glad to see you girls!" she exclaimed, spreading her arms wide.

Without hesitation this time, I ran into them, squeezing her tight. Maybe it was weird of me to hug a teacher—not to mention a goddess—as if she were family. But she kind of felt like family to me now. "I was so afraid you'd never wake up," I confessed, my face still mushed into her shoulder.

"Thank goodness you did, too," said Shani. "Because have we got a million questions for you!"

Lin entered bearing a bouquet of flowers and a "Get Well Soon" balloon. She gave Ms. Benitez a smile and immediately went about finding something to use as a vase and arranging the flowers perfectly on the windowsill.

"We're so glad you're okay," said Doli. "You look pretty good for a woman who's been in a coma for more than a week."

Ms. Benitez grinned, sitting up taller in her hospital bed, where she lay under a crisp white sheet. "Thank you, Doli," she said, glancing into the hallway and dropping her voice. "Of course, my recovery is thanks to the four of you defeating the first Chaos Spirit."

My mouth dropped open. "How did you know?" I said.

"Only that could have woken me from my coma," she explained. "When you destroyed Anubis's minion, his powers diminished and he released his hold on me."

So I was right. Anubis's powers had weakened, thanks to us. That made everything we'd gone through worth it. I quickly told her about how we had defeated the demented bat and escaped the temple. "We brought a gift for you too," I said. I pulled the green jewel out of my pocket and placed it in her hand.

She wrapped her fingers around it, took a breath, and closed her eyes. When she opened them again, I saw that their color had changed to a dark purple, like fresh plums. Looking into them was like swimming in a deep well. They were Ixchel's eyes. "You've done better than I ever imagined," she said. "You've found the first jewel."

"*First?*" Doli said, lifting her eyebrows. "So there really are more? Anubis didn't get rid of them?"

Ixchel turned to her. "The sacred gems are enchanted and indestructible. They cannot be destroyed, and if they were thrown to the bottom of the ocean, they would rise to the surface and float until they were found. However, they can be hidden in the darkest corners of the world, places mortals rarely go."

"You mean like the creepy temple we were in last night?" Lin suggested. "*Blegh.* No thank you."

Shani nodded in agreement. "I have to say, I second that 'blegh.' I was hoping that taking out the bat would send Anubis a message. You know, scare him straight so that he would just give up his evil plans and go home?"

Even as she said the words, I could tell that she knew it was wishful thinking.

Ixchel regarded her with serene eyes. "Your victory over the bat spirit was impressive. But what you killed in the temple was the Chaos Spirit's physical form. While by destroying that, you have weakened it immeasurably, given time, it could recover. This was only the first battle of many to come."

"Rats," said Shani, slumping against the windowsill.

"But what about the vase?" I asked. "I know Anubis pulverized that. Even if we find the jewels, don't we need a new vessel?"

Ixchel nodded sagely. "Yes. In order to defeat the Chaos Spirits—and Anubis along with them—once and for all, we must find the jewels and trap them in a powerful vessel. I created the first vase, I will make another. Until then, the war rages on. Only you can help me put an end to Anubis's evil."

"Well, *that's* a bummer," said Shani, moving to stand beside me. "Want us to destroy some horcruxes while we're at it?"

I nudged Shani's arm to tell her to knock it off, but Ms. Benitez, or Ixchel, regarded us with compassion. "I know this is a daunting task," she said, "but you would not have been chosen if you were not capable of completing it."

"How *were* we chosen, anyway?" Lin asked. "And do our parents know? Because mine have never once mentioned that I was half tiger."

As we watched, Ms. Benitez slowly began to transform. Her skin glowed with a supernatural light and her hair turned a shimmering black color. "Allow me to explain," she said with a voice that sounded like many voices and one at the same time. "Hundreds of years ago, Anubis, the Egyptian god of death, called forth the darkest elements of every ancient civilization in order to form the Brotherhood of Chaos. Their goal was to sow discord and confusion, leading humanity to embrace its basest nature. Death and destruction would follow and chaos would reign.

"To do this, he planned to use the Chaos Spirits to bring the other gods and humans to heel. But those of us who used our powers for good fought against him. We chose four warriors from powerful ancient peoples—Mayan, Egyptian, Anasazi, and Chinese—and created the Wildcats. The great cats have always been regarded as protectors and fierce warriors on their own. But united, they were nearly invincible. With their help, I was able to build the vase that trapped the Chaos Spirits within."

"I still don't understand," I said. "Where do we enter this story?"

"I knew that though the Chaos Spirits were confined, there could be a time when they escaped their prison. So I used my powers as a Mayan goddess to infuse the vase with strong magical protectors—the cat engravings you saw on each side, representing the four warriors. If the Spirits were ever released, a new generation of Wildcats would rise. That, Ana, is where you, Lin, Shani, and Doli come in. You are all descendants of the very first Wildcats, and each of you has answered the call. I'm very proud of you."

Shani blinked as if there'd just been an earthquake in her head. "Mind—blown," she said, perfectly capturing how I felt at that moment.

We were descendants of Wildcats? Did that mean my mom may have been one too? And were the dreams I'd had of hunting Anubis in the jungle really me seeing through the eyes of past Wildcats?

Two sharp knocks sounded and the door creaked open. The nurse in the pale blue scrubs poked her head in. "Time for lunch, Yvette." As she came in carrying a tray of food and a blood pressure machine, my heart raced at the thought that the nurse would see Ixchel lying there in all her supernatural glory, but when I glanced back at the bed, I saw that Ixchel had gone. Ms. Benitez smiled up at the nurse as if we hadn't just been talking about the end of the world.

When the cabdriver dropped us off in front of the Temple Academy entrance, I thought back to my first cab ride to the school. I knew my way around now, but in most ways, the place was even more foreign than it had been before. It turned out that the earthquakes weren't the only things that made me feel like the ground was constantly shifting beneath my feet. Thankfully, the friends I'd made were the real deal.

As we entered the lobby, Shani and Doli walked ahead and I lagged behind with Lin. Suddenly my phone buzzed in my pocket. When I looked at the screen, I saw a text from Jason, asking if Ms. Benitez was all right. I smiled. He was so thoughtful. Lin craned her neck to peer at my screen. Too late, I closed the text and stuffed my phone back in my pocket, feeling guilty.

"Another text from Jason?" she said.

I shrugged, not knowing what to say.

"You really like him, don't you?" Lin asked in a small voice that was almost a whisper.

I chewed on my bottom lip. "I'm sorry," I said. "I can't help it."

Lin nodded sadly. "It's all right," she replied. But it didn't feel all right.

I let a moment of silence pass before I said, "You know, if the rest of the year is as crazy as the first part has been, I'm going to need all the friends I can get—especially ones like you."

Lin glanced up at me in confusion. "Why would you need me?"

"Are you serious?" I answered with a grin. "You're the girl who scared Nicole so badly that she turned into a hyena. Who wouldn't need a friend like that?"

Surprising even herself, I think, Lin let out a burst of laughter at the memory, and I smiled from ear to ear. Taking a chance, I looped my arm through hers and together we followed Shani and Doli through the doors. Maybe things weren't completely all right between us yet, but for the first time I had hope that someday soon they would be.

"This is the last of it," I said as I dropped a box of my things onto my new bed in Lin's room.

A couple of days before, I'd filed all the paperwork for a room reassignment, as Mrs. O'Grady instructed, and Jason got his mom to fast-track the request for me. Turns out it pays to be close friends with the principal's son, not that I wouldn't have wanted to be his friend anyway. We'd been spending a lot of time together and I think he really liked me. I could tell that my friendship with Jason still stung Lin a little, but she seemed more okay with it now that we were all better friends. I was almost as relieved about this as I was about that fact that I didn't have to live with Nicole anymore. In fact, when Lin heard that I was filling out a room-change request, she suggested that I be placed with her. She'd arranged to have a room to herself since she'd come to Temple, but now she welcomed having me as her first roommate.

"Wow, you weren't kidding when you said you didn't bring a lot of clothes with you," Lin said, eyeing my tiny suitcase.

"Nah," I retorted. "Just the essential pieces. Like this one." I held up the Cookie Monster T-shirt. "It's the must-have item of the fall."

Lin laughed and moved to help me put the last of my things away. Just then my phone vibrated in my pocket. I pulled it out and gasped. Aunt Teppy! *Finally.*

I hurried to pick it up and shouted, "Aunt Teppy? Where have you guys been? I've been trying to get in touch with you for weeks. Where are you? Why haven't you called? I've got about a million things to tell you."

"Ana," my aunt said in a cool, detached tone that I'd never heard her use before. "We're fine. But we can't spend every waking moment catering to you, you know. We have our own lives."

I rocked back on my heels. *Where did that come from?*

"I know that," I began hesitantly. "It's just . . . I was worried. Why didn't you tell me where you were going?"

"Because I wasn't aware we needed your permission," she snapped. "We've taken care of you for a decade. Aren't we entitled to some alone time?"

Tears stung my eyes. Why was she being like this? The Aunt Teppy I knew could make me feel like I was being hugged even over the phone. I didn't know the woman talking to me now. She'd always told me that adopting me after my mom and dad died had been the best decision she and Uncle Mec had ever made, that they loved being my parents. But maybe she'd only said that to be polite, and really they couldn't wait to get rid of the burden of taking care of me. I choked back a sob.

"Can you at least tell me one thing?" I pleaded. "Where *are* you?"

"We're in Cancún." Again with that stilted, tense voice—so unlike the Aunt Teppy I knew. "I have to go now."

"*What?* We haven't talked since I got here and you have to go? Tell me what's going on, Aunt Teppy. *Please.*"

She sighed coldly. "As I said, we're fine. It's time you grew up and looked after yourself. And do me one more favor."

"Anything," I said in a broken voice.

"*Don't come looking for us!*"

Abruptly the line went dead and a dial tone blared in my ear. I stared at my phone in horror. I teetered on my feet like a tree caught in a hurricane, on the verge of having its roots ripped from the ground.

"What's going on?" Lin asked, concern etched into her face.

I turned to my new roommate. "My aunt yelled at me," I said, still in shock.

"Oh," said Lin, her eyes sympathetic. "I'm sorry. Family can be like that sometimes."

I shook my head. "Not mine," I told her. "She never yells at me. *Never!*"

"Well, why was she upset?" Lin's eyes grew wide. "Did she find out about, you know"—she hooked her hands into claws and bared her teeth—"and couldn't deal?"

"No. She would never reject me for that. I know it. Lin, something is *wrong!*"

I told her the things my aunt had said to me, things she'd never said before. I began to pace the room, wildly looking around for something—anything—that would help. Finally my eyes landed on my empty suitcase. They were in Cancún, she'd said. Not too far from here. Close enough for a jet to get to . . .

Without another thought I pulled the suitcase onto my bed and flung it open, frantically tossing in my clothes.

"Um, what are you doing?" Lin said, rising to her feet.

"I have to go find them!" I shouted. "There's something my aunt wasn't telling me over the phone. And I think . . . I th-think something's happened to my aunt and uncle. I think they've been kidnapped!" I burst into tears then, my shoulders shaking uncontrollably.

Immediately Lin flew to my side, moving me toward her bed and sitting me down. "Shhh, shhh . . . ," she cooed, doing her best to calm me.

Just then there was a knock on the door, and Doli and Shani swept into the room, giggling. "All right, we're ready to get our *Vampire Diaries* marathon on!" said Shani. But she stopped short when she saw that I was sobbing in Lin's arms. "What did you do?" she said. "Two minutes as your roommate and she's already in tears?"

Lin shook her head at her. "Shani, this is serious."

After I calmed down a little, I told my friends about the phone call with my aunt and her last words to me. "I don't know what to do," I moaned.

"You're jumping to conclusions," Doli offered. "Isn't it possible they really did just go on vacation and they're okay?"

"If they were okay," I argued, "why would they say something like, 'Don't come looking for us'? You have to trust me; I know my aunt and uncle. They're in some kind of trouble. I know it!" More tears streamed down my face.

"All right," said Shani. "That's good enough for me. We'll help you find them. Right?" She looked at Lin and Doli.

"Of course we will!" Doli exclaimed.

"And I'm sure Jason will help too," Lin added.

"And don't forget you happen to know a freaking Mayan goddess!" said Shani. "That ought to come in handy."

I nodded gratefully. "Thanks, you guys. It means a lot to know I have you Wildcats on my side."

"Looks like you might have one more wildcat who's willing to help too." Doli nodded to my bed.

I looked over to find a purring black figure curled up on my pillow. The green-eyed cat had returned! I was too torn up inside to feel happy, but it felt right that the cat was here with us. "Lin," I said, "would it be all right with you if I kept her? I mean, if she'll let me." If there was anything I'd learned from becoming a jaguar, it was that all cats were a little wild, even house cats. Though I suspected this one was no ordinary cat.

"Definitely," Lin agreed. "She can be like our mascot." I knew she was trying to lighten the mood, and even though that would be impossible until I knew what was wrong with my aunt and uncle, I appreciated the effort.

"Great, now that that's settled, let's get down to business," said Shani, reaching for my laptop. "Why don't you tell me your aunt's phone number so I can look her up. And if you've got one of her credit card numbers, even better. I can see if they've been used. Did she mention where they were in Cancún? Because hacking into hotel guest registries is easy. . . ."

As Shani started typing, Doli called Jason and asked if he could come by, and Lin brought the cat over and dropped her in my lap. I felt a wave of gratitude so strong it almost set me crying again. I wasn't alone anymore. My world had been turned upside down in a matter of weeks, and nothing would ever be the same. But at least I had friends I could count on . . . and one wildcat. I had no idea where my search for my aunt and uncle would take me, but Ixchel had told me to have faith in my powers. I would have to let them lead me to Aunt Teppy and Uncle Mec and hope that I reached them in time. I took a deep breath. Whatever came next, I was ready.

ACKNOWLEDGMENTS

I WOULD LOVE TO TAKE ALL THE CREDIT FOR THIS BOOK, but like Harry Potter said, I must not tell lies. The truth is, there were many people without whom the Wildcats would have never come to be. First and foremost, I'd like to thank the team of incredible editors who worked their magic on *Hunters of Chaos*: Brendan Duffy, Stephanie Lane Elliott, William Severs, and Ali Standish at Working Partners, Ltd., and Fiona Simpson at Simon & Schuster. Thank you all for your creativity, your great ideas, your knack for knowing what to cut and what to keep, and—most important—your patience every time I said I needed "just one more week." Thanks, also, for showing so much interest in and support for diversity in children's literature. Seriously, you guys are brilliant, and I am so, so lucky to get to work with you. I would gush more, but I don't want to embarrass you.

Huge thanks to publicity assistant Kelsey Dickson; designer Laura Lyn DiSiena; production editor Kayley Hoffman; production manager Kara Reilly; everyone in sales, marketing, and promotion; and the entire Aladdin team at Simon & Schuster. Special shout-out to Wylie Beckert for creating such an *awesome* cover. (Which features a young girl who bears a striking resemblance to my niece, Jasmine. *How did you do that?*) Thanks to my good friend Jeannie Ng, I've been a freelance proofreader for Simon & Schuster Children's Books for years, so I know firsthand how hard everyone there works on each book—even while juggling a million other things with intense schedules. Thank you from the bottom of my heart for everything you do and for showing my book (my first hardcover!) so much love.

Thank you to all the librarians, teachers, bookstore owners, and bloggers who have supported me over the years or who helped get the word out about this book. Just to name a few, Betsy Bird, Darren and Theresa Androsiglio-Fitzpatrick, Christine Freglette, Kathy Gerber, Wendi Pela-Giuliano, Tonya Johnson, Latricia Markle, Arlene Sahraie, Bina Valenzano, Ron Ventola, and Tanya Manning-Yarde. Also a big thanks to Latinos in Kid Lit, who mentioned me in their round-up for this year. I'm honored to be included!

And finally, a deep, sincere thank-you to my friends and family, who are endlessly supportive, especially my mom and dad, Madelin and Eliezer Velasquez; my grandfather, David White; and my grandmother, Guillermina White, who taught me everything I need to know about having pride in my culture and being a force for good in the world. *Te extraño, Abuela.*

THE FIGHT CONTINUES IN

Ana

WE FILED OUT OF THE DORMS AND MADE OUR WAY TO THE auditorium for school assembly at eight thirty that morning, grumbling about having to get up so early. The sky was its usual shade of cloudless blue. All around us I could see the distant red mountains overlooking Temple Academy like stone guardians.

Nothing had changed—except that the day before, my whole world had fallen apart.

Thankfully, I had three friends who were doing their best to help me put it back together: Doli Hoskie, Lin Yang, and Shani Massri. When I'd first arrived at this school, I hadn't been sure I'd ever fit in. Then I met them, and everything changed. We're all so different from one another, but thanks to Ms. Benitez, we found out that we have one huge thing in common: We are the direct descendants of ancient shape-shifting warriors—Wildcats—who were destined to fight the forces of evil.

I know, that sounds crazy. If I hadn't seen Doli turn into a puma, Lin become a tiger, and Shani transform into a lion—and if I hadn't turned into a jaguar myself—I might not believe it. But after we battled the ancient Egyptian god Anubis and the Chaos Spirits he released, there was no denying the truth. Anyway, I'm getting ahead of myself.

Last night I'd gotten a superweird call from Aunt Teppy. I was starting to suspect that something terrible had happened to her and Uncle Mec, and all I wanted was my family back.

"Tell me one more time what your aunt said," Doli whispered now, pulling us to the side of the entrance to the auditorium. She was looking at me with wide, serious brown eyes, and I realized that I must have looked totally shaken.

I took a deep breath. "She said that they had taken care of me for a decade and they were entitled to some alone time. That I should grow up and look after myself." My voice broke. The words were so upsetting, so unlike my loving aunt, it was still hard to repeat them without crying.

"Harsh," Shani said sympathetically, touching my shoulder. "And then she said that they were in Cancún and not to come looking for them?"

I nodded, feeling a lump forming in my throat. Aunt Teppy and Uncle Mec had always assured me that adopting me after my parents had died had been the best decision they'd ever made. Thinking—for even a moment—that I'd been nothing but a burden to them broke my heart. My only hope was that someone, or some*thing*, had forced her to say it—though the thought of my family in danger scared me even more. "Anubis is behind this; I know it. Aunt Teppy was lying because she had to, or was made to," I said, then added softly, "She had to be."

Anubis, the ancient Egyptian god of the afterlife, was the head of the Brotherhood of Chaos. A collaboration between different ancient civilizations, the Brotherhood had one goal: to cause chaos, both in the ancient world and, now that Anubis was reviving the Brotherhood, in *our* world. Our role as Wildcats was to defeat him.

Unfortunately, he was a very powerful enemy.

Shani pulled out her phone and started typing and clicking. "Well," she said after a moment, "maybe she was lying about the whole alone-time thing, but they really were on a flight to Cancún two days ago." She held up her phone and showed me what looked like an airline passenger list. About a third of the way down were two very familiar names: *Mecatl and Tepin Navarro*.

I gasped and reached for the phone, as if just holding something with their names on it would bring them closer to me. "There they are!" I shouted. But too soon my excitement faded and gave way to a cold fear that seemed to coat my skin like frost. Yes, they had definitely been on the plane, but *why*? I didn't care what my aunt had said on that call. I knew they would never get on a flight without telling me. Which meant they hadn't had a choice.

"How did you get that list?" Doli asked Shani.

"How do you think?" Shani said, giving her a sly look.

Doli groaned. "You hacked into the airline's server?"

Shani looked around with wide eyes at the students and teachers still streaming into the auditorium. "Gosh, Doli. Say it a little louder, why don't you?"

"Sorry. But, Shani, you know you can't afford to get in trouble for hacking again. Were you careful?"

Shani lifted her arm and combed her hand through the patch of blue hair over her left eye. "Look, boss lady, I can either be careful or I can be fast. This time I chose fast, which I'm guessing Ana doesn't have a problem with."

"You're right," I said, hugging her. "Thank you for doing that. You're a good friend." Shani had been kicked out of some other schools—according to the rumor mill it was something like eight or nine—for hacking, among other minor cyber crimes. Principal Ferris had already warned her that if she made one more misstep, she'd be out of Temple Academy, too. It touched me that Shani, who always tried to play it cool when it came to emotional stuff, cared enough about me to take such a huge risk.

Shani hugged me back for a moment and then shook me off. "All right, all right. No need to get mushy. I want to help you find your aunt and uncle, but that's not the only reason

I'm doing this. If their disappearance has anything to do with the Brotherhood of Chaos, then that affects all of us."

Lin and Doli fell silent at the mere mention of the Brotherhood. I knew it was on their minds too.

"You're right again," I said. "Wow, twice in one day. You're on a roll."

Shani began to laugh, but when her eyes caught something behind me, her expression darkened. I turned around to see Coach Lawson approaching, staring down at the smartphone she was holding. Just as she was about to pass us, she glanced up and made eye contact with Shani.

"Miss Massri, how are you this morning?"

Shani stretched her lips into a tight smile. "I'm fantastic, Coach Lawson. And yourself?"

"Wonderful, actually," she said. "My sister had a baby last night, and she just posted some pictures on Facebook. Would you like to see?"

Shani's eyes lit up, and she clapped her hands together. "Would I?"

As Shani took the phone from Coach Lawson and cooed over the pictures of the new baby, Lin, Doli, and I exchanged puzzled looks. I didn't need our Wildcat telepathic powers to know we were all thinking the same thing: *What the heck is going on here?* Shani wasn't exactly the warm and fuzzy type who went all gooey over pictures of puppies and babies.

After a few minutes Shani handed the phone back to

Coach Lawson and said, "Congratulations. She's adorable."

Beaming, Coach Lawson took her phone back. "Thank you." Then after a brief pause, she said, "You know, Miss Massri, I'm sorry you didn't make the tennis team this time. But with a little practice—"

"Yeah, thanks," Shani said, bobbing her head up and down. "You're so right. I'll keep that in mind."

"I hope so," she answered. "The team could use someone with your . . . fire." She turned to all of us. "You'd better get to your seats, ladies. The assembly will be starting soon."

The second she turned to go inside, Lin swung her incredulous gaze to Shani and said, "What in the world—"

"Hold that thought," Shani interrupted, pulling out her own cell phone and pressing a series of buttons. A few seconds later Coach Lawson cried out.

"Oh no! My phone just went black."

"Weird," Shani called. "Must be some sort of power surge. That's been happening a lot lately, since the earthquake. Try turning it off and on again!"

"All right," Coach mumbled, her brows furrowed in concern. "I'll try that." She walked away, shaking her phone as if attempting to wake it from a deep sleep.

When she had gone, Doli crossed her arms and raised one eyebrow at Shani.

"What?" Shani said, her smirk fading as she noticed Doli's glare.

"You did something weird to her phone, didn't you?"

"Who, me?" Shani pointed a finger at her chest, the picture of innocence. But we all knew her too well for that now. "All right, fine. Yes, but she deserved it."

"Why?" I asked. "Because she wouldn't let you on the tennis team? Since when do you even play tennis?"

"I don't. I just figured it would be an easy PE credit. But she blew that for me, so now I have no choice but to take weight training with Coach Hyung, and I'm pretty sure he used to be some sort of drill sergeant in the marines. For that, Coach Lawson must pay." She drummed the tips of her fingers against one another and let out an exaggerated supervillain laugh. *"Mwah-ha-ha-haaa."*

"You know there's another option, right?" Doli cut in, her voice sharp. "You could try to be mature and show a little good sportsmanship instead of killing the poor woman's phone."

"Yeah," Lin added, raising an eyebrow. "Or just *try out again next time*, like the woman said."

Shani scowled. "I could. But where's the fun in that? Besides, I didn't *kill* her phone. I simply installed a virus that'll prevent her from using Facebook's mobile app. Annoying, but not exactly techno-cide. Plus, she's the one who committed an act of attempted murder first. She tried to bore me to death with pictures of that baby." Shani closed her eyes, hung her head to the side, and let her tongue loll out of her mouth.

I bit back a laugh, earning me an annoyed look from Doli

that said, *Don't encourage her!* But I couldn't help it. Even when Shani was being downright wicked, she still cracked me up. Meanwhile, Lin, who had suffered the consequences of Shani's phone hacking in the not-too-distant past, just shrugged and said, "Better her than me."

Finally, we followed the last of the students into the auditorium. Doli hung back with me and whispered, "Let's talk about your aunt and uncle after classes. We're going to find them, okay?"

She squeezed my hand, and I nodded gratefully, trying my best to ignore the worry gnawing at my insides. I knew my friends would do everything in their power—including use their magic—to help me find my family. But for now we had to get through the school day and pretend that we were just normal kids, without a care in the world.

As soon as we settled into our seats, I groaned. My former roommate, Nicole Van Voorhies, was sitting a few rows away, and I could tell that the Wildcats weren't the only ones trying to act normal. Nicole sat at the center of a fawning group of girls. She was twisting a strand of her golden blond hair around her finger and laughing at something Tammy Winston had said. But her eyes were empty, and the rehearsed way she tilted her head back and pumped her shoulders told me that her laugh was just for show. Now that I knew Nicole was actually half-demon, the sound sent chills along my spine.

"Looks like she's recovered nicely from our run-in the other night," Lin said, following my gaze.

"Probably because she was too much of a coward to face us in the temple," I replied.

I shivered again. Everyone had thought that the temple on the far side of the campus that had been revealed after the earthquake was a Native American structure, a relic of the anicent pueblo peoples. But when we'd gotten inside a few nights ago, we'd realized it actually served as the headquarters of the Brotherhood of Chaos. It had become the site of our first battle when a Chaos Spirit in the form of a giant bat had attacked us and brought to life the nightmarish paintings on the temple walls.

If it hadn't been for all of us working together in our Wildcat guises to trap the bat under the heavy statue of Anubis, we wouldn't have made it out of the temple alive.

Outside the temple we'd caught Nicole skulking around, spying for Anubis. It turned out Nicole wasn't quite human. Whereas we were girls who could turn into Wildcats, Nicole was more hyena than girl.

"I can't even believe she's here," I whispered to Lin. "Shouldn't she be off somewhere with Anubis, wreaking havoc?"

Lin narrowed her eyes at Nicole and said, "She probably wants to lie low for a while after the way we totally ran her boss out of town. I doubt she's brave enough to do anything on her own."

That much was true. Nicole had never attacked me when we'd been alone together. Not physically, anyway. But the thing about hyenas was that they hunted in packs. Or so *The Lion King* had taught me. "Do you think she was serious when she said there were more like her at the school?"

But Lin just shrugged it off. "So what if there are?" she said. "Even in the wild, hyenas would be no match for a lion, a tiger, a puma, and a jaguar. If they're smart, they'll keep their distance."

She had a point, but the thought of a half-demon hyena posse sitting all around us still gave me the creeps. And besides, no one had ever accused Nicole of being smart.

"Good morning, students and faculty," Principal Ferris said, stepping up to the podium onstage.

Everyone quieted down and muttered a sluggish "Good morning" back. Usually she would say something like, *You can do better than that* and make us say it again. But today she looked distracted. "I'm afraid I have some rather upsetting news to share. It seems that over the weekend there was some sort of . . . event at the temple."

Shani and I looked at each other. "About time," she whispered. The battle in the temple had taken place days ago, and we'd been expecting an announcement like this ever since.

"We are not yet sure if it was an act of vandalism or the result of minor aftershocks, but several of the priceless artifacts that were excavated have been damaged. In addition . . ." Here

Principal Ferris's voice trailed off as she paused and took out a piece of paper from her pocket. She looked at it and shook her head sadly as if the paper itself had broken her heart. "Dr. Logan has written a letter informing me that he's left Temple Academy to pursue a project in Zimbabwe. He . . . he won't be returning."

At this last bit of news, the room began to buzz with conversation. Jessica, who had a not-so-secret crush on Dr. Logan, cried out, "No!" Of course, I doubted she would have been quite as upset if she'd seen Dr. Logan in his true half-man, half-jackal form, his perfect white teeth and neat hair replaced by jagged fangs and matted fur. "Dr. Logan" was just the human form Anubis had taken to get onto school grounds.

Principal Ferris folded the note and slipped it back into her pocket. "As a result of these developments, the temple itself has been sealed, and the historical foundation has halted any further exploration for the time being. This means that the plans to relocate Temple Academy have also been canceled."

This time everyone cheered and applauded. No one had wanted the school to move—not the teachers and not the students—so this was great news for them. As for Lin, Doli, Shani, and me, we cheered because we had succeeded in ruining Anubis's plan to take over the campus and use the temple for his own sinister purposes. In fact, the only person who didn't seem thrilled by the news was Principal Ferris.

Shani leaned over and whispered, "By my count, that makes Hunters of Chaos two; Anubis a big fat zero."

Principal Ferris moved on to less exciting announcements, and then the choir got up to sing the national anthem. Finally the assembly came to a close. Doli stood and said, "Let's hurry. We have to squeeze in our appointment with Ms. Benitez before class."

I rose to follow her, but then I saw Jason Ferris standing near the back of the auditorium. "Ferris" as in Principal Ferris's son. What was he doing here? "Uh, I'll meet you outside," I said. "I'll just be a sec."

Doli followed my gaze to Jason and snickered. "Fine."

Shani shrugged, and my friends disappeared into the cluster of students leaving the auditorium. Only when I saw them exit the room did I sidle up next to Jason and say, "Hey."

Jason turned to face me, and for a second I forgot how to breathe. Sure, those incredible blue-green eyes and that dirty-blond hair streaked with gold made him seriously cute. But now I also knew how brave, kind, and selfless he was. He'd risked his life in the temple to help us defeat the bat Chaos Spirit. As far as I was concerned, Harry Styles had nothing on Jason Ferris.

"H-hey, Ana," he stammered, giving me an awkward hug.

"Were you waiting for me?" I asked when I pulled away.

"Well, yeah. I, um . . ." He bowed his head, then scratched the back of it, peeking up at me so only a hint of blue showed beneath his long eyelashes. "I just wanted to ask you, you know, how you are."

"Oh, uh, I'm okay, I guess." I twisted my fingers together behind my back, urging myself to be cool. "How are you?"

"Good. Good," he said. "How are you?"

I giggled and bit my lip. "You already asked me that."

"I did?" he said, his eyes widening. He stared down at his sneakers. "Oh yeah, I guess I did." He winced and smacked his forehead, whispering, "Stupid, stupid, stupid" to himself.

I laughed and grabbed his hand. "Hey, that's my friend you're hitting," I said.

He let out a shuddering sigh, looking at our joined hands and then up at me with a half smile. "Sorry I'm being such a dork. It's just—it's really good to see you."

I nodded, feeling my stomach tingle. "It's good to see you, too. It's nice to have something to think about besides my aunt and uncle."

Jason's eyes darkened with concern, and he moved closer to me. Doli had called him the night before to let him know about the phone call. "Has there been any news since last night?"

I shook my head. "We're working on it. We're actually on our way to see Ms. Benitez now, if you want to come with us."

"I would," he said, "but I should really go check on my mom."

We both glanced toward the stage and saw Principal Ferris just standing there with a faraway look in her eye.

"She seems kind of down," I noted. "Is everything all right?"

Jason sighed and shook his head. "Believe it or not, I think she's just missing that creep Dr. Logan. She carries that note around with her all the time. I've caught her taking it out to read every once in a while, like she's hoping this time it'll say something different. I wish I could tell her he was actually a force of ancient evil so she would get over him, but she still thinks he was a stand-up guy. How messed up is that?"

"Pretty messed up," I agreed, "but it's not her fault. He had weird power over some people. But now that he's gone, maybe she'll get over him."

"I hope so," Jason said. "I really want her to be as happy as I am." He squeezed my hand and gave me a shy smile before walking away. How could I feel so good about Jason, I wondered, and so bad about everything else at the same time?

Outside, Shani, Lin, and Doli were waiting for me.

"Sooo . . . how's Jason?" Doli asked with a knowing smile.

I felt my face warm. No use trying to deny it. "He's fine."

"Then why do you look so confused?" Lin asked.

"Because boys are confusing," Shani answered for me. "And relationships are already hard enough without your crush knowing that you're an evil-fighting wildcat who occasionally turns into a jaguar."

We all burst into laughter. It was funny because it was true.

Crystal Velasquez is the author of *Hunters of Chaos*, the Your Life, but . . . series: *Your Life, but Better*; *Your Life, but Cooler*; and *Your Life, but Sweeter*; and four books in the Maya & Miguel series, based on the television show—*My Twin Brother/My Twin Sister*; *Neighborhood Friends*; *The Valentine Machine*; and *Paint the Town*. She holds a BA in creative writing from Penn State University and is a graduate of NYU's Summer Publishing Institute. Currently an editor at Working Partners Ltd. and a freelance proofreader, she lives in Flushing, Queens. Visit Crystal's website at crystalvelasquez.com, visit her blog at yourlifebutbetter.blogspot.com, or find her on Facebook at Facebook.com/CrystalVelasquezAuthor.